GOOD H|E|ART

I

II

GOOD H|E|ART

Book 1

L. Marie Thomas

Printed in the United States of America

First Printing, 2019

ISBN-13: 9781689228626

Also available as an ebook.
www.Amazon.com

www.LMarieThomas.com

Acknowledgments

For a first book, I feel like I need to thank everyone who has been involved in any part of the process. Please excuse how long this is about to be....

First of all, I would never have been able to do any of this without God. Seriously. I have a hard time accomplishing anything without Him. Thank You, Jesus, for rescuing me from darkness and depression and fear and anxiety. I can't get through a single day without You.

And then, my gorgeous, strong husband. The man I respect and admire and can't get enough of. You are my best friend and my leader on this whole crazy adventure. My heart belongs to you always, since we are one. Yay! You're my favorite!

My beautiful girls...What can a Momma say? It makes me cry just thinking of you. God brought us all together for a reason. You are His STRONG LITTLE WOMEN. I am blessed beyond words to be your mother, and I can't wait for you to discover what all is in store for you. There are plans for you, and a purpose for every little thing about you.

To my parents...Mom, you are such a strong woman and I've looked up to you every day of my life. Thank you for helping me plot this whole thing. We get even more excited than Samantha and her mom do. It's been a joy. Dad...we almost lost you during this whole journey. It taught me so much about what a limited time we have here. But you have always prepared me for that: There is a purpose for my life and limited time, and goals I must set to achieve what I'm supposed to do. I love our talks, our meetings about all of it. I love that you're still around for it now. I can't thank God enough for that.

My sister – you get me. Thank you for supporting all of this. The sister relationship in the book and the fun in all of it is dedicated to you. I am a writer and you still love me and my hermit-ness. ;-) That's awesome. I love you more than the sand in the sea and the stars in the sky.

To my wonderful Mother-in-Law, you've been a huge part of this process and so supportive. Same goes for everyone on my husband's side of the family. Could a girl ask for better in-laws?

To everyone who's been there since the beginning, you know who you are. My bestie, my family, my friends, my church family...Thank you.

Everyone who helped raise our children before we even knew them: You are all a part of this journey, and so dear to my heart because you kept our kids safe. We could never thank you enough for all you've done.

To my editor – Sarah Tehuiotoa – you brought my writing to a new level. Your insight goes beyond what I can describe. I can't help but want to send you every email and text I ever write.

To Natascha M., who helped with all of the private security agent lingo. You are amazing and sweet, and extremely gifted and professional. I am your biggest fan.

To Jaime Slover, who designed my logos and book cover and put up with all of my flakiness: God has gifted you bigtime. Thank you for blessing me with your gifts!!

To my photographer and stylist and sweet friend Taylor Cornell. You are such a light in my life! Here's to more adventures in creating art together ;-)

To Kali, who loves me no matter what. My dear friend, assistant, agent, and everything in between…you are the best. You help me to be smart with every dime that comes in and every second I have in my schedule. I don't know what I would do without you.

And to all of you who are my warriors who have been praying fiercely for all of this: I hope someday to be half the person you all are. I am so blessed to have you in my life.

Everyone involved – What can I say? Let's see what God has for all of us and GO!

To my husband, for truly loving me…

Part I
30 days and counting…

When I find her beneath the tree, she is curled in a ball and bleeding. I slide to a stop and kneel down beside her. She looks up at me, her big eyes peaceful despite what happened.

She's in shock.

"I found her!" I yell into my radio. "She's alive!"

A crackling voice says something back to me, but the words are jumbled.

I glance around, hearing distant shouts echo, but no one can be seen through the trees. I wave my flashlight, making a sweeping beam. No one responds. Waiting for them isn't an option.

I bend and carefully pick her up. A whimper of pain escapes her mouth. Her body is so light in my arms. I turn in a full circle, looking around, confused as to where I am and where I came from. Panic settles in.

"Help!" I yell. "Help!"

Suddenly, something cold touches my face. I look down. It's her hand. She's touching my cheek, as if she's the one telling me that everything's going to be alright.

"It's okay," I tell her. "You're okay."

Her eyes roll back into her skull and her hand drops.

I start running.

Lyla Brooks
Chicago, IL

My throat hurts from screaming. My heart is pounding so hard that even the tips of my hair seem to pulse, throb. My hand is up on my scar on the back of my neck which is slick with sweat. In the nightmare, it's blood. My other arm is wrapped tightly around my curled-up legs. I woke up like this a second ago, in the corner of my room, rocking back and forth on my carpet. Like usual.

"Everything will be okay," I whisper to myself, crying, rocking. "Everything's okay. You're okay."

Tears stream down my legs in little warm rivers because my eyes are pressed to my knees. I can't look up. I can't. I'm trying to remember what I normally do to calm down. I can't think. I can't breathe. I can't stop crying. Dogs rip at me in the nightmares and I can still feel them tearing at me, causing familiar ghost pains to flicker down my neck and back. I can still hear them snapping and barking, their echoes bouncing off the trees in the nightmare.

"It's okay. You're okay."

But I'm not okay. This has been happening for years. I don't know how much more I can take.

…Singing. That's what I do to calm down. Mom used to sing to me every night when she and dad would burst through the door whenever this happened. I told them to start wearing earplugs. Their lives don't have to be wrecked by this. Just mine.

I start singing my mom's favorite song, an old hymn called *It Is Well With My Soul*. The words are muffled against my knees and sound terrible, but my heart starts to slow down. The sound of dogs barking and snapping stops. All the flickers of pain fade. I let go of my scar and slowly look up.

When I wake up like this, I am always surprised when there are no dogs in here. I'm alone. I blink against yellowed brightness. I always sleep with the lights on. My room is calm and quiet. Mom and I decorated it a couple years ago with things that might cheer me up: Dried flowers and leaves and lots of twinkle lights. Painted happy faces smile at me from every inch of my dresser. We even hung up some of the sundresses we've been collecting for a while. If my nightmares ever stop, I'll wear a casual dress every single day because it's the opposite of pajamas.

There are no pictures of friends on my walls, just a few of my parents and me. One of my brother. I look at the clock on my nightstand. It reads two in the morning, meaning today is my eighteenth birthday. I haven't really been dreading it, and I haven't really been excited for it. I don't know what to feel about it. No one will call me. My brother Will hasn't come home in years and never talks to me. That's what hurts the most.

I swallow and sing a little more, shivering now. Then I wipe my tears and force myself to stand up and get back into bed. I don't let myself check the closet or underneath the bed or in the shadowy spot under my desk. I know I'm alone.

I'm very alone.

"Everything will be okay. Everything's okay."

I pull my sheet and blanket up to my shoulders and curl into a ball. My scar is exposed. I reach back and touch the mangled skin that starts at the base of my skull and spreads like an upside-down tree down my back. I keep my hair long to cover it, because I don't let anyone ever see it. Not since what happened with Justin.

I squeeze my eyes shut.

"Everything will be okay," I whisper again. My mantra. "Everything's okay."

But it really isn't.

Will Brooks
That evening

Gripping the steering wheel, I pull the rental car up to the house and cut the engine. I sit for a minute, unmoving, reluctant to get out. I don't know how this is going to go. I don't know how Lyla is going to react. She might hate us after today.

I look down at the small box in the passenger seat. It's wrapped in yellow paper, my sister's favorite color, and it's full of pictures of our old life. She'll finally be able to see them now. She'll understand why I've been so distant all these years, so mad at our parents. She'll know me now. She'll know herself.

That's what makes me grab the box and get out of the car.

I don't even glance at the yard as I walk up the driveway and step up to the ugly green door my dad asked me to paint about a thousand times. I didn't get around to it before I moved out. I pause for a second and look at the doorbell, then over at the flower box beneath the window to my left. Some pink flowers stare back at me. I remember rolling my eyes the first time I saw my mom trying to plant flowers on her own, acting like she was a normal housewife and mom.

I swallow. I think I laughed at her that day.

I focus on the door again and take a deep breath as I tuck the yellow box tightly under my arm. Finally, I ring the doorbell. My palms are wet. Probably because I haven't been here in a while – maybe a couple years. I have my reasons.

Soft footfalls approach the door and I brace myself to see my family and the inside of this house and all the little things that will remind me of the past – the anger, the arguments with my parents, the miserable teen years I spent here.

The door opens and only my parents are there – my mom with her short hair dyed blonde now and my dad with his graying hair and beard. Blonde hair for my mom, a beard for my dad. Both are so that no one will recognize them from the past.

Mom steps forward immediately and hugs me. She clings to me for a long time. She's in sweats and smells like orange cleaner. I look at my dad over her shoulder. His eyes are guarded. I haven't seen him in so long. He has more lines around his eyes, more gray in his beard.

"I'm so glad you're here," my mom says as she lets me go.

Dad gives me a curt, uncomfortable hug. "How was your flight?"

"It was fine."

"I'm sorry this was so last minute," he says.

I shake my head. "It's important that I'm here."

He looks me in the eyes. "Yes, it is."

We start down the hallway together, passing the pictures of our "normal" family on the entry table. There are a couple of me playing football. Guess my parents just can't bring themselves to put them away and move on. One is of Lyla and me on a beach when we were little, before things changed. She has no clue where the picture was actually taken.

The orange cleaner smell is stronger in here, mixed with the mustiness of a vacuum. We sit down together at the kitchen table. My dad and I built it when I was in high school, and we carved our initials and the year into the side of it right where I'm sitting. That summer was one of the only good ones with him, which is ironic because he worked me to death when he found out about the drugs I was doing.

I don't touch the carving and decide not to look around at anything else. I set the yellow shoebox on the table and slide it to the side.

My parents are both silent, watching me carefully, maybe waiting for me to speak first.

"What's the plan?" I ask quietly. I glance at the staircase.

"She's asleep," Dad says. "She won't be up for a while."

That's strange. It's close to dinnertime. Maybe she's sick.

"Then let's talk about what we're going to say to her."

Dad clears his throat. "Sure."

"I was thinking on the flight here that you should do most of the talking. Mom and I will chime in when we can."

Silence hangs and my parents look at each other. A concerned message passes between them. My muscles tense up.

"What is it?" I ask.

They don't answer.

"You're kidding me," I say.

Dad sighs. "Will –"

"We're not telling her today?"

"No."

"You lied to me."

"Yes, we did."

My hand curls into a fist beneath the table. "Why?"

"Because it was the only way we could get you to come home."

I stare at them, disbelieving. My mom still hasn't spoken, just watches me worriedly.

"For her birthday?" I ask. "You lied just so I would come home this year?"

"Of course not," Dad says. He clasps his hands together and leans forward, looking at me intently. "We got word that a reporter might be onto us."

I blink, taking in this new information. We've been in hiding for fifteen years. The press gave up looking for us a long time ago, or so I thought.

"How do you know?" I ask.

"Someone's been digging into us. A couple red flags were raised recently. We think they might have found us."

"When is the story getting out?"

He shakes his head. "It won't."

"But we *have* to tell Lyla everything, in case it does – "

"It won't, Will. This isn't the first time someone's gotten close. We have people handling it."

I try to appeal to my mom, since my dad isn't listening. "What if it gets out this time, Mom? Do you really want Lyla finding everything out on the six o'clock news?"

She shakes her head, eyes teary. "Of course not."

"If the story leaks," Dad says, "we'll call you and warn you. Don't tell her anything until we can get there."

"What do you mean get there? Where will she be?"

"We'll have to handle the press here, Will. We can't just - "

"Where will Lyla be?" I say too loudly.

My dad looks at me intensely. "She'll be with you," he says. "In Good Hart."

I stare at him, not understanding. "I'm sorry, what?"

He speaks slowly, carefully. "That's why you're here. You'll be flying back home with Lyla tonight and she'll stay with you for as long as it takes for us to track down this reporter. Maybe a few weeks or so. Or the rest of the summer."

"The *summer*?"

"We're not sure. But it would be best for you both to lay low in a small town in case the story does get out. Which it won't."

My mouth is open in shock. "You're serious."

"Yes."

I let out a harsh laugh. "I don't believe this."

"Please, Will," my mom says. "Lay aside any bitterness you have against me and your father and think of Lyla. I know it's sudden, but we don't have a choice."

"There's *always* a choice. We can finally come out of hiding. People will know we've been living as the Brooks all these years, but so what? They'll get over it within a matter of weeks, when the next big story hits."

They don't respond.

I slowly stand to my feet, palms flat on the table. "We could call her down here right now and show her what's in this box," I say, shoving my finger at it. "We could tell her the truth. Right here, right now. She deserves it."

Silence.

I look at my mom and ask quietly, "How long are you going to beat yourself up about what happened?"

Her eyes fill with tears.

"If I had been there," she says, like she always does. "If I had been a better mother...maybe the dog wouldn't have gotten to her."

My jaw clenches because I agree with her.

"She won't blame you," I say.

"I know."

"You can't just keep the past from her forever because of it."

8

"Yes, we can, because we're her parents," she says. "It's our decision."

"That's not fair."

"I don't want her knowing any of it!" she shrieks and gets up from the table. She walks out through the kitchen and out the garage door. I start to follow her, livid. She's so dramatic sometimes. It's annoying.

"Sit down," Dad says.

"She's being selfish."

"Sit down, Malcolm!"

The use of my legal name makes me pause. Breathing hard, I sit slowly, staring at the stupid box that Lyla will apparently never get to open.

"Will, listen," Dad says.

"I'm *listening.*"

"We're waiting for the right time. It's not today. Trust me."

"You're a coward," I tell him before I think better of it.

Dad's eyes ignite. "Excuse me?"

"I'm just saying Lyla can handle it!"

"Oh, I see," he says. He leans back and folds his hands on his stomach in feigned calm. "And you know this for a fact?"

"Yes. She's eighteen years old now– "

He sits up. "And still wakes up every night screaming bloody murder!"

We both go absolutely silent at his outburst, listening for any movement upstairs. There's nothing.

I stare at him. "What are you talking about?"

"You know what I'm talking about."

"That's still going on? It's been years."

He sighs and rubs both hands down his face tiredly. "If you called every once in a while, or came home, you'd know."

I remember the sound of her screaming every night whenever I'd come home for a visit. When she was fifteen, she started to have nightmares about the dog that attacked her when she was three. She doesn't know it was a guard dog from the place we were staying at in Brazil. She doesn't know that our mom blames herself for it because she was a terrible mom back then and was never around.

"Has she seen a doctor about it?"

"Many. The best of the best. We've tried medications, therapy, everything. Nothing's worked."

"Is it still about the dog attack?"

Pain flickers in his eyes and he nods. "Your mother's been homeschooling her since her freshman year."

I try to picture my mom teaching anyone anything. I can't.

"She sleeps a lot throughout the day and has a hard time functioning. Her friends stopped coming around. We wanted to tell you but..." He trails off.

But I never call or come home anymore. He doesn't have to say it. I keep my distance from my sister, just like I keep my distance from most people.

"Who knows how she'd react to something like this right now," Dad says. "If we can avoid telling her, then we will. For a little while longer."

I don't respond because I still don't want my sister to come back with me to Good Hart. I hardly know her for one because she is nine years younger than me and we haven't been close at all since we were little – a time she doesn't even remember. Her being at my house will be awkward. Not only that, but apparently she'll be up screaming all night, every night. I don't want to have to hear it.

"I can't do it," I say. "I'm sorry."

I'm not sorry. My parents have woven a web of lies for fifteen years and now they're trying to drag me into it. Again.

"Why won't you do this for us?"

I frown at him. "Are you seriously asking that?"

"Yes."

"You said it could take all summer. I'm too busy."

"Doing *what*?" he snaps.

My back stiffens.

"After all we've done," he says. "It was all for nothing." He leans forward. "You're living exactly the way we didn't want you to."

I let out a slow breath through my nose. It takes all the self-control I can summon to not take a swing at my own father. I've been pretty successful at flipping houses in Michigan, but I'll never tell him that. I never touch my inheritance. I don't want to end up like my parents used to be.

"I live modestly," I say, "because you asked me to."

"You think that's what I'm talking about? We care about you making a way for yourself. Working hard. You did it with football but then you gave it all up when – "

"Yeah, okay," I say sarcastically. "*Great* time to bring that up, Dad."

He stops himself, takes a breath. "At least *pretend* you have a job while Lyla's there or else she might suspect something."

I laugh humorlessly to make it seem like his words didn't cut me. "You think I'm actually going to agree to this?"

He stands to his feet and walks around the kitchen island. I watch him, blood pounding through my ears. The old hurt and rage and sick need for his approval are warring inside me.

"I didn't want it to come to this," he says.

"Come to what?"

He takes a large envelope out of a drawer, and I'm reminded of what happened on my eighteenth birthday. I laugh harshly. "You trying to pay me off?"

He comes around and hands it to me. "Open it."

Shaking my head, I grab it from him and tear it open. I slide an embossed paper out.

"What's this?"

"The deed. To the Manor."

I stare at it, my mind clearing.

"And there's access to a trust with enough money to get it up and running and keep it that way. You can hire the staff again, or you can let it sit there and rot. We don't care. But we decided we'll give you the choice now. We can't protect you forever."

I slide the paper back into the envelope and set it down on the table. "Done."

He lets out a breath. "Just like that?"

I look away. "Just like that."

He takes the envelope back. "You'll get it when this is all over."

"But – "

"If you tell her anything, you won't see any of it."

I stand to my feet again. "I wouldn't do that behind your back."

"Don't act like you hadn't already thought about it, son."

Taking the envelope with him, he heads to the garage door, probably to go console Mom and tell her I accepted their offer. He looks at his watch.

"Your sister usually wakes up in about half an hour. She'll be happy to see you. Try to pretend like this was your idea for her birthday." He nods at the yellow box I brought for her. "Put that in a cupboard or something before she sees it. Your flight's in two hours."

After that, he leaves me here in the kitchen.

I turn and rake my hands through my hair because he's right about what he said: in the past few seconds since seeing the deed, I pictured myself telling Lyla everything tonight, in Good Hart. I pictured taking her straight to the Manor, showing her who she really is, and why I've been so distant. She hasn't known who I really am for all these years, who *she* really is. How do you have a relationship based off that? Without my parents around, what would be keeping me from telling her everything? Nothing.

But now, the Manor hangs in the balance. It's the only part of my inheritance from my grandfather that I actually want, and my parents have kept it from me this entire time. It's the only place I ever had any good memories. It's where I told Alexandra I loved her when I was only twelve; where I played with my sister for hours and watched her take her first steps; where Juanita, our nanny, and some of the staff, raised me whenever my parents weren't around. If I want the Manor, I'll have to keep up with this twisted charade for a while longer, like I have for fifteen years.

The difference is, now I won't be able to avoid Lyla like I've been doing. It'll be just me and her, every freaking day for weeks…or months, and I can't tell her anything.

All because some good-for-nothing journalist found us.

Samantha Foster
Down the street

I found them. The infamous Bailey family. I can't believe it. No one has been able to find them for fifteen years, except for me – a boring twenty-five-year-old from Chicago who runs a coffee shop with her mom and younger sister. Any journalist would kill for this story, and yet *I'm* the one who found them. At least, I'm pretty sure of it.

The Baileys. They are right down the street from me.

I'm hidden in my car with my eyes glued to the front door of their house. It's gray outside, the kind of day that makes random echoes of thunder without rain, but I still have big sunglasses on. I lift them every once in a while, to get a closer look at the house through my binoculars.

If I'm right and this house belongs to the infamous Baileys, then this is not what I expected to find at all. Middle class suburbs. Not even a gate at the entrance to the neighborhood. The house is simple, white with red brick, and the front door is a nice deep green. Pretty pink flowers overflow from a box in front of one of the windows. I wonder if they have someone who takes care of their flowers and gets them to look as full as they do. I've never been able to do that.

In the driveway sits a rental car that a man pulled up in a while ago. It's way nicer than my car, but still not the best he could have chosen. I'm hoping the man is their son, the heir.

The Malcolm Willard Bailey the Fourth.

I have a picture of Kathy Bailey pulled up on my phone. It's one of the last pictures ever taken of her, fifteen years ago. She has long, dark hair and she's holding a three-year-old daughter with the same dark hair, but bright blue eyes. I still haven't seen a daughter yet. She would be around seventeen or eighteen, and she would have those blue eyes.

If she exists, then I just might be onto something.

"You have to see if we're right," my mom said when we first discovered all of this.

My sister pushed me towards the door of our coffee shop.

"And then write about it!" Nell said.

I've only ever written one book about what happened to me. I don't post on my blog anymore, and I never even finished my journalism degree. There are a thousand reasons why I should just drive away and act like none of this ever happened.

As I think that, I pull my journal out of my purse and start writing.

Lyla Brooks

I walk all the way down the stairs with my eyes closed, hand on the railing, my body feeling heavy. This is normal for me. In about twenty minutes, I'll be awake enough to put a smile on my face for my parents, who I know will try to do something fun for my birthday. We'll have yellow lemon cake. They'll give me a few presents. Then we'll eat dinner later and I'll try to keep my eyes open long enough to watch a movie with them. I'm determined to not let them worry about me today. I'll act as normal as possible.

I yawn and rub my eyes as I reach the bottom of the stairs, hearing my mom in the kitchen.

"Morning, Mom," I say to her, turning the corner. My stomach is tight and cramping with hunger. "Do we have eggs?"

"It's not Mom," a deep voice says.

I stop in the doorway of the kitchen, blinking.

My brother is standing by the kitchen counter.

Will Brooks

I stare at my sister, trying not to show my shock. She's still pretty with her long, nearly-black curls and her bright blue eyes, but she is pale and has lost probably fifteen pounds since I last saw her.

"Will," she breathes.

"Hey, Lyla." I scratch behind my ear. "Happy birthday," I add, half-heartedly.

"Thanks…" She's flustered.

We stare at each other. Her pajamas are way too big for her. Her eyes are wide with shock but tired, the skin around them dark from lack of sleep. And there is a trace of sadness in them that I've never seen before.

Lyla reaches up and touches the hidden scar on the back of her neck, a habit of hers when she's nervous. I feel bad for being so surprised by her appearance. She laughs, soft, and looks down at herself, her other hand going to the hem of her shirt. She tugs. "I probably look a little different."

I swallow and shake my head.

She smiles. "Yeah, I do. It's okay."

I don't say anything because for the first time in my life, I am thinking that maybe my parents are right. She isn't ready to hear it. Maybe it is best to send her away for a while.

"I've missed you," she says. "I…"

She presses her lips together. Then, without warning, she heads straight over to me and throws her arms around my neck. I grunt because the wind is knocked out of me.

"Sorry," she whispers.

"It's okay."

"Hi," she says.

"Hi." I hug her back, all the tension draining out of my body. It feels good to hug her, like this is normal, like we're close. I can't remember the last time we hugged, but she definitely feels different in my arms. Fragile. Like she's a little girl again. My throat suddenly grows tight with emotion. I don't know why. I clear it out and let her go.

She backs up. "What are you doing here?"

Looking at my sister – at her tired, sad eyes – I feel something give way inside me. My pride, probably. Sure, I don't understand why my parents have never told her, but I can understand why they're not telling her now. Until the nightmares stop, we'll put it off.

I take a breath, and then I tell her that I'm taking her back with me to Good Hart for a while, for her birthday present.

I try to sound like I've been planning this for weeks.

I try to sound like I'm looking forward to it.

Samantha Foster
Down the Street

Nothing has happened at the house for the past hour. I'm still just staring at it, waiting for some sort of movement, and waiting for my mom to answer the phone. Mom is even more excited than I am about this. While I was only ten when the Baileys dropped off the face of the earth, my mom – like the rest of the world – followed every news report about them until the press finally gave up looking for them. She knows more about the story than most, and she's been telling me and Nell all about it since this first began.

My phone rings and I jump and grab it from the center console. It's my mom.

"You're not going to believe this," I say immediately.

She gasps. "What happened?"

"A guy pulled up in a rental car a little while ago. From the way Kathy hugged him, I think he's their son. He's about my age."

"You're kidding!" she says excitedly. "Nell! Come in here! Someone pulled up to the house. Samantha thinks he's the son." There's a pause. "Hold on, Nell wants to talk to you."

There is a fumbling sound as my sister grabs the phone. Her voice is too close to the phone, too loud.

"Is he cute?" she exclaims. "He'll be the most eligible bachelor in *America* when you write this."

I roll my eyes. "Nell, really?"

She waits for an answer.

"Alright, yes," I admit, pinching the bridge of my nose. "He's sort of cute. But I couldn't see very well from here."

"I knew it. Rich people always have attractive kids."

I shake my head. That is so something my sister would say. It's why I won't tell her just how attractive the man actually is. When he pulled up to the house and I watched nervously, sitting low in my seat, I found myself studying him with my binoculars. I told myself it was just so I could detail him later in my story about this. He had work boots on with jeans and a button up shirt rolled up at the sleeves. There was a small yellow shoebox in his hands. His hair was dark and a little messy, his jaw stubbly.

I couldn't see his eyes. The dad and two children were known for what people called their "Bailey blues."

"I'll put you on speaker," Nell says.

A second later, I hear the low rumble of customers behind them. I feel slightly guilty for not being there for the evening rush, but they're the ones who told me to do this.

"So, what do we do now?" Mom asks.

"I don't know. I'm hoping something will just happen on its own. They've been in there for a long time."

"You should go peek through the windows," Nell says. "Maybe they're drinking expensive champagne and eating caviar."

I laugh. "I'm not about to get caught looking in their windows." I pick up my binoculars and look through them again. "I already feel like a stalker."

My mom sighs happily. "I can't believe this is happening."

"I know," I say excitedly.

"Have you seen the daughter?" she asks.

"Not yet."

"She'd be around eighteen," she tells me. "And the son would be twenty-seven."

"Yep." I went to the library and collected every article and book I could find on them. The stacks of research are in the car with me, filling up the seats like faithful passengers.

When the first article was published about the elusive Malcolm – who always went by Mark – and Kathy Bailey having a boy, it was twenty-seven years ago. People speculated that they named him Malcolm Willard Bailey the Fourth because he might possibly be named after the men on his father's side. Nobody knows for sure. Then, another article came out fifteen years ago with that picture of Kathy Bailey out shopping in Brazil, holding a three-year-old girl – a daughter the press didn't know about. Then they disappeared.

Nell says, "He's probably around your perfect dating age."

"Nell..."

"What? I'm just saying."

My sister has been trying to set me up with someone for months, but I am keeping my distance from guys right now. I'm not ready for a relationship again.

"The shop's busy," Nell says. "I'll handle it. You two talk and update me in a little while."

I hear my mom take me off speaker, and I can picture her sitting on the desk in the office next to the coffee bar.

"I just can't believe this is happening," she says again contentedly.

"I know. It's crazy." I open a yogurt and spoon some into my mouth.

"What are you eating?" she asks.

I end up talking with a full mouth. "Yogurt." I swallow. "You should see me. I have a cooler stocked with food and a thermos of coffee. It's a very official stake-out I have going on here."

"Good for you," she laughs. "Hat and sunglasses?"

"Hoodie, sunglasses...binoculars," I tell her.

"You're kidding!"

"I told you I can't get too close to the house."

"I think you're being a little paranoid, honey." She pauses. "Hold on. Let me call you back. Your sister needs help. She looks flustered."

Even though Nell was running the shop all by herself when my mom and I came into her life, Nell has some issues dealing with stress, we've noticed. It comes from a long, hard past. Some days are harder than others. Sometimes she makes random decisions or comments without seeming to connect a consequence to it. I'm still getting to know her, and so is my mom.

I tell my mom I'll call her if anything changes. We hang up, then I stare at the house some more, eating my blueberry yogurt. If something doesn't happen soon, maybe it would be best to just go home, back to my normal boring life...avoiding Brian, trying to heal, trying to be happy.

I pick up the binoculars again, telling myself that if I don't see a teenaged daughter within the next hour, I'll leave. No matter what.

Lyla

Even though I am as slow-moving as always, I am very excited as I pack my things with my mom. I decided to wear my favorite yellow-flowered sundress with white sneakers, because I am eighteen years old today and I'm going on a plane for the first time ever...with my brother. I have wanted to do this for so long, and my parents know it, but they always change the subject whenever I bring it up, or they say, "Yeah, maybe," which always means no.

Then, all of a sudden, my brother shows up here to take me back with him. This is the best birthday ever.

My mom is quiet as we start to pack. I wonder if she's worried. I'm a little worried about how things will be too, but way more excited than anything else.

I close some dried leaves into a book and put it into my backpack, telling my mom that maybe Will would like the leaves sitting out for decoration. They're from the tree in the backyard, the one that Will hung a tire from to practice throwing a football through. After that, my mom and I decide to pack even more decorations. I wrap some framed pictures of our family into socks and tuck some candles and jars into sweaters. By the end, we have filled an entire suitcase with decorations. We pack my dresses into another one, always optimistic that the nightmares will go away and I'll be a normal person. We pack lots of pajamas, too, because we know that won't happen. Also, a few pairs of earplugs for Will.

By this point my mom is laying down some ground rules: Calling daily to check in with them. Never going anywhere without Will, unless I get permission from Dad to go out with friends, or especially with a boy.

I laugh. "Yeah, Mom, I'm sure I'll make lots of friends and start dating a boy immediately."

I'm being sarcastic, because as excited as I am about all of this, I know that not much is going to change. I will still be asleep most of the time during the day and won't have much energy or time for making new friends. Especially going out on a date with a guy. I've never been out with a boy. Ever. Not even Justin. We didn't get that far before he wrecked everything.

"You never know," my mom says, grinning. "I met your father when I was eighteen."

I smile. "So I've heard. A thousand times."

She smiles back at me for a second, and then it slowly fades as she takes my hand.

"I love you," she says urgently. "No matter what happens, you know that, right?"

My mom has always been slightly dramatic. It hits her like a flareup sometimes. Still, though, I blink at her, concerned. "Yeah. Of course. I love you too."

"And I love your brother. So much. I hope you can…bring some light to his life. I don't think he has anyone else."

I nod, wondering about the grip of her hand on mine, the look in her eyes.

"I've always wanted to do this," I remind her, although now I'm starting to question things.

Was this Will's idea, or theirs? Is there something else going on here?

I hug her, and when she pulls back gently after a second, she wipes a tear away. I smile, immediately trying to make her feel better. It's a reflex of mine, maybe from years of trying to convince people that I'm okay. Trying to convince myself of that, too.

"I'll try to make him some friends," I tell her. "Maybe I can even get him a girlfriend."

She laughs and swipes at another tear. "Right. I'm sure he'll be all for that."

A few minutes later, we start to walk out with my three suitcases, two duffle bags and my backpack. I stop and look back. I won't be here for a whole month. Maybe even for the rest of the summer, like Will said. It's crazy. I love my room; it's small but so cozy because I spend so much time in here. It feels strange leaving it now, like it's really sinking in.

I look over at the corner of carpet where I always wake up screaming and rocking back and forth, and then I turn and walk out without looking back. I try not to worry about what my room in Will's house will be like, what corner I'll wake up screaming in.

I have a feeling that things are going to be different there. I don't know what that means, but something is changing. For better or for worse, I don't know.

But I'm about to find out.

Samantha

The front door of the house suddenly opens. I gasp and toss my journal back into my purse, fumbling for my phone. I call my mom. "Pick up, Mom. Pick up. Pick up!"

It's that man again, the one who pulled up in the rental car. He's walking back to it with suitcases.

"Sorry about that," Mom says casually when she answers on the fourth ring.

I practically scream at her: "He's coming out of the house!"

She gasps. "Who?"

"The son."

"Oh my gosh."

I hear some shuffling, and then my mom quietly calls Nell back into the office.

I watch carefully, eyes wide behind my binoculars. "He's got big purple suitcases and duffle bags. He's putting them in the trunk."

"Purple?" Nell asks, intrigued.

"Yeah." I duck down when he pauses and glances around. But there's no way he can see me. My car doesn't stand out from any others on the street.

"Are his eyes blue?" Mom asks.

"I can't tell from here."

"Of course they are!" Nell says frantically.

I see a flash of yellow as someone else comes out of the house. I swing my binoculars over there. "Wait," I say. The yellow I saw was a teenaged girl in a sundress. "There's a teenaged girl! She's coming out too. Okay, okay. She's probably his sister. You guys, she has the same exact hair her mom used to have!"

"Oh my gosh," Nells says. "It's them. It's the Baileys. Nobody panic."

"It still might not be them," I tell her.

"It's them! Tell us everything!"

I list off the details in a rush. "Okay, there's Mark and Kathy. It looks like Kathy is crying a little. She's hugging her kids."

"Don't you know their names?" Nell asks.

Mom answers for me. "The son is probably Malcolm, or maybe he goes by Mark like his dad. But no one knows the daughter's name. It was never released to the press."

"They're getting in the car!"

Nell and Mom are both in a panic. "Okay, okay…"

"They're driving away. What do I do?"

"Follow them!" Nell says.

"Really?"

"*Yes*," Mom agrees.

"What about the shop?"

"I can handle the shop without either of you," Nell says anxiously, not knowing how that comment sounds to us.

"Samantha Marie, you *have* to do this," Mom says.

"Okay, okay, okay, okay…" I am nodding and buckling my seatbelt. Then I start the car once Mark and Kathy go back inside.

"They're probably going to the airport since he's in a rental car," she says. "You have to find out where they're flying to."

"What if they're going to Australia? Or China or something? It could be anywhere."

Mom ignores me. "Make sure to count to five before you follow. Don't be too obvious."

I count to three and then throw the car into drive and pull out into the road, breathing hard. "Okay, okay, okay, okay…This is happening."

"Calm down," Mom says, although she's just as frantic. "I don't want you to crash. This is no big deal."

"Mom. I'm following the *Baileys*. This is a *huge* deal! What will I do when I get to the airport?"

There's a long pause. "You'll follow them," Nell says. "No matter where they're going. Your story depends on it."

Sienna Rodriguez
Chicago O'Hare Airport

My hands are clenched tightly together behind my back as I wait for my new clients to arrive at their terminal. I've scanned the small group of people waiting for our flight, and I've decided no one is suspicious, nothing is out of the ordinary. Although, there is one man who is rather large and would be difficult to take down if I had to. If he ends up sitting next to my clients, then I might try to arrange getting his seating assignment changed...

I try to relax and remind myself again that there is no overt threat to my clients. No one even knows they are the kids of a multi-billionaire.

Even so, I have made my opinion very clear to my team leader that it will be almost impossible for me to provide adequate protection for the siblings under these circumstances. Usually, I would have a team of at least three right now, maybe even five. The Baileys could afford it. We would have driven our clients to the airport after sending at least one officer ahead to run recon. We would get the siblings through check in, security, and then onto their private jet without being more than five feet away from them the entire time. Depending on the airport, we might be armed.

As it is, I am alone. I am unarmed. I did not drive them here, or even follow them. I was asked to wait for them at the terminal, and I reluctantly followed orders. On the flight, I will be sitting in the very back of the plane, while they will be four rows from the front. This is all so that they won't know they have protection.

My neck and back muscles are all knotted up because I have absolutely no control over, or eyes on, my clients right now. This case is going to be harder than I thought. I've gone from overt close protection, to covert. No, this is just surveillance, really, and it's a far cry from the professional experience I've had since starting in this industry.

I have traveled to the farthest countries and most remote islands in the world, ridden in private jets and helicopters and even on the back of an elephant in Thailand, and occasionally been in more danger than I was during my time in Iraq – all while guarding Tessa Lands, the daughter of billionaire oil mogul Richard Lands. She was the first client I landed as an executive protection officer. I went everywhere she went. I heard everything, saw everything, even saved her life multiple times…from situations she brought upon herself.

After just three years, I couldn't take it anymore. I quit a few weeks ago.

Her parents understood but Tessa was affronted, asking me just who I thought I was and all that, that I would quit working for *her*. She tried to fire me herself, screaming the words at me, but her parents just rolled their eyes at her and apologized to me and then I walked out of their 20,000 square foot summer home for the last time, with my last, generous paycheck.

At twenty-nine years old, I was extremely wealthy but unemployed, and questioning the very purpose of my life. My dream had been to start my own company of executive protection officers that are solely women. High profile parents can trust women with their daughters, no questions asked. If I were a rich parent with a daughter, I would prefer to have a woman guarding her, and properly trained women are few and far between in this industry. My plan was to fix that problem. Unfortunately, Tessa caused me to rethink all of it.

Until I received a phone call last week that changed everything.

I am back on the job now, but this time, I am assigned to an heiress who has no idea she is an heiress. In just thirty days, give or take, I will be paid more than I used to make in a year. Not only that, but there are two female officers who have heard of me and want to work for me when this is over. If all goes well, I'll actually have a company soon.

That is, if I can adequately do my job guarding clients from an uncomfortable distance like this.

I glance down the hall through the sea of people, and my senses suddenly quicken. I have spotted them – Malcolm Willard Bailey the Fourth and Lillianna Elizabeth Bailey. In the flesh. They are going by Will and Lyla now.

I watch as they find seats, and I memorize what they're wearing so I can better keep track of them. Will's in cargo pants, work boots, and a light button up shirt rolled up at the sleeves. Lyla's in sneakers and a yellow sundress that stands out like a beacon of light. They sit down together not far from me.

I casually turn away and pull my phone out to contact Emil, the only other officer assigned to them. He's already in Good Hart.

I text, **I have eyes on.**

A response text comes within seconds. **Sounds good.**

I frown. *Sounds good?*

I send another text. **Flight scheduled to depart on time.**

No response. I send the same information to our team leader – Carlos Sanchez – who is unfortunately staying behind in Chicago. He sends an appropriate, professional response, and I slide my phone back into my pocket.

I'm starting to wonder about the officer in Good Hart I'm going to be sharing a house with and working with. All I know about him is that his name is Emil Alanovic and he's been living on the property next door to Will's for five years, watching over him from a distance without Will's knowledge. I've been looking forward to working with someone who must be the best of the best, since he's been with the Baileys for so long. I'm hoping he'll be willing to share some of his knowledge and experience with me and maybe even use some of his contacts to spread the word about my company.

Lyla says something to Will, and he nods and points down the hall. Lyla stands to her feet and heads towards a bathroom that's about twenty yards away. Straightening, I glance around. When Lyla disappears through the doorway, I casually follow her. I hate this. Tessa could never walk through an airport unguarded. People would recognize her immediately. With Lyla, though, no one knows who she is. Not even her.

She might find out soon, though. If her parents can't stop what's been set into motion, the whole world might.

Samantha Foster
Chicago O'Hare Airport

I am officially a stalker. There is no other way to put it. I can't even call myself a writer because I'm *not* a writer. Not really. Just because I've written one book and have an old blog doesn't mean anything.

I glance over at them. I am pretty sure they're the Baileys now. They both have the Bailey blues. When I saw that as we stood in line at the check in counter, I almost gasped out loud.

Thankfully the woman behind the counter was enthralled by the brother and asked intrusive questions. I can't blame her. He is one of the most attractive men I've ever seen in real life, especially with those blue eyes and his hard jaw lined with dark stubble. Because of the woman's nosy questions, I found out they are traveling to a town called Pellston, Michigan. The woman asked if that's where he lives, and his sister answered for him when he didn't.

"He lives in Good Hart," she said happily.

I've never even heard of Good Hart, but at least it's not in Australia or China. Michigan isn't too far. I stepped up to the counter, shaking, and I bought a one-way ticket for an insane amount of money.

So now we are all waiting for flight 2158 to Pellston, Michigan. But I – being paranoid and stressed out – am sitting at another gate so it looks like I'm waiting for a different flight heading to Phoenix.

Workers wave their glow sticks around outside the big window next to me as others load luggage onto the plane heading for Phoenix. Some of the people sitting around me are dressed in shorts and button-up shirts dotted with palm leaves. Most look retired or close to it. The man next me to shifts his weight and is too close to me now. Abruptly, I stand up and go to the window, feeling like I can't breathe. I can't believe I'm doing this. I just cannot believe it.

I stop in front of the window, sliding my ticket into my back pocket. I risk a glance over my shoulder at the two people I'm stalking. The girl is glancing around excitedly. She yawns every so often, pretty in her yellow dress that's a little too big for her. Her brother just sits there, not talking to her, not looking at his phone even, just sits there. He seems unfriendly to me, like he thinks he's better than everyone else, his sister included. He's ignoring her.

Suddenly, he looks right at me.

I gasp and quickly face the window. This is crazy. I am crazy for doing this. Maybe I should get on this plane to Phoenix instead. I could trade in my ticket at the counter nearby. Maybe what I need is a vacation where I can think things through about Brian and come to terms with everything. It'll be hot in Phoenix this time of year, but it would be like that feeling of getting into a hot car after you've been in a cold grocery store and you just sit there for a second while it warms your blood. That sounds nice right now. Comforting.

My phone dings with a text and I pull it out of my purse. It's my sister.

Not many places to stay because it's so last minute. But I found this cottage. Check it out! It's on the beach!

I stare at my phone. Am I really going through with this?

She sent the link, so I hesitantly press it and it goes to a page about the cottage. It's small and white, two story. It looks well-kept. There's only one picture of the cottage and the rest of the pictures are of the town of Good Hart. A little red-faced general store. A small highway running beneath what they call the Tunnel of Trees. The gentle waves of the massive Lake Michigan with white beaches and tall, wind-blown grasses stretching for miles.

And it all makes me feel like I'm welcome there. Like I should go there. I don't know why.

I decide to just call about the house. It can't hurt. And if I'm going to do this, I might as well stay in a cottage on the beach. I find the number for the caretaker and I dial it. Someone picks up on the first ring.

"Hello, this is Dorothy," she says.

She sounds exactly like a Dorothy would sound.

"Um, yes," I whisper. "Hi, Dorothy. I was calling about your cottage for rent?"

"I'm sorry, what was that?"

I repeat what I said, above a whisper this time.

"Oh, yes!" She goes into all the details – one bedroom with a loft, great views, small kitchen with appliances and utensils, fully furnished.

"Great," I say. I close my eyes. I can't believe I'm about to say this. "I'll take it for the week."

If nothing happens in one week, I'll come home.

Dorothy takes my credit card over the phone. "Oh, and the key's in the light by the door."

This is happening. A week in Good Hart, digging into this family's life to see if they're the Baileys. I'm crazy.

"Enjoy yourself!" Dorothy says.

"I will." I hope. "Um…before you hang up…" I lower my voice and put my hand over my mouth as I speak. "Do you happen to know a man who lives in town with the last name of…Brooks?"

There's a hint of curiosity in her old voice now. "Will Brooks?"

I sigh. Will? I look back at him and his sister. His name would be Malcolm. I'm almost sure of it. Although, maybe he goes by Will because of his middle name - Willard. "Maybe we're not talking about the same guy. He's, um, tall, dark hair."

"A little unkempt? Blue eyes?"

"Yes. And he's – "

She cuts me off. "A real cutie?" She's starting to sound twenty years younger.

"Yes, he's…sort of attractive."

"Yes, I know him. As well as anyone can, I guess. He keeps to himself."

"And…how do you know him?"

"Well, everyone knows him, but he bought my house a while ago and he's renovating it right now."

Renovating?

"I've heard he's planning to sell it soon. He flips houses in the area, although I think he might keep the one he bought from me. He's been in it five years while he's been fixing up some others."

He flips houses? My heart sinks. Maybe this was all for nothing. It's not them.

"Is he a friend of yours?" Dorothy asks.

"Oh," I say quickly. "Yeah, no. Not really. My…mom knows his mom…"

"And is he the reason you're coming for a visit?"

"No. I just…I thought he was – never mind."

"Ah, I see," she says curiously. "Well, you're right. He is."

"He's what?"

"Single."

I give an abrupt laugh.

Dorothy giggles. "I'm serious. Maybe you'll be the one. He doesn't date, dear, and people are starting to talk."

"Oh!" I shake my head. "No, no. That's not…Anyway, thanks! My plane is boarding so I have to run." It's true. Everyone is in line already, including the two people who are definitely *not* the Baileys. My palms start to sweat. Am I still going? Should I still do this? I frantically shove my wallet back in my purse with my free hand. I'll be the last one to board.

"Let me know if you need anything else," Dorothy says. "I know the area and the locals better than most."

I pause, biting my lip, then ask, "Would you be…willing to give me his address?" My heart is pounding. "I mean…I might as well stop by and say hi, if I get a chance."

"Of course, dear. From what I know, he could use a friend."

I don't know what she means by that, but I don't think much about it because I'm frantically grabbing my notebook with all my notes about the Baileys out of my purse. I start writing as Dorothy gives me Will's information. But the whole time I'm thinking this is pointless, this is stupid, I am crazy.

We end the call, and after I shove the notebook back in my purse, I stand here, frozen, staring at the line that is slowly diminishing as people board our plane. I see the two siblings in line. They hand their boarding passes over, and the sister's yellow dress is absorbed into the small crowd as they disappear.

I don't move. My phone is still in my hands. I think of calling Mom and Nell and telling them we were wrong. They aren't the Baileys. This was a complete waste of time. The only thing it really served to do was to prove to me that I need therapy.

And I'm definitely not going.

But then, as if a sign from heaven drops down into my hands at that very moment, I get a text. From Brian.

Please talk to me. What are you so afraid of?

I'm going.

I throw my phone into my purse and stride towards the gate.

I feel rather bad for the woman who scans my boarding pass because it is slightly damp from my clammy, shaking hands. She eyes me curiously, and I walk quickly past her and out the door that leads outside. I stop immediately when I see our little plane with a metal staircase leading up to it. It's devastatingly small. It's also about to have its door closed by a flight attendant.

I quickly start over to it.

"Wait!" I yell, and the woman stops and looks at me, then waves me over. I hurry up the steps, glancing back at the airport just once.

And then I'm actually boarding the plane.

The pilot greets me with a flight attendant. I choke out a hello and turn to see that the plane is not only devastatingly small, but also devastatingly empty. The left side of it has rows of two seats, and the right side has rows of only one seat. And there they are; the man who is possibly Malcolm Willard Bailey the Fourth, and his little sister. They are four rows back.

"Ma'am, please take your seat," the flight attendant says behind me.

Evidently, I've stopped in the middle of the aisle.

"Right. Sorry."

I glance at my ticket and slowly walk down the aisle, looking for my seat while trying to keep my face turned away from them. My feet come to a stop when I see my seat assignment, and so does my heart.

My seat is right across the aisle from them. Of course.

"Ma'am," says the flight attendant again.

I can't help it – I look down at them and see that the man named Will is staring at me. He's in the window seat, and his sister is in the aisle seat across from mine. For one short second I imagine myself running back down the aisle of the plane and jumping out the door. But in reality, I clumsily sink into my seat, put my seatbelt on, and turn to face the window. I can't breathe because my purse is clutched so tightly to my chest. I try to relax but can't. If they see me around town now, they will recognize me from the plane. Will they suspect I followed them?

"You'll have to store your purse beneath the seat in front of you," the same blasted flight attendant tells me.

I nod and bend over to store it, seeing out of the corner of my eye that the girl is looking at me now too. The corner of my journal that's filled with notes about them is poking out of my purse, and I quickly shove it back inside and make sure the whole thing is stored safely beneath the seat. A little turbulence could mean the entire thing spilling out into the aisle. I should've gotten a purse that zipped.

Okay, breathe. You're fine. They hardly even noticed you. They don't know you're following them.

But all ten of my fingers are clamped around the armrests. The flight attendant goes into her happy speech about what to do if the plane crash-lands and we all happen to survive.

All of a sudden, I'm afraid to fly.

No, I'm not afraid to fly, I'm afraid of *everything* right now – the Baileys finding out they've been followed, my whole plan being shot because they've seen me, crash-landing into Lake Michigan and having to use my seat cushion as a flotation device as the Baileys splash around beside me in the dark water...

I shake my head and snap out of it. We start rolling down the runway and then our tiny plane is taking off. We lift into the night air with nothing but wings and engines holding us up. This is ridiculous. Why am I so scared? I've never been this afraid to fly. I close my eyes, my face turned towards the window. My ears pop. I feel a little sick.

Suddenly, a warm hand covers mine on the armrest. I open my eyes and look across the aisle. The girl is holding my hand.

She smiles.

"What's your name?" she asks.

It takes me a second to answer. "Samantha."

"I'm Lyla," she says.

Lyla Bailey, I think. *Lyla Brooks.*

Her arm hangs across the aisle like a bridge. I notice that her brother is leaning his head against the window with his eyes closed, seeming asleep already.

"Everything will be okay," Lyla says.

Her calm words make me blink at her. She said it so matter-of-factly, with a smile you can't help but smile back at. She's comforting me. The girl who might be Lyla Bailey is comforting the woman who followed her.

"I'm a little nervous, too," she says. "This is my first time on a plane."

I stare at her. "It is?"

"Yeah. I'm so excited!"

Two possibilities rise up in my mind. Either this is not a Bailey and her brother isn't either, or…this girl has no idea who she really is.

Suddenly, I feel linked to her. I didn't know who I was either for a very long time.

Still holding my hand, Lyla looks straight ahead. I take the opportunity to study her out of the corner of my eye, and I see myself in her, although we look nothing alike. Lyla has more hair than anyone I've ever seen. It's beautiful – dark and thick, curling down over her shoulders and past her elbows, resting on the yellow of her dress. There are faint circles under her eyes, and her skin is pale. But her lovely blue eyes dance with excitement because she thinks this is her first time on a plane. If I am right and these two are members of the infamous Bailey family, then this girl has no clue about any of it.

Maybe that's why this happened to me, of all people.

I squeeze Lyla's hand.

"Thanks for comforting me," I tell her. "I feel better."

And I do. Lyla has some sort of peace about her. It seems to spread from her hand and all the way up my arm, to my heart. She smiles at me again warmly and lets go of my hand. I should feel embarrassed about a teenager having to comfort me – especially her in particular considering why I'm even on this flight. But all I feel is…peaceful now.

Her brother is watching. I meet his eyes. They might be the same sparkling color as his sister's, but they're harder. His expression makes me think of a wall.

My nerves tighten again and I feel exposed and vulnerable and scrutinized by this very attractive, very off-putting man.

Lyla smiles at him and then looks back over at me. I turn to face the window, thinking maybe I did the right thing by following them.

Or maybe this was a terrible idea.

Will

My sister falls asleep eventually, which I expected. Her head rests against my shoulder, her dark hair covering my arm and some of my shirt. Her expression is slightly troubled in sleep.

I sigh and try to loosen my jaw, opening it like I'm popping my ears. It's tight from stress. Or anger. Or both.

Rubbing my neck, I find myself glancing across the aisle at the attractive woman who held Lyla's hand when we were taking off. She still hasn't moved, just sits stiffly looking out her window even though there's nothing to see except darkness. She must be afraid of flying.

Although part of me wonders if she was holding Lyla's hand because my sister was the one who was nervous, because she thinks this is her first time on the plane. Maybe the woman noticed and reached out to comfort her.

I wouldn't know. I was pretending to be asleep, and I'm not sure why.

I look down at Lyla, feeling this warmth in my chest I haven't felt in a long time. When's the last time she was close to me like this? Asleep on my shoulder like this? Probably when she was little.

I was nine when she was born. Lillianna Elizabeth Bailey. I remember thinking that if my parents loved her more than they loved me, I would run away or something. I thought my mom would carry her everywhere she went, like people normally do with babies. But once I saw that my parents simply handed her off to Juanita and went about their normal, extravagant lives, I felt for this little girl. I wanted to be around her constantly. I decided I would teach her everything, since my parents clearly wouldn't. Juanita was a good woman, loving but very strict and firm. I wouldn't be that way with my Lills. She had me wrapped around her finger until she was three.

Then everything changed. New life, new name. After a while it became apparent that my parents saw no need to ever talk about the past with Lyla. The distance grew between us, and I got angrier and angrier.

Now, here we are. I hardly know my sister. Damage has been done and I don't think it can ever be repaired.

A sudden panic rises up in me. What am I going to do with her in Good Hart?

A bump of turbulence makes Lyla shift in her sleep, but she stays there on my shoulder. I rest my head back and close my eyes for a second, remembering what it was like to hold Lyla when she was little, and feeling bad for not letting myself come home. But it's not like my family's come out to visit me either. It's a two-way street.

I turn my face to the window again and look out into the night, restless. We must be over the lake now. It's like an ominous, black sea…fitting for the beginning of our journey. I'm not looking forward to getting back to Good Hart with Lyla. There are things laying around that'll need to be hidden tonight before she sees them, so I'm hoping she'll be asleep when we get home. I'll wait to wake her up so I can put it all in my garage that I keep locked. Part of me wants to leave it all out and show her immediately when we arrive. This is who we are. Or used to be. You're a Bailey.

But I know I can't. Not if I want the Manor.

Maybe I'll go there later tonight. Just before we left today, my dad said to leave Lyla alone when she wakes up from the nightmares because she gets embarrassed. She won't even know I'm gone.

I look down at Lyla again, then glance over across the aisle. I'm surprised to see that the woman is looking at me now. Her expression has calmed slightly. Her eyes are a stunning light brown, lighter than her skin. Her hair is straight and black. I wonder what ethnicity she is. She blinks a few times, but she doesn't look away. Then her eyes go down to my sleeping sister, and she turns and faces the window again.

For some reason I think of Alexandra. I think of my mom never being around. I think of Juanita never reaching out to find me after all these years.

My jaw flexes again. I turn to face my window too, deciding to not look at the beautiful woman again.

Sienna Rodriguez

The flight to Michigan is uneventful. I couldn't even see Will and Lyla the whole time since I was in the back row. Ridiculous. I've never done anything like this.

After landing, the plan is that I will be the last one off the plane, and I'll head straight to the house before Will and Lyla get home, which I don't like, either. I'll see my new headquarters, meet Emil, and get things set up before the Baileys arrive home.

The Pellston airport is like a log cabin. There are stuffed bears and mountain lions at baggage claim and a stone fireplace that sits as the center piece of the small airport. Lyla is taking it all in like she has just woken up to a dream world. She grabs about ten tourist brochures from a stand and then looks around at everything while Will waits for her luggage. That's where I reluctantly leave them. I walk out to the dark parking lot and look for my car that Emil said would be sitting in the west corner. It's nothing flashy, but I don't mind. I text Emil that I am on my way, and then – going against all of my training, all of my experience – I head out without my clients.

Twenty minutes later, Emil isn't outside to meet me when I pull into the driveway of the house that's on the property next to Will's. I am slightly annoyed when I have to knock. I texted him my ETA, and he makes me knock? There is a big pot that's been tipped over on the porch, the soil spreading to the front welcome mat. Welcome indeed. There are boards on the windows that a lot of locals put up for the winter, but I wonder if Emil has them up year-round. The siding of the house is a dark wood that looks to be cedar.

I knock again. It takes more than thirty seconds for Emil to answer. When he does I see a tall, well-built man a little older than me. From his file I know that he is thirty-three, and he was in the army before he became a professional private security agent. His military background shows in his build and shortly cropped dark hair. He's in a white t-shirt and jogging pants. It looks like he's just woken up. I think maybe his shirt is on backwards, like he pulled it on in a hurry. In fact, he is still tugging it down over his torso.

I clear my throat and look up at his face.

"Hey," he says.

Hey? "Hello," I return professionally.

He squints. "You're a woman."

I groan inwardly. It looks like he hasn't seen a woman in six months. And I'm about to be his roommate.

"We've been texting all day," I remind him.

"Yeah, but Carlos introduced you as Rodriguez. I pictured a big Mexican guy."

"Spanish," I say, curbing my temper. "And yes, I'm a woman. Sorry to disappoint."

"I'm not disappointed. Just surprised." He laughs softly. "Sorry. I've heard I don't always give a great first impression."

No kidding.

"I'm Emil Alanovic," he says casually, extending his hand.

"I know. Sienna Rodriguez." I shake his hand quickly before stepping past him into the house.

"Come on in," he mutters under his breath as he shuts the door behind me.

"The Baileys will be arriving within thirty minutes," I tell him. "I last saw them at baggage claim. Carlos told me to get settled in before they get home and my shift starts."

"Your shift?"

"Yes. I can take night shift tonight."

He laughs, and then he must realize that I'm serious because it dies off. "Sure, that…sounds good." He clears his throat and gestures for me to lead down the bare hallway.

"I'll give you the grand tour of our lavish headquarters," he says sarcastically. He pushes a pair of French doors open on our left. "This is the fully equipped workout center."

It is a makeshift, disorganized gym. There is a punching bag in the corner with no mat beneath it, just the carpet, and a single bench with free weights strewn around it. Even the weights on the stand aren't in order by size and weight.

"And on down this way," he says, passing me, "is the kitchen and living room." He hurries to pick up a few TV dinner boxes that are out on the counter and he stuffs them into the overflowing trash can. There is a smell in the air, cologne mixed with something moldy.

"I would've cleaned up if I'd known…you know," he says, stacking two pizza boxes.

I look away to survey the living room that adjoins the kitchen. There is a tall bookshelf filled with books by Vince Flynn, Tom Clancy, John Grisham, but mostly by Louis L'Amour. A big TV is connected to a gaming console and two wireless remotes sit on the coffee table, next to three empty beer bottles.

"You have friends here?" I ask.

"Yeah. A couple guys from around town. They were here tonight."

"Do they know what you do for a living?"

"Of course not. They think I'm renting my parents' house and living off their money."

He scratches his stubbly chin. It's ironic, I think, that to get to where he is, he has to be the best of the best. Seeing him as he is, you'd never know it. He is guarding the heir to one of the most massive fortunes in America. But he comes off like a frat boy.

"And where is Will's house?"

He points to the north-facing window and I go to it and look out.

"You won't see much," he says. "We're on a few acres. So is Will."

All I can see is the dark forest of thick trees. No lights. I suddenly feel very secluded and very uncomfortable being here alone with this strange man I've never met before tonight. Dark memories start to return but I push them away. No need to be paranoid. I can take care of myself. I straighten and come into the kitchen with Emil.

"Do you want a beer or anything?" he asks, opening the fridge.

"No thank you. I'm on the job." I didn't mean for that to sound so condescending, but it did.

"Right," he says, and I think he is trying not to smile as he grabs a beer and pops the cap off on the corner of the linoleum counter.

He leans back against the oven and takes a sip of his beer, eyeing me. The muscles in his arms are very defined, and he has a tattoo of a cross on the inner bicep of his left arm. There's a big scar right next to it. Looks like a bullet wound.

"Lyla knows Carlos, right?" he asks.

"Hmm?"

He is amused. "Carlos. Lyla knows him? Or else he would've come here himself."

"Right," I say quickly.

I tuck my hair behind my ears self-consciously. I am not used to feeling self-conscious. It annoys me.

"Carlos couldn't come here because Lyla would recognize him," I tell him, referring to the Bailey's Head of Security – our team leader – who has been watching over Lyla from a distance back in Chicago for 15 years. "She doesn't know he works for their family, obviously. She thinks he lives in her neighborhood, that's all. But he couldn't come here and have her seeing him. So, he hired me."

Emil stifles a yawn. "Well, welcome to the most boring job you'll ever have."

I don't know what to think right now. "My things arrived yesterday?"

He nods. "They're upstairs. First room on the right is yours. Wanna see it?"

"I will later. Where's the hub?" I ask him.

"The what?"

"The room with monitors that are linked to the cameras covering Will's house? I was told there are cameras mounted all around the exterior of his house, and some on the inside too. We have access to them?"

"Yeah." He nods towards a door in the hallway. "Downstairs."

We head down the cement steps together and I stop at the bottom to take in the mess. There are old candy wrappers strewn about and a thick sheet of dust over the entire desktop. But there are four large monitors and top-of-the-line surveillance equipment, which is what I was hoping for.

"I haven't come down here in a while," Emil says. "No need."

The monitors aren't even on. Probably haven't been turned on in years.

41

"You don't check in on who comes and goes from his house?" I ask, trying to keep my tone normal. I am recalibrating, taking in the reality of my surroundings and the situation. None of it is what I had hoped for, and this case is difficult enough as it is.

Emil laughs. "I haven't seen anyone come over in months. The last guy was there for some sort of delivery, and I'm sure he was treated with the utmost respect from The Caveman," he says, referring to the name some of the locals have given Will. Carlos informed me of this when he prepped me for this case.

Emil looks at me and groans, his beer hanging at his side in his hand. "Don't tell me you're actually going to watch them and follow them wherever they go."

"That's my job."

"You'll feel that way for about a day."

"You don't follow Will whenever he goes somewhere?"

"He's twenty-seven years old. He can take care of himself. Nothing has happened because nothing *happens* in this town. Trust me, you'll see."

I run my finger along the dust on the desk. "Why do you do this, if you hate it so much?"

"Why else?" he asks. "The massive paycheck. You?"

I dust my hands off and look around some more. "I needed a change of pace." I turn to Emil. "Do you know Carlos very well?"

"Of course. I trained under him."

"Then you know that he's a very big man and you don't want to get on his bad side."

He shakes his head angrily. "And you're going to tell him about how I do things around here."

"Of course not." I shrug. "I'm not about to come in here and tell you how to do your job. There's been no need for heightened security until now."

He is surprised. When his eyes trail down over me curiously, I turn and sit in the swivel chair. I find the power button on one of the monitors and press it. Then I turn on the others. Each screen shows a different shot of Will's house, inside and outside. Four different views. I study them, memorizing the way Will's house is laid out.

I don't tell Emil this, but I can't blame him for not wanting to watch them this closely. The surveillance system is another part of this job that is very unusual. What I'm looking at here breaks every unwritten rule of privacy in the book. Without it, though, we would be sitting blind, waiting silently, watching nothing at all because of the distance between us and our clients. At least this way, we can know of their plans and hopefully get to one of the cars in time to follow them.

Thankfully, as far as I know, they won't be going out much. Will is reclusive, and Lyla will be asleep most of the time throughout the day because of nightmares I'm told she has. Even so, I'm hoping the Baileys will figure things out on their end within a matter of weeks. I don't know how long I can do this.

Emil breaks into my thoughts by leaning over and taking the mouse controller from me. I can smell his cologne, and for some reason it doesn't repulse me, not entirely.

"If you click here," he says, "it shows a different view for each one."

"Eight cameras," I say mostly to myself.

"And all the sound equipment you could ever need," he says, pointing at a few pairs of headphones that are worth probably a thousand dollars each. He laughs softly. "A little crazy, don't you think? All of this for two kids who nobody even knows are rich."

I would agree with him, if I didn't know the whole story. It's time to tell him.

I stand up and lean back against the desk, crossing my arms. Emil backs up, looking at me curiously.

"Carlos wanted me to brief you," I tell him.

He straightens, setting his beer on the desk. "On what?"

"On what's going on. Your job just got a whole lot more interesting, like one of your books upstairs."

His face changes into a childlike eagerness. "I'm listening."

"What I'm about to tell you cannot be repeated to anyone."

He nods. "Of course."

"Will thinks that there is a reporter who might possibly leak a story with their whereabouts," I tell him.

"Right," Emil says.

"There's no story getting out. That's just what his parents told him to get him to bring Lyla back here with him."

"So, what's really going on?"

"Her parents are buying time while they try to get around the terms of her grandfather's will." I level my gaze at him. "As of today – Lyla's eighteenth birthday – she is worth eighty million dollars."

Emil blinks at me.

"And they have thirty days before they have to tell her about it."

Lyla

I finally have to give up looking for Samantha when Will and I reach his car in the airport parking lot. It's dark out, with only the moon and a few lights on the tops of poles above us. I don't see her out here, and I'm disappointed. She wasn't at baggage claim, or in the bathroom, or anywhere else in the tiny airport that was more like a log cabin. The chances of seeing her again are probably slim, even in a small town. I can't help but feel that I missed an opportunity.

I really wanted to introduce her to my brother on the plane after we talked, but with the way she sat – totally motionless and tense and with her body turned almost completely away from us – I decided I didn't want to disturb her again.

Minutes later, as much as I tried not to, I started feeling tired. I couldn't help it. The gentle movements of the plane and the white noise made me feel like a tired kid in a car seat. I fell asleep. My first flight ever and I slept through most of it, until the landing bounced me awake.

And then, as soon as the seatbelt sign went off and people started standing up, Samantha hurried to be one of the first passengers off the plane without saying goodbye to me. Feeling slightly disappointed, I wondered where she was going, and why she was so nervous. Will stared after her too. I grinned up at him, and when he noticed, he cleared his throat and looked away. He's definitely attracted to her, and I thought maybe he could talk to her in the airport.

But she was nowhere to be found, and when Will realized what I was doing when I searched the restaurant and bathroom and car rental area, he got annoyed and said we needed to go.

It's only a twenty-minute drive to his house and I look out the window as we start off, trying to see the area. But it's really dark out here. Very remote. And then it gets even darker when we take a turn onto a little

45

twisting road that doesn't even have a line down the middle of it. Will says it's actually a highway, and this part is called the Tunnel of Trees. I look up through my window, trying to see the trees, but I'm barely able to see the moon anymore except when it pokes through branches and leaves, making them into little black silhouettes.

At one point, our headlights swoop across a fence that lines the edge of a farm. In very pretty, purple letters someone has painted the word *Remembrance*.

"What's Remembrance?" I ask Will.

He looks at me curiously and I point. He shrugs.

"I don't know."

That's all we say for a while. I rest my face on the door and the heat from the vent makes me feel cozy as I look out at the dark trees above me.

Will wakes me when we reach his house. He is already out of the car, leaning into the open driver's side door. I didn't even know I was asleep.

"This is it," he says. He seems irritable.

I rub my eyes and look up at the house through the windshield. It's nicer than I expected. It's blue with darker blue trim and has a wooden porch with a fun two-seater swing to the left. The house is lit up from the headlights of Will's car, and the lights are on inside, the front door open.

"It's bigger than Mom and Dad's house," I say.

Will either doesn't hear my comment or he ignores me and shuts the door. I get out and walk around to the trunk to get my luggage.

"I already brought it all inside," says Will.

"You did? Sorry."

"It's fine. I had to…clean up a little anyway."

We walk up the porch steps and through the front door. The first thing that hits me once we're inside is the smell of saw dust. The second thing that hits me is the fact that the whole inside of the house is being remodeled. Will tells me to be careful as we both navigate around shards of wood in the hallway with rusty nails sticking out. I trip on an electric drill and slap my hand against the wall before I lose my balance. Didn't he say he cleaned up?

"Wow," I say when we reach the kitchen.

The cabinets have been ripped off one of the walls and the countertops have tools all over them. The refrigerator is in the living room, right next to the couch.

It's almost as if Will hadn't planned on me coming here. I don't know what to feel about that. I am really trying to sound optimistic when I ask how long the work will take.

He clears his throat. "Probably another month or so."

We turn down the hallway to the right and he shows me his office, then the closet where I can put some of my jackets and shoes, and the laundry room that has paint cans and dirty socks on the floor and clothes on top of the dryer. There's a door in there and I try to open it, but it's locked.

"What's this?" I ask.

"The garage," Will says. "That's where I…work out. I keep it locked."

"Oh."

Any particular reason you would lock your workout equipment in there?

But I don't ask. I figure he'll tell me if he wants to, which he won't. Still, though, I can't help wondering about it.

Will heads towards the staircase by the living room. "I'll show you your room."

The upstairs is better than the downstairs. There are four bedrooms, and mine is about twice the size of my room back home. There is a queen bed pushed against the wall and a big green desk beneath the window. A dresser sits by the door that leads to a big walk in closet.

"Wow," I say. "This furniture is really nice."

Will rubs his neck. "Yeah."

I love the bathroom. It's down the hall and has a claw-foot tub with a little stained-glass window above it. Will says it's rare for a house this old to have so many bathrooms. The best part is this one is all mine. Will has his own bathroom attached to his bedroom, which he doesn't show me, and I don't ask him to. If he keeps the garage locked, I'm guessing he doesn't want me in his room either.

He leads me back downstairs through the living room and out the back door.

"This is the best part," he says as we step into the darkness outside.

He flips a switch and these little lamps light our path like a star chart down through the trees. I can't see much past the lights. There are so many trees and so many stars that it feels like we're in the middle of nowhere. We must be on a few acres because I can't see lights from a single neighbor. He walks me down the wooden path that splits the trees and opens up to tall grasses and miles of beach, white in the moonlight. There is a fire pit made out of stone with lawn chairs around it. I wonder if he hangs out with his friends here.

"This is why I bought this place," Will says, looking out at the water.

We stand here for a while with the huge blackened lake in front of us, the little waves breaking silver. The wind blows my hair and I hold it down – a habit – to keep my scar covered. I glance at Will a couple times. I want to hug him, but of course I don't. Even so, I think I will remember this moment for a long time.

I am too tired to unpack or even change, so the only things I take out of my luggage when I get back upstairs are some cozy socks and my bag of toiletries. I pull the socks on and bring my toiletries down the hall with me to the bathroom, feeling at least a little settled when I set the bag beneath the mirror. I'm about to brush my teeth when I remember I haven't eaten dinner.

When I come back downstairs, I can't find Will. I look over at the laundry room with the locked garage door, but I don't go in there to open it. Maybe he's working out.

I raid the fridge that's in the living room and am surprised to find some really nice food. I expected pizza, maybe a carton of orange juice or something because he used to be obsessed with orange juice. But Will's fridge has things like Kalamata olives, goat cheese, raspberries, fresh peaches, butternut squash cubes. I actually find a thing of caviar in the back – a little black jar of it. I take a taste because I've always wanted to try caviar, but I quickly spit it in my hand and scrape my tongue. It must've gone bad.

I am rinsing my hand in the kitchen sink when Will comes downstairs wearing a white t-shirt and gray sweatpants. His shaggy dark hair is wet, and I realize he was showering.

"I threw away your caviar," is the first thing I say to him.

He stops. "Why?"

"It went bad." I spit again in the sink.

Will walks around the counter and pulls out the small trash from beneath the sink. He digs out the black jar and wipes it off with a towel that's lying next to a pile of drill bits. I make a mental note to never touch that towel.

"I just bought this," he says.

"Really? It's awful."

"You can't just eat it; there's a lot you have to do to prepare it."

"Oh." I feel my brow crinkle. How does he know this stuff?

He walks back into the living room and puts the caviar back in the fridge. He gets out a plastic container of something and comes back into the kitchen.

"We can have leftover chicken parmesan," he says quietly.

"That sounds good," I say. I step out of his way and he puts it in the microwave. "Do you cook?" I ask lightly.

He punches the buttons for three minutes. "Yeah."

"Wow," I say.

"What?"

"Nothing, I just pictured you...not cooking." I smile. "Maybe you can teach me."

He doesn't really respond except to say, "Yeah, maybe..." and then he starts picking up some of the tools and gathering them to one spot in the corner.

I look through the bottom cabinets for plates, but there are only pots and cutting boards and mixing bowls. There are no other cabinets to look through since they've been ripped off the wall so I just sort of stand here for a second.

"Um, do you have plates?"

He stops and looks at me. "They're in the garage."

"Oh. I can get them."

"I'll do it." He sets down a hammer and some other tools and then walks over to the laundry room. He glances at me as he stops at the door. I look away and pretend to be uninterested, but I am really wondering what kind of a person keeps their garage door locked. What's in there?

He comes back in with a stack of plates that are really nice – heavy with blue rims – and once the chicken parmesan is heated up, we end up on the couch with our plates on the coffee table. I tell him it's really good and he says thanks and then we're silent. After a minute, I can't take much more of this, so I glance around for the TV remote and find it on the little table next to me. But when I pick it up and press the power button, Will snatches the remote from me and shuts it off.

I stare at him.

"My cable is out," he says quickly. "So is the internet. I forgot to tell you. I'm…fixing it."

"Oh. Okay." He's avoiding my eyes. "Do you…want to watch a movie? We don't need cable for that. I brought some of my own."

After a second, he says, "Sure, yeah."

I stand up to go get them, glancing back at him before I go up the stairs. Is he acting weird? Or is this how he always is? Maybe this is an off day for him. Or maybe this is an awful foreshadowing of what my time with him will be like. No wonder he isn't dating anyone, according to Mom. He probably doesn't have any friends at all.

Hopefully I can help him with that.

I find my case of movies in my striped bag along with my cozy gray blanket I packed. I take them both with me when I go back downstairs.

Will is still tense about something as he waits for me. I pick out a movie about football, so we can bond about it. We both love football. It was when we were watching games at home as a family that Will seemed to not be so annoyed with our parents for some reason. He and Dad would actually almost get along.

I put the movie in and sit back down next to Will, pulling my gray blanket over my shoulders. I try to put him at ease when the movie starts, telling him I am never on the internet or watch TV much anyway.

"It's fine that they're not working," I tell him. "I don't even own a phone. I accidentally dropped it in some water."

"Dad told me. Why don't you replace it?"

My face flushes a little. "I'll get around to it."

No need to go into the fact that I have no friends. I'm not allowed to be on social media, either, so I don't really see the point of getting a new phone.

We eat our chicken parmesan together, leaning over the coffee table as the movie plays on the TV above the fireplace.

The TV is huge – something else that surprises me. We grew up with a modest TV that my parents refuse to replace with a flat screen because it "still works just fine." It's the same story with the family car we've had for ten years. Will, on the other hand, has a newer car, a bigger TV, bigger house, nicer couches. He cooks with expensive food. There are boat magazines on the coffee table and an expensive-looking red guitar on a stand in the corner. I'm learning that my brother lives differently than our parents, and I like learning that about him. Sure, he is quiet and kind of rude to people and he's very awkward with me, but maybe I'm misjudging him. I want to learn more.

I think of what my mom said when she was helping me pack. She said she hoped I could bring some light into his life, because she didn't think he had anyone else. I told her maybe I could even help him get a girlfriend.

I glance at Will. That's my plan. It would've been nice if we could've talked to Samantha some more. I wonder if she lives here. I wonder if she's single.

Will and I eat in a silence that isn't very comfortable at all and then we sit back and focus on the movie. He doesn't mention anything about football, or say a word in general to me, which is fine, I guess. After a while my eyelids feel like they weigh ten pounds each. I haven't made it through an entire movie without falling asleep in so long. I try really hard to keep my eyes open because it's my birthday and I want to hang out with my brother more. Mostly, I don't want to have the nightmares.

But I can feel myself losing the battle. *Please, please, don't let them come tonight. It's my birthday.* I can't stand the thought of waking my brother up with my screaming. He told me he has earplugs, but will he wear them? I don't know where they are, but I'm too nervous to ask. *Please. Please. No nightmares…*

I drift off, thinking that I haven't brushed my teeth or even changed out of my dress, but I just don't have the energy. The cold leather couch presses against my cheek. The fridge hums loudly beside me. The movie plays without me watching. My gray blanket offers some comfort, and a scent of home.

But I know what's to come.

I dread it.

Samantha

Two hours after leaving that tiny airport, I finally pull up to the cottage. I drove down Harbor Springs first to buy a few essentials and get dinner, and then I got a little lost on my way to the cottage. But I'm here now. That's all that matters.

It's so dark that it's hard to see it even with my headlights on. But it's a two-story house, small and white. It looks just like the picture on the website, just more…falling-apart. I sigh and stare at it, a little disappointed. No wonder this house was still available when all the other rentals were taken.

There are spiders living in the corners of the porch. I can see them in their gleaming webs illuminated by the light of my cell phone as I walk up the porch steps. My body tries to shrink in on itself so none of them can touch me. I hate spiders. And these are the big kind, too, with the big round abdomens and crab-like legs. Poisonous, probably. The kind that nests in one of your ears at night. This does not bode well for whatever waits for me inside.

It takes a good fifteen seconds before I finally get up the courage to stick my hand in the light by the door where Dorothy said the key would be. I hold my breath as I feel around in there, imagining a giant spider dropping down on my fingers, but there is no spider and also no key. I check beneath the doormat and find nothing but flattened leaves. And there is no key beneath any pots on the porch because there *are* no pots on the porch. Grumbling about small towns, I check my phone to see if I have service and pump a fist in the air because I do. I call Dorothy.

"Oh yeesh!" she says. "That's right. I left it beneath the brick by the gate. Sorry, dear. Haven't been there in ages."

No kidding? I almost say out loud. But then I silently scold myself. I'm not normally this snippy, but it's been a long day during which I've questioned my sanity about a thousand times. I walk to the gate, find the brick, and pick it up with two fingers. A key is stuck to the bottom of it, held there by mud.

"Here it is," I say. "I found it."

"Oh good," Dorothy says. "And honey, let me just say that you are so sweet, I can already tell. Such a sweet, sweet gal. Just Will's type, I'm guessing. Not that it's any of my business."

I am blushing. "Oh thanks, Dorothy, but – "

"And your secret's safe with me," she adds. "I won't tell a soul."

"My secret?"

"That you're here to see him. I'm rooting for you."

"Okay. Thanks," I say, face flaming. "I'm inside now and the place is really nice."

And it is, actually. The inside is blessedly better than the outside. I feel my entire body relax.

"Welcome to Good Hart, dear," Dorothy says. "Enjoy a pleasant stay."

When I thank her and end the call, I am smiling.

I go back to the car and bring the groceries and clothes inside, then take a look around. The living room is tidy, with crocheted pillows on the couch and a red rug beneath the coffee table. Everything has brown bears on it. Wait a second…are there bears in Good Hart? I am staying in a cottage all by myself in the middle of the woods, and there are bears. I'll have to buy bear spray tomorrow.

In the master bedroom there is a handmade quilt on the bed – also with bears all over it – and a nice-sized bathroom. No spiders, as far as I can tell. Not even in the tub. I let out a relieved breath. My night is looking up.

The loft upstairs has only three things in it: A chair, a lamp and a desk. A writing desk, just like the one I have back home. Maybe it's a sign.

I put the groceries away and hang up my new shirt in the closet. I text Mom and Nell on our group text to tell them I made it okay. Mom says to make sure all the doors are locked, and to call first thing in the morning. Nell says to go write about all of this.

I'm exhausted, but my mind is buzzing. I brush my teeth with my new toothbrush, wash my face with the hand soap from the dispenser that's shaped like a little brown bear holding a red heart, and crawl into bed beneath the blanket of patterned bears and trees. After checking for spiders, obviously. The sheets are freezing, the mattress lumpy but still comfortable. I lay here with the blanket up to my chin, looking around at the strange shadows and hearing just about every creature that's awake in the forest outside.

I don't sleep. I can't. But I only try for about ten minutes. And then I find myself tiptoeing over the creaky wood floors to my purse and pulling out my notebook along with a pen. I head upstairs to the loft and turn on the lamp, then sit down at the writing desk and blink until my eyes adjust. I pick up the pen, take a breath, and open the notebook.

I start to write.

First, I write about how this whole thing started. My mom thought she recognized Kathy Bailey at the coffee shop, although her hair is very different. She definitely had similar features. Then, when she used her credit card and Nell saw that her first name was Kathy but her last name was Brooks, she and my mom looked up old pictures of her while I made her coffee. When I came back into the office, they showed me the picture they found, and Nell handed me my purse and my keys and told me to follow her, just to see if it was her. She told me to write about it. "We might have just found the Baileys after fifteen years!" she said. "This story would make your career!"

I did follow her, just for fun. Then, because I'm apparently crazy, I followed their kids all the way here.

…Or maybe I did it because I'm still running from things in my own messed up life.

Pushing that thought away, I write about Lyla next, her warm eyes and smile and gentle spirit. Then I detail Will, his good looks and quiet manner and his judgmental stare. I decide that I'll go to his house first thing in the morning, just to look at it. Then maybe there will be a chance to ask the neighbors discreet questions, see if these siblings are the Baileys.

I get that feeling as I write – a warmth in my stomach that means a story is taking shape.

Sienna Rodriguez

It's past eleven now. I'm in the cold basement of the house next door to Will's, watching the screens in front of me. I am enthralled by these siblings. So far, I can tell that they're not like other rich kids, which makes sense because Lyla has no idea she's a Bailey and Will has to live like he's not.

I find myself thinking of Tessa. Already, the differences between this case and my last case are obvious. Tessa wasn't an easy client. In the three years I guarded her, I had to rush her four different times to the hospital in the middle of the night for overdosing. Another time she got drunk on champagne and broke her nose on the side of the pool at two in the morning. I happened to be in the bathroom when it occurred. Her friends came to get me, and I found Tessa laughing and backstroking through swirling lines of blood that filled up half the pool. Another time she posted the address to her family's Aspen home to her online followers just so she could host a party there while her parents were in Dubai.

And now, I'm watching over two quiet, calm siblings in a very quiet, calm town.

Lyla is asleep on her brother's shoulder on the couch. She's wrapped in a gray blanket, her yellow dress showing only around her bent knees. Her feet, in knitted socks, are tucked up closely to her.

I wonder when she'll start to wake up screaming.

Will finishes the movie and turns the TV off, then pulls his phone out and scrolls through something – the news, I'm guessing. Probably wondering if the non-existent story got out. He looks down at his sister. I study him. What kind of man is he?

He slides his phone back into his pocket and tilts his head back on the couch, looking up at the ceiling. He rubs a hand down his face and then looks at his sister again. Then slowly, he starts to get up. He carefully leaves a pillow in his place so Lyla doesn't wake up. And then he does something that surprises me. He lightly touches her hair and stands over her for second, just looking at her.

The heir to the Bailey fortune is not who I thought he'd be.

Will straightens and then goes to the back door, locking it. He walks over to the kitchen counter and writes a note on a napkin, then grabs his keys and his jacket off a hook in the hallway. He heads to the front door.

I sit up. He wouldn't leave, would he? On his sister's first night here? He's leaving her alone, when he knows she's going to wake up screaming?

Sure enough, he walks out, and on an exterior camera I can see him on the front porch, locking the door behind him.

Panicked, I get up and take the basement steps three at a time. I hurry down the hall and find Emil's bedroom door. I pause, wondering if this is a bad idea, and then I knock. No answer. I knock louder. I hear some rustling. He's probably waking up, remembering he has a roommate now.

"Yeah," he says groggily.

"Sorry to wake you, but Will's leaving the house."

It's silent for a second. "And?"

"Emil," I say testily. "He's leaving Lyla all by herself."

"Good thing she has two bodyguards next door."

I cross my arms on my chest. "Shouldn't you follow him to see where he's going?"

The door suddenly opens, and I blink and back up. Emil is there with no shirt on, squinting against the light in the hallway.

"I know where he's going," he says. "He does this sometimes in the middle of the night."

I frown. "Does what?"

"He's taking his boat out."

"His boat?"

He yawns, nodding. "He's going to the Manor."

Will

The cold, dark air rips against my hair and skin. It feels good. This is my favorite thing to do. Since I can't exactly have people knowing that I own a yacht and a speedboat, I only go out at night. Sometimes I cruise miles out and cut the engine and sit in the wind and the quiet. Other times, like tonight, I go to the Manor.

The thirty-thousand square foot mansion was built during the Gilded Age of America, and then bought and restored by my grandfather in the 1960's. It's on a thousand acres in a hidden cove off Lake Michigan and has a dock and boathouse for six boats, staff housing, stables for award-winning horses, and a farm on the back hundred acres that supplied anything our family or the staff could possibly need. It was pretty much an entire village when it was up and running. It's still known as the Carson Manor, because my grandfather had his rich friend buy it under his name – Henry Clive Carson – so that no one outside of the family and the staff would know it's a Bailey mansion.

Now it's empty, one of the most extravagant abandoned mansions in the world.

And it's going to be mine.

After just ten minutes on the lake, I come to the cove and slow down to turn into it. The property stretches before me, dark and motionless except for the hundred-year-old trees blowing in the wind. The moon hangs low over one of the chimneys, looking like a marshmallow on a stick. I pull the boat up to the dock and cut the engine. Grabbing a flashlight from a waterproof compartment, I turn it on and step out and tie the boat to a dock cleat.

There are old curled leaves that have gathered at the front door. I haven't been here in a few months. Brushing them aside with my foot, I get my keys out of my pocket and unlock the front entry door. The marble floors reflect my flashlight as I push the heavy door open with a loud creak. I stop in the massive four-story foyer and stare up. Cobwebs interrupt the thin beam of yellow from my eager flashlight. The colorful paint on the trim everywhere still annoys me. My parents wanted this house to feel "European," while I always wanted it to feel American, and still do. Trim work is tedious and costly, but well worth it.

My eyes drift over to the marble stairs. There were countless times that Alexandra and I talked right there. She was always three steps above me. We wanted to run this place together.

Unfortunately, it didn't turn out that way.

I blink and force my thoughts away from her, seeing the windows now. They are dirty and probably completely un-transparent by now, but they are historic and extravagantly detailed with iron and gold. Magnificent.

Before, I never really knew why I came here. I was technically trespassing. Guess I still am, since I won't get the deed until all of this is over.

But tonight, my pulse is fast and my mind is whirring…because I have a reason to be here. It's about to be mine.

There's a lot of work that needs to be done. I'll have to start hiring people back…

And then, if the story gets out, this is the first place I'll take my sister to.

Part II
29 Days and counting…

Voices crackle through my radio, still unclear. I can't switch channels. I'd have to put her down, and there's no time. Branches scratch my neck and face as I sprint through the trees, but I barely feel it.

A voice finally comes through clearly. "What's your location?"

I stop and shift her so I can reach up and press the button, but I pause. I look down at my chest, thinking it's warm from all the adrenaline. But it's dark, almost black and wet. I bend over and set her down carefully, feeling for a pulse. It's there, but it's weak.

I grab my radio and press the button. "She's bleeding out!" I say frantically.

"What's your location?"

I look around, but I still can't see the lights from the ambulance. I squeeze my eyes shut, trying to calculate. Then I press the button again. "We're at least three miles from the command center."

"Stay right where you are. We'll come to you."

"I don't think she'll make it."

Christian Freeman

I woke up this morning with the usual heaviness in my chest. It's making me drive faster right now. My heart feels like it weighs fifty pounds and is pressing on my stomach. I shift in my seat and Estes, my German shepherd, whines beside me, but I don't look at him. He can sense when I feel this way. It always gets worse the closer I get to Remmi's neighborhood.

Something else always happens too. The deputy on the side of the road at Hilltop turns a blind eye to my speeding. I'm going twenty over on this road that is very dangerous to speed on. But the heaviness is what's weighing down my foot, it seems. Lame excuse, and I've never said it out loud, but I feel it.

Sometimes though, like today, the blue and red lights catch my eye in the rearview mirror. I don't have the old adrenaline rush I used to get whenever I got pulled over. Nothing gives me much of a rush anymore. The heaviness doesn't make room for anything else.

I just look in my mirror and sigh, then pull over on the gravel shoulder as far as I can. I glance over a few yards and see that, ironically, I pulled over right near the fence where her name is painted in purple. *Remembrance.* No one knows who painted it. My jaw flexes and I look away from it.

It's Sheriff Crawford today. I wonder what mood he'll be in. Ticket or no ticket? Lecture or no lecture? Pity? Disappointment?

Disappointment. It's all over his face when I roll down the window.

"Freeman," he says.

"Crawford," I say, looking straight out the windshield now.

Estes wants him to pet him. He used to be his dog before he gave him to me. For a therapy dog or an emotional support dog or something, which

I wasn't happy about at first. But either way, he's mine now. I give Estes a look and a small command with my hand and he immediately goes still.

"You could get killed. Or kill someone else," Crawford says.

Same old speech. "Sorry, sir."

He waits for me to look at him, but I don't.

"I can't keep letting you off," he says, giving up. "I'm ready to fire Stanley for letting you off so much."

But Stanley dated Remmi's mom a while back, so he cared for her. He knows the heaviness.

Crawford sighs. "Don't make me regret the soft spot I have for you, Freeman."

"I won't, sir."

I glance at him for only a second. Long enough to see him nod and look over at Estes, whose ears perk up but other than that he doesn't move.

Crawford walks away with a crunch of gravel beneath his boots. I notice he looks over at the fence with her name on it, then shakes his head and walks on.

Jaw clenched, I pull back out into the road when it's clear. I roll up my window immediately because I never drive with the windows down now. I don't want to think about Remmi sticking her head out whenever we drove this road, to look up at the Tunnel of Trees as if it was her first time seeing it.

Or her last...

I keep my speed down to just five over the limit. Then I pull into her neighborhood, telling myself this will be the last time I do this. Because she's not coming back.

Estes licks my elbow and I pet him behind his ear, trying to take slower breaths. Trying not to think.

Lyla
Will's house, down the road

I am really confused when my eyes flutter open. It takes me a second to remember where I am. I'm in my brother's house on the couch in his living room. My gray blanket is over me. I'm still in my dress. The giant TV is off. The house is completely still. A light that was left on in the downstairs bathroom casts a wedge of yellow across the room.

I rub my eyes. There's a clock beneath the TV, its glowing green numbers telling me it is seven forty-eight. Seven forty-eight in the morning? It has to be. The sun isn't over the lake in the window next to me; it's on the other side of the house, where it's rising in the east.

Because it's morning.

My heart jumps and I sit up, looking around frantically. I can't believe it. It's seven forty-eight in the morning, meaning I actually slept through the entire night...without a single nightmare.

A loud, wild laugh escapes my throat. I cover my mouth and sit here listening, hoping I didn't wake Will. I don't hear anything. Tossing the blanket to the side, I get to my feet and run to the back door. I unlock it, throw it open, and step out onto the porch. I stand here for a second, looking out at the whole world in front of me, before I sprint down the massive deck to the yard where I follow the path down to the beach. When I reach the water, I run into the lake in my dress and socks, jumping around and kicking the small waves. I lose a sock, but I don't care. I dance and laugh and splash, all by myself.

If someone were to see me, they'd think I'm crazy. But they wouldn't understand it unless they've gone every day of their life for the past three years being tired all the time because of nightmares. My arms flail and I spin around and around. Drops splash on my face, wetting my eyelids, my cheeks, my hair. I dance like a child. Like someone who finally has legs to dance. Or like someone who is finally free. Because I am. I'm free.

I dance and dance and laugh and stop, catching my breath, and then dance some more. I have never felt this way. Still breathing hard, I look up at the sky and reach my hands up. I'm awake. I am *awake*!

But then, a question punctures the back of my mind. Will the nightmares come back? Is it just for one night that I've gotten a break?

I shake my head. I can't think that way. Right now, I will enjoy this day. I'll *live*. I'll bake muffins and make friends and I will help my brother with whatever he needs around the house because I am awake to do it. I'll swim in the lake. I'll build a bonfire on the beach. I'll start a garden. I'll make tea and drink it on the porch with Will and all the new friends I'll have. There is so much to do.

I wrap my arms around myself. My legs are soaked and so is my dress, but I don't care. Everything is perfect. The water is smooth, the air still. I smile, feeling energized for the first time in so long. I start dancing again, laughing and even shouting. I can't wait to tell Will and Mom and Dad. We'll all celebrate because this is really, truly miraculous.

My life starts today.

Christian

I'm parked at her house, but I haven't gotten out yet. I look over at Estes.

"This is the last time," I tell him. He cocks his head to the side like he does when he's trying to figure out what I'm saying. "The last time, okay?"

He doesn't believe me. I don't believe myself either.

There's another teddy bear in front of the door. A bright green one this time. A card too. When I first came here a few weeks ago to see if they were home yet, I found that people had left a bunch of cards and flowers and a pile of these bears in all sorts of colors, like a sad, crumpled rainbow. I decided to start collecting it all in a cooler, to keep it safe for whenever they return. I do this every day, but this is the last time, because they're not coming back.

I get out of the truck and so does Estes, and we walk up the porch steps. I slide the card into my back pocket and pick up the bear so I can add it to my collection in the cooler in the bed of my truck. I knock on the door, ring the doorbell, although I know no one is home. No one has been home for weeks. Still, though, I have to check. Audree's not answering her phone and I don't know where they went, so the only thing that's in my control is to come here every day and check if they came home or not.

"Audree?" I call loudly. "Mrs. Tyler?" I know there'll be no answer, but I knock again. "Hello?" I look through the front window.

There's the magazine lying open on the couch, untouched for weeks. One of them was reading it the day their world ended.

I stare into the dark room. I am breathing hard now, thinking of banging on the door and looking into this exact window that night. But I was too late.

Estes whimpers and nudges me incessantly until I pet him. My fingers dig into the soft hair behind his ears. It's somewhat comforting. I step back and he moves with me as we head around to the back of the house like we do every day. It's the only time I leave home. But like I said, today is the last time because this isn't healthy.

Estes is beside me the whole way around the house, closer right now because he senses my mood. We walk down to the beach and stop on the sand. Estes sits tall next to me. I slide my hands into my pockets and stand here looking out at the water with the green teddy bear tucked under my arm. This is the only place I let myself think of her. Nowhere else. I picture her long red hair, her freckles. And I think of how I loved her. I can still hear her laugh. It's distant, but I can hear it.

I take the bear and look down at it, twisting it in my hands until it tears a little. The white stomach is embroidered with her name, Remembrance, because that's what all the elementary school kids decided to do. Remmi would bring them these teddy bears whenever she came to read to them at school and now these kids are giving them back to her with her name stitched into the little stomach, along with cards that say things like "We'll always remember you" and "We miss you" and "We love you, always and forever."

I groan, tearing the bear more. Then I cock my arm back and throw the bear out into the lake, expecting it to go far. But it gets caught on my finger in the release and splashes pretty close by, which makes me so mad that I think I should've strangled the bear instead or ripped its head off. That would've been more satisfying. But I didn't. So, I just watch it get tossed by the small waves until a bigger one comes and then it is gone. Like Remmi. Gone. My hands are in fists so when Estes whimpers I can't pet him because I don't want to and I can't relax my hands enough to. *Why her?* I ask for the thousandth time, maybe the millionth. Why her?

And then, when I hear her laugh again, I think I've really lost my mind now. But that's when I notice that Estes isn't whimpering because of me. He's looking down the beach, his ears turned in that direction. There's the laugh again, and Estes perks up, really looking now, and then...I see her.

She's far down the beach, around where my grandma's old house is. I squint, looking closer. It's a girl with dark hair. She's wearing a bright yellow dress. I find myself taking a few steps out towards the water so I can see her better, and then I stop just to stare.

She's dancing.

Estes stops beside me. We're totally entranced as we watch her, this girl who's by herself, dancing all crazy on the beach. I've never seen dancing like this, at least not from anyone my age. It's wild and careless, like a kid. That's where the laughter is coming from. It floats over to me and everything else is momentarily forgotten because I can't take my eyes off her. She shouts a couple of times with her hands flung high in the air, and then she spins around and kicks the waves and laughs some more. I'm totally frozen, just watching…until Estes does something I normally wouldn't be okay with. He starts slowly walking over to her, forgetting me.

I don't stop him yet because he's being so calm about it. In fact, I follow him. I don't know why. It's not like I want to talk to her or anything because she looks like she might be nuts. But I'm moving towards her, closer to the trees than Estes is so she won't catch me watching her. I was right about her being on my grandma's old property. A guy named Will Brooks bought it a few years ago. I spent a lot of time out on this beach growing up. So did Audree and Remmi. My stomach quivers as memories start coming up inside me. There used to be a fort somewhere in the trees. I wonder if it's still there. Maybe Will took it down.

Estes is still ahead of me, walking calmly. The girl's laughter is loud now, and suddenly Estes picks up the pace. I do too so I can catch him before he takes off or something, not like he would.

Wait a second…I'm wrong. He's running towards her all of a sudden.

"Estes!" I whisper harshly, but he doesn't even pause.

He has never disobeyed me. Not once.

My heart pounds as I watch. I hide behind a tree so the girl won't see me. Maybe she'll think he's alone. Estes reaches her and starts bouncing around with her, excited and wondering why she's so excited. It's kind of entertaining to watch – this strange girl dancing, not even aware that a dog is dancing beside her.

But then, Estes barks once, and that's all it takes. The girl whips around and sees him…

…and lets out the loudest scream I have ever heard in my life.

Emil

When we hear the scream, Sienna doesn't even falter for a second. She opens the back door and pulls her gun. I fumble for my gun that's on the table beside me. Only a fraction of a second has passed during my hesitation, but it's a fraction of a second that could mean life or death for my high-value clients. Sienna is just ahead of me, vaulting over the railing of the back deck. I race after her, my feet barely noticing the thick brush and exposed roots of trees.

This might be it.

Christian

Before I can even react, the girl turns and dives into the water. Estes follows her.

"Get away from me!" the girl screams, kicking and splashing as she swims deeper out.

I run out of the trees without thinking. "Estes!"

The girl looks over her shoulder, seeing me. She's swimming frantically. "Get him away from me!"

"Estes, come!"

He isn't listening. They're both farther out in the water now, the girl trailed by Estes as he dog-paddles. I have no choice but to run in after them before the girl drowns from panic or something. The water is like liquid ice. It engulfs me, taking my breath away as I make my way towards them.

When I'm close enough, I grab Estes by the collar and drag him back towards the shore. He fights me the whole way.

"What are you *doing*?" I yell at him.

We splash through the water until I can walk. I have to wrap my arms around his chest and drag him to shore.

"Are you possessed?"

I finally put him down on the sand, still holding him by the collar. But then he shakes the water off his body so fiercely that I have to let go. I bend over with my hands on my knees, catching my breath because that was insane. What just happened? Why did he do that? And more importantly, why did the girl freak out so much about it?

I look out at her, pinching the water out of my eyes. She's still far out there. All I can see is her pale, frightened face, her dark hair plastered to her cheeks.

A twig snaps somewhere behind me and I turn, but no one's there. Estes whimpers, looking over there.

"It's all right," I call to the girl. "He won't do that again."

She doesn't respond.

"You can come back now."

I'm freezing. My back muscles are starting to shake. If I'm this cold, she must be even colder out there in the water, considering it's still early in the morning.

Dark memories start to come up when I think of the cold water, what happened to Remmi. I shake my head.

"You should come out before you freeze." That sounded angry.

"I'm scared of dogs," she calls to me.

"Yeah I caught that."

"I'm not coming out until he's gone!"

I sigh and look down at Estes. I grab his collar again and walk him back into the trees, where I tell him to sit. He obeys immediately, and he even looks up at me like, *"What? What's wrong?"* Like I'm overreacting.

"Stay," I tell him. "For real. Stay."

Whenever I've told Estes to stay, he would sit there all day unless I told him otherwise. Seriously. Not even someone else could get him to move. But today, I'm not so sure he'll be that good, not after what just happened. I slowly walk away from him, glancing back to make sure he's obeying me. I would tie him up if I had a leash, but I don't.

When I get back to the beach, I see that the girl hasn't returned to shore yet. She hasn't moved a foot.

"It's okay," I tell her, glancing back at where I left Estes to make sure he's not rushing out of the trees. "You can come back."

"Is he tied up?"

"Yeah," I lie, because at this point, I'm thinking she'll never come back and I'll have to go after her.

I shiver as I watch her begin to swim back. I have this uneasy feeling in my stomach, and I wonder if it's because Estes isn't next to me.

The girl stands up when the water is shallow enough and starts sloshing towards me. She's holding the back of her neck, and I wonder if she hurt herself. Her yellow dress is heavy and soaked, clinging to her body. When she reaches the shore, she grabs her sock that's floating nearby. It doesn't match the one she has on her foot.

She straightens and comes to me, pulling off her other sock and wringing it out. I expect her to be embarrassed about what just happened, but instead, she seems serene. Still happy like she was when she was dancing. Like none of it happened at all.

She smiles all wide at me, even as her wide eyes glance over towards where I left Estes. They are as blue as the lake. "Hi! I'm Lyla." She reaches out her dripping hand and shakes mine. Her fingers are like icicles.

"Christian," I say.

I can see her chin quiver slightly in a shiver. "That's a cool name."

"Uh...thanks."

She laughs musically. "Sorry I screamed at you."

I shake my head dumbly. "It's okay."

"Were you watching me dance?" she asks. It's not accusatory, just curious.

My neck gets hot. I'm about to say no, but something in her eyes makes me think maybe it's okay to tell her the truth.

"Just for a minute," I admit. "Then Estes went all psycho. Sorry about that."

"It's fine." She blinks her big eyes.

"Why were you dancing?" I ask before I can stop myself.

Lyla smiles and looks out at the water. She is trembling with cold but seems to not care.

"Because," she says quietly. She looks back at me and she's biting her lip like she is trying to contain some sort of uncontainable excitement.

That's it? Is dancing on the beach a normal thing for this girl? "I've never seen you around here before."

She shakes her head. "I'm from Chicago. I just got here last night. I'm visiting my brother for a month, or maybe longer."

I nod, realizing who she is. "Is Will Brooks your brother?"

He's known to be a recluse around here, but I don't tell her that.

Her face lights up. "How did you know that?"

"This used to be my grandma's house."

"Are you serious?" This is very exciting news to her.

"Yeah."

"Then you have to come inside and see it! And say hi to Will!"

73

For some reason, I get this strange feeling, like a sudden terror at the thought of seeing the inside of this house with all the memories. Before Will lived here, Remmi and Audree and I spent countless hours here with my grandma. It never bothered me before to think of all of it. But that was back when Remmi was alive.

I roll my neck and try not to come off as frantic. "I have to go, actually."

Lyla shakes her head. "It'll only take a second. It'll be fun. And I'll give you a tour of it because he's doing all this work to it and he says it's really different now. Will's asleep, but we should wake him up anyway. It's late, isn't it?"

"It's like eight."

"Oh, oh yeah."

She laughs softly, and I find myself staring at her in silence while she looks out at the lake again, all happy.

"Your lips are blue," I tell her.

With her pale skin and blue eyes and lips, she looks kind of corpse-like. And she's too skinny.

She lightly touches them. "Are they?"

"You should get inside. And I should get back home."

"You seem pretty cold too," she tells me. "You're shaking."

I try to relax my muscles but can't.

"I think my brother's clothes would fit you. There's probably something you could borrow."

She turns towards the house without another word. I stare after her for a second, then I find myself following her – this girl I've never met before. Her hair is almost black and straight from the water now, and she's holding it down over one shoulder. Before it was curly and dark brown. It hangs far down her back like a wet curtain. I've never seen so much hair. She looks back with her blue eyes and smiles at me. I've never seen someone so happy either. Except Remmi.

We're halfway up to the back door when I snap out of it and realize where my thoughts are going. I can't do this.

"Actually, I need to go." There's no denying the shaking in my voice. Maybe she's still thinking I'm just cold.

Lyla stops, confused. "Let me just get one of my brother's sweatshirts so you don't freeze to death."

I'm slightly panicked now, and angry at myself for coming to this neighborhood again. Remmi's gone and she's not coming back. Neither is Audree.

"What's wrong?" Lyla asks.

"Nothing," I say. "I just have to go."

But Lyla is adamant about this sweatshirt. "Just give me a minute and I'll find one."

"Fine," I say harshly. I try to calm down, glancing over towards where I left Estes. I don't see him. I wish he was next to me. "I'll wait out here."

"Are you sure? It's pretty cold."

"Yeah, I'm sure."

She turns to go inside but pauses. "Do you want some tea?"

I squint at her. "Tea?"

"Yeah. And some toast or something? Are you hungry?"

I find that my mouth wants to tilt up slightly in a smile. This in itself is pretty shocking.

And not good.

"No. I'm alright. Thanks."

"You sure?" Her face brightens when she thinks of something else. "I could make us my mom's raspberry pancakes to celebrate!"

"Celebrate what?" I say, frowning.

She shrugs one shoulder, smiling a smile that makes my mouth go dry. "Life."

There is something almost contagious about how she's being...all happy. But the ability for me to be happy died a month ago. Remembering that, remembering everything, makes me back up from her.

"Just the sweatshirt," I tell her.

I shouldn't even borrow the stupid sweatshirt. I should leave right now.

Her smile fades a little, but not in a sad way. It's because she's studying me. I look away from her and walk over to a long bench beneath the window and sit down. Lyla goes inside without offering me more tea or food.

My wet shirt and pants are stuck to me, making me shiver pretty bad. A few minutes pass. I look around at the yard – the place where my grandma forced me to bury the bird I killed with my bb gun, the place where we built a fort, the spot where I used to have a tire hanging so I could practice throwing a football. Remmi would always retrieve it for me.

My heart speeds up and I sit on my hands, trying to warm up and forget everything. I'm starting to wonder if I should just leave right now and never talk to this girl again, but she comes back out. I stand up quickly, anxious to go. That's when I see she doesn't have a sweatshirt or anything else for me.

"I put it in the dryer for a minute," she says, "so it'll be warm for you."

I grit my teeth because I need to get out of here.

She's in a different outfit, I notice. That's probably what took her so long. But instead of wearing warm, comfortable clothes, she's in another casual dress. Orange this time, with a black butterfly pattern. It drapes over her loosely, like it's a little big for her small frame.

I realize too late that I'm staring when she looks down at herself.

"I'm never able to wear dresses, really," she says cheerfully. "I've been waiting for this."

There's some story behind that, but I don't ask about it. When I realize that she might've wanted to look nice for me, I back up towards the railing.

"You don't need to warm the sweatshirt."

She smiles, completely at peace. "Relax, Christian. It'll only take a minute."

My jaw clenches at the way she said my name. I want to get out of here.

Lyla comes to the railing too and leans over on it, looking out, completely at ease. "Sorry you had to get in the water. I hope you didn't have your phone on you or anything."

"It's in my truck," I say.

I don't carry it on me because I'm sick of all the phone calls and text messages, except from my parents. And they know where I am right now, back in grandma's old neighborhood. Remmi's neighborhood.

I suddenly remember something else I was carrying. I sigh and pull out the soaking wet card from my back pocket.

"Oh, no," Lyla says. "What's that?"

I try to shake it out, knowing it's pointless.

"It was for a friend."

This one was for Audree. I wonder who left it, and what it says.

"Is it ruined?"

"Probably."

"I'm sorry."

I look at her. "It's not your fault."

Lyla and I go silent for a few seconds. I set the card down on the railing, thinking maybe I can dry it out. I lay it face down so Lyla doesn't see the bleeding name scrawled on the front of it. I don't feel like answering any questions about any of it right now.

I lean over on the railing too, hoping Lyla can't tell how cold and uncomfortable I am right now. But she's looking at the card, not at me.

"Do you know people around here?" she asks hopefully.

"No." There is a bite in my tone that I can't help.

"But didn't your grandma live here?"

"Yeah." That's all I feel like offering at the moment.

"Oh," she says awkwardly.

I can tell she wants to ask more about that, but I'm thankful when she doesn't.

She clears her throat and laughs at something. I'm not sure what.

"Where do you live?" she asks.

"Harbor Springs. About thirty minutes from here."

She smiles at me. "You probably do fun things with your friends all the time," she says kind of dreamily.

It's a strange thing to say. "I don't, actually."

Lyla blinks at me, smile fading. "Why not?"

I shrug. "I just don't."

Again, Lyla looks like she wants to dive further into this like she's a shrink or something, like my dad. But she's smart enough not to. She tucks some wet hair behind her ears. Her lips are still blue, and again I wonder why she's in that dress.

"Do you know my brother?"

I laugh harshly without meaning to. "No one knows your brother. People only know *of* him."

She looks down, nods. "I'm starting to see that." She looks back up at me with her blue eyes. "So what are you doing here?"

I try to shrug casually. "Estes and I were just…walking the beach."

Lyla's staring at me again, like little kids do when they've just met someone. I think she gets the sense that I'm keeping something from her.

I push off from the railing. "I need to get going," I say for the thousandth time.

"Let me get Will's sweatshirt from the dryer," she says.

"It's okay – "

"I'll just get it real quick," she says and she's already walking inside the house.

I groan and find myself trying to catch a glimpse into the living room. Lyla was right, the house has changed. For some reason the fridge is in the living room, right next to the window. It looks almost nothing like it did when Grams lived here. Maybe someday it wouldn't be so bad to go inside and see it.

I shake my head. Not with this girl being here now.

She comes back out with the sweatshirt and another smile. "Here," she says.

I take it quickly. "Thanks."

I peel off my soaked t-shirt and drape it on the railing. Then I pull the sweatshirt over my head, feeling warmer instantly.

I didn't think it was a big deal to take my shirt off in front of her – because it's not – but when I pull my head through the sweatshirt I see that Lyla is now pressed against the wall with wide eyes and a red face. Her hand is up at the back of her neck. It's like she's never seen a guy without a shirt on before.

This girl intrigues me.

I turn away from her and start down the deck steps with my wet shirt in my hand.

"Thanks for the sweatshirt. I'll get it back to you."

I don't know how I'll do that without seeing her again, but I'll have to think of something.

"It's no problem," she says.

I raise a hand in the air in a slight wave without looking back.

"Christian!" Lyla calls when I reach the sandy grass.

I reluctantly stop and turn, walking backwards towards where I left Estes. I can't wait to see him.

"What is it?" I ask.

She smiles, looks down at her hands, then at me again. "Everything will be okay," she says.

I pause, wondering if I heard her right. "What?"

"I said everything will be okay!" she almost yells. Then she calms herself. "Whatever you're upset about, I'm sure it'll all be okay in the end."

I feel my jaw muscles tighten, my shoulders flex, because she doesn't realize what she's saying.

"That's not possible," I mutter under my breath, but I give her a small nod of fake gratitude and I walk away.

Twice, I want to look back at her, but I don't let myself because whatever it is that I'm feeling about her right now as I tread heavily through the trees, it isn't good.

Sienna Rodriguez
Next door

The kid is finally gone. Emil and I came back next door once we realized the situation – that Lyla screamed because of a dog. Emil's upstairs now, most likely looking through the fridge, while I'm downstairs watching the screens, shaking.

Lyla is still on the back porch. I watch her turn to head inside, but she notices the yellow card that the kid accidentally left on the railing. She picks it up and looks at the front of it for a second, then goes inside and sets it on the kitchen counter. She immediately picks up the phone and calls her parents. I listen as she tells them that her nightmares didn't come last night. She is so excited that she doesn't hear the concern in her parents' voices. If she is out living life, it's more complicated to guard her.

Maybe I'll get my team of five now.

I hear Emil come down the basement stairs and I stiffen slightly. He stops behind me, silent.

"What's up?" I say without turning to him, trying to sound light.

He waits, then leans against the desk next to me with his arms crossed. Does he have to get so close? I hate the smell of him. No, I actually hate that I sort of *like* the smell of him, that's what it is. I look up at him sharply and lose some of my careful control.

"What is it?" I snap.

He shrugs. "Nothing. It's just…that was crazy." His perusal makes me uncomfortable. "You okay?"

My stomach sinks at the look in his eyes. I let out a quiet breath. "When did you look me up?"

"Just now, upstairs," he says, not denying it. "I didn't expect to find anything."

I nod. "But you found out about my sister."

"Yeah."

I look up at him. His eyes are soft, and it annoys me. "And?"

"And I think I understand you a little better."

I grit my teeth, silent. He doesn't understand me at all. I rub my face, exasperated, then realize my hands are still shaking so I clench them in my lap beneath the desk.

"It's okay," Emil says.

He kneels down next to me. I look at him and I hate the pity I see there in his eyes.

"It's why you're so good at what you do," he says. "It's part of your story."

I shake my head, defensive. "And you're terrible at what you do. What's your story?"

He makes a soft, hurt sound and nods, looking down at the unfinished floors. "Yeah, alright. Thank you."

He doesn't move from where he is.

I feel bad for a second, but I can't bring myself to apologize. I hate that he looked me up. He had no right. And I hate that anyone with my name can look up the headlines about my sister being murdered when she was sixteen. Two years younger than Lyla.

I am focused on the screens, avoiding looking at him. There is a car across the dirt road from our house, just the front bumper visible on the cameras. I've been waiting for it to move.

"Can you go see who that is, please?" I ask shortly.

He sighs and looks at the screen. "Who?"

"That car's been sitting across the road for a while."

His jaw flexes. "Sienna – "

"Fine," I say and start to get up.

"Alright. I'll do it."

He stands to his feet, then pauses there next to me while I avoid looking at him, and then he quietly goes upstairs. When he is gone, I let my breath out and clutch my arms around my chest, trying to stop the sounds of my sister's screaming in my head.

Samantha
Across the road

I am pretending to be lost. Actually, maybe I am lost, in a philosophical sense. Because once again I am sitting down the street from a complete stranger's house, in a different state this time, watching it. Somehow, I'm going to try to find out a little bit more about them if I can.

I stare at Will's house, feeling a sense of de ja vu from yesterday back in Chicago. His house is barely visible through the trees but I can see that it's blue and it backs up to the lake. It's bigger than his parents' house, but still, it's modest compared to what you'd expect from a Bailey. His car in the driveway is modest too, like his rental car was. Nice, but nothing flashy. I can see a pile of debris on the south side of the house. Dorothy was right. He's renovating it. Is he doing the work himself? It's not like I've never heard of a billionaire doing manual labor. There are plenty of rich people who've given up their fortune to charity because they've realized money can't buy happiness.

But for the Baileys, money seemed to buy plenty of happiness fifteen years ago. They were the furthest thing from modest that a family can be. They were famous for traveling to the far ends of the earth, living extravagantly, hosting lavish parties, although it was hard to get a photo of them. That was the only admirable thing they seemed to spend money on back then – their privacy. Who knows how many millions they spent to make sure hardly any pictures were published of them or their children?

There is still no movement at the house. They probably aren't even awake yet because it's pretty early on a Saturday morning.

So, what do I do? I am tempted to take pictures of what I can see of Will's house and send them to my mom and Nell because they asked me to. I look around. I'm surrounded by forest. The dirt road is small enough to make you nervous if someone came at you in the opposite direction in their car. You'd have to pull over and let them pass. It's quiet here, peaceful. No one is out. No one is watching. I could just take one quick picture…

But then, there's sudden movement. Not from Will's house. It's from the brown house on the next property from his. There are boards on the windows and a big pot tipped over on the front porch, so I didn't think it was occupied. I thought I would go unnoticed if I pulled over across the road from it. But I was wrong.

A very large, muscular man in his thirties walks out the front door. When I realize he's heading towards me, I quickly pick up my phone and open my GPS just as the man gives me a small wave. I glance around the car. Nothing out of the ordinary. I left all the research about the Baileys in my car that's currently parked in the Chicago O'Hare parking lot.

The guy crosses the dirt road and I roll down my window, smiling nervously.

"Hello," I say, trying to keep my voice even.

"Hi. I just wanted to make sure you were okay. I couldn't help but notice you've been out here for a while."

"Yeah, thanks, I'm fine," I say. "Just a little lost."

"Where're you headed?"

"Harbor Springs." It's the only other town I can think of.

He frowns. "That's pretty far south of here. Take a right when you leave and just follow…"

He goes on and I pretend to be taking mental notes when really, I'm wondering how to ask him if he knows anything about Will.

"Great," I say when he finishes giving directions. "Thanks."

He glances down at what I'm wearing – jeans that I wore yesterday and a t-shirt I got from the grocery store last night because no clothing stores were open. It says, *I Heart Good Hart.*

"Are you visiting?" he asks because I clearly look like a tourist.

"Yeah. Just for a little while."

"Where are you from?"

"Phoenix," I blurt. I don't know why I lied or why I'm so nervous. "You?"

"L.A.," he says.

"Oh, that's nice."

He nods. "Bit cooler here."

"Yes!" I say too loudly. I clear my throat. "Yeah, it's true."

He glances around. "It's a nice area. Peaceful compared to L.A. I like it."

I nod, feeling that the conversation is coming to a close. I try to think of a way to ask him about Will.

"Is this just a summer home for you? It looks ready for winter."

"No, I live here year-round." He gives a small laugh and rubs his neck. "I keep meaning to take the boards off the windows."

That's weird, I think. But I say, "Do you like this neighborhood? And...the neighbors and everything?"

He glances towards Will's house, only for a second. "I don't really know anyone. I came here to get away from things."

I sigh inwardly. "Oh." I think of something else. "Do you know Dorothy Freeman?" Dorothy knows about Will's reputation.

"Yeah," he says. "You know her?"

"Just because I'm staying at her rental house."

He nods, not responding with more information like I wanted him to.

Dangit. That didn't go very far.

He leans over more, and I catch the scent of his cologne.

"What are you in town for?" he asks.

I suddenly regret dragging the conversation on. I'm not good at lying. I start rambling nervously.

"I, um, I'm here, yeah, for fun...you could say. Just a vacation."

He smiles kindly. I really need to calm down.

"I'm Emil Alanovic," he says.

I nod excessively.

"Wow," I say. "That's some name."

"Family's from Poland."

"I'm...Samantha Foster," I say. I cough as I lightly shake his hand. "I should get going. Thanks for the directions."

He nods. "See you around."

"Yeah," I say too loudly. "Okay, bye."

I start rolling up the window too soon. He straightens, amused. I give a small wave and he nods and then heads back to his house. It still smells a little like his cologne in here.

I look straight ahead, gripping the steering wheel. Now what? Do I just drive away? Emil glances back at me, so I start the car up and pull out into the road, driving super slow because I have no idea what to do.

I turn out of the neighborhood towards the two-lane road, and then I notice a little sign on the side of the road. *Music and Arts Festival.* It's today in Harbor Springs. If Will is going to do something with his sister today, I'm guessing he'll take her to the festival. Maybe I'll see them there if they go.

And then…maybe…I'll be brave enough to bump into them.

Will

It is utterly silent when I wake up, like I'm deaf. There's no ticking furnace or birds at the window or the sound of waves off the lake, like there usually is. I roll over, confused, touching my ears. That's when I remember the earplugs.

And my sister.

I sigh and roll to my back again, digging the earplugs out. I lay here for a second, taking in my new reality. Maybe it won't be so bad. She'll be asleep most of the time.

Then I hear a sound coming from downstairs. I sit up, listening. She's awake.

I let out a long breath, rubbing both hands down my face. Then I check my phone, seeing a few texts that came in from my dad. I didn't hear them because of the earplugs. I blink at the time of day on my phone, unable to believe that I slept past ten o'clock. Must be stress.

Lyla's going to be awake today, the first text says. **No nightmares last night. Try to lay low.**

I groan. How does he expect me to do that?

I am slow to put on my button-up flannel shirt I wore for painting the other day. It's still pretty clean. So are the pants I've worn a few times recently, even though there's a stripe of white paint down the side. I grab new socks and put my work boots on. I'm determined to still have a normal day, no matter what Lyla chooses to do around the house. And I'm in more of a rush now to get this house finished and move on. The Manor is there, waiting for me.

Lyla's rummaging through the freezer in the living room when I get downstairs. She's wearing an orange dress today with little butterflies on it, and she's standing on her tiptoes in knitted socks – one purple, the other one white. Her face lights up when she turns around and sees me. She must have showered because her long hair is wet and hangs down her back, probably so I don't have to see her scar. I'm relieved about that.

"Hi!" she says, smiling so wide that it looks painful.

"Hey."

She spreads her arms. "So…?" she says expectantly.

"So."

"I'm awake!"

I nod and try to sound positive. "Yeah. You…slept through the night."

"Isn't it great?"

"It's…awesome."

"Right? Mom and Dad are so excited. Mom especially." She touches her dress. "And I can finally wear something other than pajamas!"

I rub my face tiredly. "That's…pretty cool."

"I have all these things I want to do today."

I stifle a sigh. "Great."

She nods slowly, studying me now. Maybe she can tell I'm not as excited about it as she probably thought I'd be. Silence falls over us. She goes back to looking through the freezer when I don't say anything else about it.

"What are you looking for?" I ask.

"I'm making a list of what we need at the store, but we don't need much. You have really fancy food in here." She stops and looks at me. "But where's your tea kettle?"

I shake my head. "I don't have one."

Lyla blinks at me, like she can't imagine a world where some people don't own tea kettles. "So, you probably don't have tea either."

"No."

She glances around, looking lost. "Where are the cabinets for that wall? Just curious."

"I'm sanding them… to paint them."

"Are they in the garage?" She looks over at the laundry room that leads to the locked door of the garage.

I scratch behind my ear. "Yeah."

"Do you want help? I like doing that kind of stuff…I think."

"Nah, I'm good."

Her expression falls, and I feel bad for a second. But she can't see what's in there.

You shouldn't even be awake right now. This wasn't the plan.

I glance around the kitchen and living room, realizing there is absolutely nothing for us to do together, since she can't help me with the cabinets in the garage, and I don't want her helping with anything else. Plus, I'm pretending that I have no cable or internet.

"Maybe you could give me a tour of the town today?" she asks.

I stifle a sigh, thinking of my dad's texts. "I have too much to do around here."

"Oh, come on. Just for a little while. We don't have to be out for long."

"Lyla –"

She grabs my keys off the counter. "Let's go. It'll be fun. We can get breakfast somewhere." She heads off down the hallway towards the front door, pausing. "Are you coming?"

Working my jaw, I glance around at all the things I was hoping to get done in the kitchen this weekend. And I'm thinking about the fact that I have to keep her from seeing the news.

"We won't be long," she says. "Maybe an hour or so."

I let out a breath. What are the chances that the story will get out in the next hour anyway? Lyla is smiling at me, waiting.

Seeing her blue eyes that are dancing like they used to when she was little, I say, "Yeah. All right," and tell her she should probably get some shoes on.

"Oh yeah," she laughs.

She heads to the closet and – after she pulls off her mismatched knitted socks – she slips on some flip flops.

I find that I'm slightly amused by this.

"Can I drive?" she asks, closing the closet door.

My amusement disappears. No one else has ever driven my car.

"Or…I don't have to," Lyla says awkwardly, seeing my reaction.

I force myself to say, "It's fine."

"Are you sure?"

No. "Yeah, I'm sure."

And then, minutes later, we are driving down Lake Shore Drive, going seven below the speed limit. Lyla insisted on having all the windows rolled down and the music playing too loudly for this time of day. She sings along, but she doesn't know the words and she's off-key.

I feel my quiet life slipping through my fingers.

"You can speed up a little," I say, trying to sound light.

"I'm a little nervous," Lyla says. "Isn't there supposed to be a line down the middle of the road? It's so twisty. But it's so pretty. Is this the Tunnel of Trees?"

"Yeah."

She leans forward to look up through the windshield, but then gasps and slows way down as a biker goes past us in the opposite direction.

I turn to her, only now realizing something. "Do you have your license?"

She laughs. "Of course. I just never drive. Ever. This is probably my fifth time driving since I got it."

Well that's fantastic.

Lyla turns down the music a little. "So, what do you do for fun around here?"

It takes me a second to think of what I usually do. "I work on the house, mainly. Sometimes I go into town and pick up supplies or get some food...to-go."

Lyla's expression barely masks her worry. "And all your friends? Where do they live?"

I clear my throat.

"I'm still meeting people," I say. "I haven't been here long enough to get close to anybody."

As if five years isn't long enough to do that.

She nods and doesn't say anything. I know what she's thinking. If my sister had a normal life, she would probably have about a thousand friends. She would be just like our mom, always inviting people into the house and bringing food to the neighbors and volunteering her time to help the poor. Although unlike our mom, she wouldn't be doing it all so that she can try to come off as a normal person.

"What do you do for a living?" Lyla asks. She glances sideways at me and laughs softly. "I should probably know this."

I hesitate, wondering if she's going to tell Dad. I doubt he would believe her anyway.

"I flip houses," I tell her. "I've done a few in the area."

She nods, interested. "That's great. It must pay really well."

"Yeah." I look away.

"Where do you want to take me first?"

I frantically search for ideas. I'm not prepared to have a day like this with her. It was simple before, when I thought she'd be asleep.

"We could stop at the General Store. Get some cinnamon rolls for breakfast."

"Okay," she says excitedly. "Then what?"

"I thought you said we'd only be out for an hour."

"How far is the General Store?"

I pause. "About five minutes away."

Twenty if she keeps driving this slowly.

She laughs. "So, then what?"

I look out the window, annoyed. What else is there? How am I supposed to keep a teenager busy in a small town?

"We could...go to a few shops in Harbor Springs," I tell her. "I think there's a music festival going on today in town. There'll be live music."

Her eyes widen. "I've never seen a live band before."

I stare at her. She's serious. Sure, she's had nightmares for years, but that doesn't mean she can't do things. What do my parents do with her all the time? Don't they want her to have a normal life? Isn't that one of the biggest reasons they live the way they do and lie to her like this?

An uncomfortable thought occurs to me next, and I push it away as quickly as it comes: If I had been around more, maybe I could've helped Lyla have an actual life.

Shaking my head, I look out the window and don't say anything else for a while.

When we finally arrive at the General Store, Lyla parks my car ever so slowly into a space and turns it off, looking up at the small red building with a wide smile.

"This is so fun," she says. She takes her seatbelt off. "Look at all the motorcycles."

"Yeah. Exciting." I suppress a yawn.

The little shop is full of bikers. I've never seen it this packed. We get into a long line to buy our cinnamon rolls.

90

"I like your tattoo," Lyla says to the big biker in front of us.

The man looks down at her for a second, as if deciding whether she's being sincere or not. Lyla only smiles at him.

"Thanks," he says.

He has a long, stringy beard that's black with a white stripe down the middle of it. A patch on his leather vest says *Skunk*. I can't believe my sister's talking to this guy. She's tiny compared to him, and her orange dress next to his black leather makes her look like a sunbeam.

The door jingles and someone steps into the line behind us. I glance back and see a small Hispanic woman with her hair pulled back tightly in a bun. She's looking down at her phone as she tries to squeeze into line behind us, between us and the door.

"Do the birds represent something?" Lyla asks the biker.

"Yeah." He holds his arm out so she can see it better. "My grandchildren."

And that's all it takes. For the next few minutes while we stand in line, the big biker tells Lyla all about his six kids and fourteen grandchildren. Lyla listens intently, asking their names and what it's like to be a grandparent.

I find myself studying my sister as she talks to him. Is this what she's like? All this time, I've never known what type of person she is. She was so young when I lived at home, only nine when I moved out. I can't think of any good memories with her at the house in Chicago because I wasn't exactly an exemplary older brother during that time. The best memories I have of her are from our childhood at the Manor, before everything changed. I've never been able to share those with her.

By the end of their conversation, the man is like a new person, smiling and laughing with Lyla. He pays for his hat and keychain and before he turns to leave, he moves to actually hug her.

Before I can stop him, the woman behind us moves forward and steps between them to grab a postcard from the front counter. She bumps into the biker and the man is forced to back up.

"Oops!" the woman says, smiling. "Excuse me. I'm sorry."

But she doesn't move, just stands in front of Lyla, looking down at her postcard. I frown slightly, watching.

The biker is annoyed, but he smiles down at Lyla. "Good talking to you."

"You too," Lyla says. "Have a good trip."

He turns to leave, and the woman gets back into line behind us. She's still looking down at her postcard, unconcerned. I study her for a second. That was strange.

Lyla's face is bright and cheery as we step up to the counter and ask for two cinnamon rolls. She puts her hand on my arm.

"I can pay for us," she says. "I have some allowance saved up that I haven't been able to spend."

I look down at her hand and am suddenly struck with a memory from when we were younger...Lyla toddling up to me when she was two and jumping into my arms so I could spin her around. She loved it when I threw her above my head and caught her. We'd do it over and over until she was tired from laughing and my arms were killing me. We'd usually be at the Manor. Lyla knows nothing about it.

"Will?"

Annoyed by the sudden memory, I say, "No. I'll pay," and I move away from her touch by pulling my wallet out.

She doesn't notice. I get my change and we leave the store together.

Halfway to the car, I stop and look at her, frustrated. "You can't just talk to everyone like that."

I don't know why I'm so mad. Maybe it's because I prefer to keep to myself but now my teenaged sister is here and she's talking to bikers and making me think of the past and stirring everything up.

"Why not?"

"Because."

To my surprise, Lyla smiles. "I'm just talking to people, Will, making friends. It's not going to kill me."

I get into the car in the driver's seat this time, and Lyla doesn't say anything about it, just hands me the keys. She eats her cinnamon roll and so do I, using it as an excuse not to talk the whole way to Harbor Springs.

We end up going to four or five little shops together in town. Lyla makes conversation with almost every single store clerk we come across. She introduces me to them like she's campaigning for me. I know what she's doing. She probably heard from Mom about my reputation around here.

That gives me an idea.

"Let's go in there," I say, nodding towards a tourist apparel shop.

I look around when we get inside and immediately spot Tricia near the back, talking to a customer. She's in her fifties now, still tall and stalky. She's a hard worker. I leave Lyla by the women's sweatshirts, telling her I'll be right back.

Tricia sees me coming, and she turns away.

"Tricia," I say, annoyed.

She grabs two stacks of t-shirts and starts taking them to the back.

I follow. "Tricia, come on."

I glance over at Lyla. She's discreetly watching us, trying to pretend that she's not.

Tricia doesn't even turn to me as she says, "I have the right to refuse service to –"

"You wouldn't do that to my sister, would you?"

She whips around, craning her neck. "She's here?"

"Yes."

Her face changes, only slightly. "I haven't seen her since she was three." Then she focuses on me and looks me up and down. "Sober?"

I roll my eyes. "I was never a drunk."

She rolls her eyes too and starts walking away from me again.

"I need you to come back," I say.

Tricia stops. "Back to what?"

"I'm getting it up and running again. I need you. Double the salary."

Years ago, Tricia ran the garden and had twenty employees under her, supplying fresh produce to every worker at the Manor and our family.

She turns to me. "When?"

"Probably end of the summer, I'm not sure. But you have my word."

"Can I get my team back?"

"Of course. Whatever you need."

Eyeing me just as intensely as the first time, she says, "Keep your money. I'll take the same salary as before."

I smile, and we shake on it.

When I get back to my sister, I feel like I'm on a high, like I have a purpose again.

Lyla holds up a sweatshirt to her torso and asks me if I like it.

"Yeah, it's great. You should get it."

"It's kind of expensive."

"How much?"

"Forty dollars."

I grin and start taking out my wallet. "I'll get it."

"No, I have my allowance," she tells me again. She smiles, folding the sweatshirt over her arm as we walk up to the counter to pay for it. "Who was that?"

I shrug. "An old friend."

Tricia is over fifty, so I know Lyla is only excited because I know somebody.

She nods, and refrains from asking more.

Tricia's response has given me hope that everything will work out. I'm picturing the Manor more and more and mentally making a list of everyone I need to hire back, everything that needs to get done. It's extensive.

At another shop Lyla buys me a smiley-face magnet for my fridge, because she says my house is "kind of sparse," and she buys me a blue tea kettle and about a thousand types of tea.

Before I know it, we've been out for hours. We even have to stop for lunch. Our conversation is becoming stunted and the thrill of talking to Tricia is wearing off. Lyla keeps asking me questions about myself – when's the last time I dated someone? Am I interested in anyone in town? Would I go on a date with someone local if I thought she was pretty? I can't very well tell her that I keep my distance from women and most people in general.

But Lyla won't stop asking. Is this what it's going to be like the whole time she's here?

"We should go home," I tell her as we walk out of the café.

"Can we get some ice cream first? It's just down here. Is mint chocolate chip still your favorite? It's still mine."

By the time we get to the ice cream shop I am so bogged down by thoughts of the past and frustrated at my parents for putting me in this whole situation that I stop answering her questions all together. She finally takes the hint. We take our ice cream down to the pier, where the Music and Arts Festival is going on. We sit on a bench and eat our mint chocolate chip ice cream together, people-watching in silence.

A band starts playing from one of the booths. Lyla's all excited about it, having never seen a live band before.

"Do you dance?" she asks me.

"No." That came out too harsh.

"Oh." Her face falls, and she goes back to eating her ice cream, turning away from me.

My jaw flexes as a pang of regret hits me.

Hanging from the awning to the right of us is a flat screen TV. I don't think much of it until two words come up on the screen that make my heart start pounding.

Bailey Enterprises.

Our family's company.

My stomach immediately drops, and I stare at the screen, frozen. I don't know what to do. Wouldn't my parents have called me first if the story got out? Wouldn't they have warned me? I pull my phone out to check, but there's nothing. A newscaster appears on the screen. I'm waiting for the words explaining that the Billionaire Baileys have been found, living as the Brooks family all these years. I'm half-excited, half-terrified. Lyla's attention is on the screen now too because she's probably wondering why I'm so focused on it.

Say it, I find myself thinking. I'll have to tell Lyla everything, right in the middle of a festival, but the thought is a relief. *Say it.* Her nightmares didn't come last night. She's so happy today. Now's the time to tell her. She'll finally know why I've been so distant all these years. She'll finally understand the strife between me and our parents. Her questions will change from being about my life now to what *our* lives were like back then. We'll finally actually talk.

But the story is about a branch closing down in Texas. All the adrenaline goes out of me so quickly that I feel dizzy.

"That's sad," Lyla says, because a bunch of people were laid off. She doesn't know it's her own family's company.

"Yeah." I wish I could tell her right now, but my parents would ask her how she found out and she'd say I told her, of course.

"You okay?" Lyla asks.

"I'm fine."

"You sure? You seem a little…"

Lyla trails off, and I look at her. Someone in the crowd has caught her attention. Her face lights up. I turn and look, and my adrenaline spikes again when I see who it is.

It's the woman from the plane.

Lyla stands up. "I'm gonna go say hi."

"Lyla, wait."

"It's okay. I'll just say hi real quick. I'll be back."

She starts to leave but I catch her wrist.

"*Wait*," I say firmly. "You can't just…you can't just talk to everybody like this."

She stares down at me, trying not to smile. "Will," she says calmly, "I'm going to go talk to her. You can come with, or you can stay here. But I'm going."

"Lyla – "

"No, Will. Nightmares have pretty much wrecked my life, and they might come back tonight." She pauses, swallowing. "But today? Today I have lots of energy so I'm going to talk to people. And *live*."

I stare at her, my grip loosening on her wrist. She has our father's talent for negotiating and our mother's gift for getting what she wants.

I let her go.

Lyla smiles.

"Thanks," she says. "I'll be right back."

I watch her walk away. She goes to a trashcan first to throw away her napkin, then heads for the woman I hoped to never see again. I keep my distance from women, especially women like this one – someone who keeps popping up in my mind ever since I first saw her yesterday. It just makes things easier when I keep my distance, less complicated, because people can't know who I really am.

I crunch up the napkin in my hand and stare down at it.

My sister is turning my life upside down, and it's only been one day.

Emil

Irritating music thumps from three different booths near me. Jazz from one, alternative from a second, and bluegrass from a third. It's a mix that sounds like mud. I watch the people who are standing in Lyla's path, making sure she's safe as she walks over to something or someone. Sienna is across the street, casually walking in the same direction as Lyla. She bumps into a guy with a violin in his hands, and she gives an apology but keeps going, surreptitiously following. I like her. She's intense. She has a reputation for being the best of the best, and there are deeper levels to her that she's not willing to let me see. Not yet, at least.

My eyes scan the crowd. I recognize most of the people around here, of course. There's Bruce Andrews, running a tasting booth for the Pier Restaurant where he's the bartender. He used to be on the security team for the Baileys at the Manor, so he and I can safely chat about Will's antics when I get a chance to have a drink out, which is almost every Saturday night. Then there's Theo Lorkowski a few paces away, Marty Alcott across the street, and Melissa Freid, who gives me a nod in greeting as she takes her almost-teenaged daughter into the candy store. I nod back. They are all former employees of the Baileys at the Manor. All still well-compensated by the Baileys for their loyalty...and their discretion, of course. All legally gagged too, just in case.

I grin. With so many people around here who used to work for the Baileys and are still ever-loyal to them, there is no safer place on the planet for Lyla to be. Soon, there will be a buzz around town between those in the inner circle. Lillianna is here, they'll say. And Malcolm is getting the Manor up and running again. They'll have to wait and see who he hires back. Some won't be pleased if they find they've been left out.

Finally, I think. *Some action.* I feel like I'm in a Grisham novel.

There is someone else I recognize in the crowd. It's the beautiful woman from before – the one who was on the side of the road in her silver rental car, lost outside my house. Samantha Foster, I remember. From Phoenix, Arizona. She is trying to see through the crowd, looking over towards someone. Lyla's walking up to her, I realize. I wonder how they would know each other, but I don't think much about it. There is a group of teenaged boys who are eyeing Lyla as she passes, and Sienna looks ready to brawl.

Rolling my eyes, I head over there to dissipate the situation in case Sienna talks to them or something. I'm starting to wonder if this is going to be a problem with her.

Lyla

I try to control my excitement as I head over to Samantha, but this is just too good to be true. I wanted to introduce her to Will yesterday and I didn't, but here she is again. What are the chances of running into her like this? It has to mean something. But I have to be careful because a lot rides on this conversation. She might possibly become my friend or even my brother's future girlfriend. I can't seem too excited or desperate.

As I make my way over to her, I see her gaze stop on someone and I realize it's my brother. He's looking right back at her through the crowd, but then I see Samantha suddenly make a U-turn and hurry back towards the parking lot.

"Hey, wait!" I say loudly, hurrying over to her. She doesn't turn. "Samantha!" I call out.

Samantha jumps and whirls around. Her eyes widen when she sees me. I walk up to her, trying to smile in a friendly and not overly eager way.

"Hi!" I practically yell. I calm myself as I stop in front of her. "Hi," I say casually. "How are you?"

She is blinking a lot. "I'm...good, you?"

Maybe she doesn't remember me. "Do you remember me?" I ask. "From the plane?"

"Um..." She glances at my brother again, then back at me. "Yes, of course. Lyla, right?"

"Yes!" I laugh. "I held your hand and probably made you really uncomfortable."

She seems to relax a little.

"You didn't make me uncomfortable." She smiles. "It calmed me down, actually."

"Oh good," I say, relieved. "I'm glad."

Then we stand here for a second, neither of us knowing what to say. Two guys lugging guitar cases pass us, their hair flowing down and mingling in their long beards. I try to think of what normal people ask when they've just met someone. I'm a little out of practice.

"Do you live around here?"

I thought that sounded pretty good, but her face turns a little pink.

"No," she says. "I'm visiting."

"Me too. How long will you be staying?"

"I'm...not really sure. A week, maybe. You?"

"The rest of the summer, probably. This whole trip was a surprise for me for my birthday yesterday. I've never visited my brother before. Or been outside of Chicago, ever. That was my first time on a plane yesterday, but I think I told you that already."

And I think I might be talking too much. I press my lips together.

Samantha frowns slightly at something I said, but she doesn't say anything. The wind picks up and I hold my hair down casually so I don't make her uncomfortable with my scar.

"How old did you turn yesterday?" she asks.

"Eighteen."

She smiles and nods, like she's thinking about that. "Happy birthday."

"Thanks!"

She glances at Will again.

"Do you want to meet him?"

"Who?"

"My brother." I glance back at him through the crowd of people. "I think you make him nervous."

"Why would I make him nervous?" she asks quickly.

I almost say, *"Because he thinks you're gorgeous!"* but I stop myself just in time. "I don't know. But I can introduce you."

"Oh, I don't think..."

But she stops talking when I lightly take her arm and walk in front of her through the crowd of musicians and artsy people towards Will. He has finished his ice cream and is now looking down at his hands that are clasped between his legs. He doesn't see us. He seems very remote as he sits there, although we're surrounded by people. He makes me think of an island.

"Will," I say when we get close. He looks up, and when he sees I have Samantha in tow, he stands up. "This is Samantha. She was on our flight."

Will nods, looking like a businessman as he shakes her hand even though he's in a dirty work shirt and pants that have a streak of something white down the side. Maybe paint. I'm sort of embarrassed that he's wearing this right now. It doesn't help me with what I'm trying to accomplish here. Although, I guess Samantha is wearing a t-shirt that says *I Heart Good Hart* and jeans. Maybe she doesn't care.

"Nice to meet you," Will says.

Samantha smiles and lets go of his hand pretty quickly. "Nice to meet you, too."

They both sound very professional. Samantha looks over the crowd like she wants to leave. Did I cross a line? Was it rude to bring her over here when she's clearly nervous right now?

My brother doesn't say a word, so I take over.

"So where are you staying?" I ask. I look at Will. "She's visiting for a week." Maybe longer if they start dating.

"A little cottage on the beach," she says.

"In Good Hart?" I ask, hoping she'll say yes. That would make things very convenient.

"Yeah. Off Sun Way Circle."

"Are you visiting family?" I ask.

She looks at Will. "No. Just…getting away from things for a while. I don't have any plans or anything." She clears her throat. "A friend of mine told me this area's really beautiful."

My brother nods casually. "What friend?"

"Um…Dorothy. She owns the cottage I'm staying in."

"Dorothy Freeman? I know her."

"Oh. Yeah, she mentioned that."

Will's eyes flicker. "You talked about me?"

"No," she says quickly, giving a nervous laugh. "No, I mean…yes. I guess we did. She was…telling me about some of the locals around here. She, um, mentioned you're renovating her old house?"

Will studies her. "Yeah. I bought it a while back."

"That's what he does," I say. "He flips houses. He does a great job."

Will glances at me, his jaw flexing. I give him an innocent look that says, *"What?"*

"Is that right?" Samantha studies him, swallowing. "Good for you."

"It pays the bills."

"Mm." She keeps her eyes on him for a second, then she looks over at the flat screen hanging from the awning above us. The newscaster is still talking about some huge corporation closing down a branch, letting go of all those poor people. Will glances over at it too, then at me. He clears his throat and looks at Samantha. She is studying him. There is some pretty serious eye contact going on. I think they like each other. This is so great. Maybe they've been thinking about each other since yesterday.

Suddenly, Samantha turns to me. "We should hang out while I'm here," she says. "What do you think?"

What do I *think?* I think I'm going to pee my pants.

"Sure," I say, trying to sound casual. "What about tonight? We could go out to dinner. I wanted to go to that restaurant on the pier later." I point at it down the street.

Will tries to break in. "I don't – "

"Sounds great," Samantha says. "And it'll be my treat. For your birthday yesterday."

"Yay!" I say before I can stop myself.

Will sighs quietly, but I don't think Samantha heard it.

"I have a few things I need to do beforehand," she says. "I'll meet you guys there. Should we say 7:30?"

I nod excitedly. "That's perfect." It'll give Will and I more time to see the town.

I refrain from hugging her as we say goodbye. Will turns to me when she walks away.

"What?" I say because his eyes are annoyed and his mouth is working. He shakes his head without saying anything and we head back to the car.

We decide to drive through different neighborhoods, so Will can show me some of the houses he's fixed up and sold.

"It's beautiful," I tell him.

The last one is especially. He told me he re-finished the brick on the outside and painted the rest white. I imagine him working on this house for months by himself. This one reminds me of our house back home in

Chicago. There is a family playing outside on the lawn with their little boy toddling around. Will watches them pensively.

"You're really good at this," I say, and he blinks and looks at me. "You made a cozy home for them."

He clears his throat. "Yeah," he says. "Thanks." He pulls away from the house.

We drive around quietly after that. The town of Harbor Springs is really pretty, with houses that range from small to massive, almost all of them nice no matter the size. There are trees everywhere, especially up on the hill with houses built up the side, overlooking the bay.

In the center of a neighborhood is Harbor Springs High School. I look up at it as we pass, wondering what it's like to go there. Is this where Christian went? The building is all brick and there's a grassy field next to it, cut short. There are two pop-up dummies out there. That's what you practice tackling on.

I ask Will to pull over so we can get out for a while. He stops the car on the side of the road by the field and we get out. I go to the back of the car and ask him to open the trunk.

"What for?"

I smile. "It's a surprise."

Earlier, I snuck my football and two nerf guns into the trunk of the car, just in case. We used to have nerf wars when he was in high school, so I brought them with me. It was the only thing I could do to get him out of the bad mood he'd be in most of the time growing up. That, or playing football.

When he sees them now as I pull them out of my striped bag, he sighs.

"What?" I say.

I take the nerf gun and shoot a dart at his arm. It sticks there.

He shakes his head and plucks it off. "Lyla."

"No nerf war? Then how about football?"

"I don't play anymore."

"Oh, come on," I say. "Let's just toss it for a minute."

He rubs his neck, looking around as if he's afraid someone will see. "I haven't played in years."

That makes me sad. He used to be so gifted. He played in high school and then was supposed to go on to college with a full scholarship. The

103

NFL was already interested in him. I still remember my dad being really upset when Will turned eighteen and moved out, deciding not to go to college at all. They argued on his birthday – like the worst argument I've ever heard between the two of them, which says a lot. My dad kept saying something like, *"This is exactly why we never told you about it, Will! You're becoming the exact person we didn't want you to be!"*

I didn't know what he was talking about. I was around nine years old. Now, I still don't know, but I do realize what a big deal it was for Will to give up everything he did. And he did it to live like this, alone, flipping houses in a small town where no one likes him.

I toss the ball at him and he catches it against his stomach. He shakes his head and puts it back in my bag in the trunk. "I told you, I don't play."

I take it out again and back up about ten feet. "Come on. Don't think about it too much."

He groans quietly and I toss it again. He catches it, but only so it doesn't hit him in the face. He looks down at it in his hands and turns it over a couple times, silent. I don't want to have to play the card about how I finally got some real sleep last night and this is the first day of my new life. But seriously, it's true.

Maybe Will realizes this because finally, he clutches it in both hands and angles his elbow back, nodding for me to go further out. I clap my hands and run out into the center of the field. I turn around just in time to see him throw it in perfect form. It lands in my arms without me having to move an inch.

I laugh. "This is so fun!"

Will loosens his arm out. When I toss it back to him, it spirals through the air in a high arc. I guess throwing a football is like riding a bike. I haven't done it in a long time, but my arm remembers everything.

Will grins when he catches it. "Nice spiral."

"You taught me, remember?"

He frowns. "I did?"

"Yeah. The summer before you moved out."

He tosses it back to me with more force than the last one. "I don't remember that."

He doesn't? It's one of my favorite memories of him. One of the only good ones. I was obsessed with learning how to throw a perfect spiral after that. I wanted to show him the next time we played. I never got the chance. He only came back for two days every Christmas, and the weather was never good enough to be outside. Then after a while, even those visits died off.

We toss it back and forth a few times.

"So why don't you coach or something? Like Dad," I ask.

"Don't want to."

"But you'd be so good at it!" I say as I catch it and throw it back.

He shakes his head and doesn't respond. He doesn't throw the ball back either.

I watch him, then I start to come back over to him. "Does Dad know you renovate houses?"

He laughs angrily, picking at the laces of the ball. "He wouldn't believe it."

"Can I tell him? He'd be proud of you."

"I doubt that," he says.

"Why?"

Will looks off to the side, tucking the ball beneath his arm. He scratches his neck and seems reluctant to answer.

"Lyla," he finally says, "there are things that happened a while ago that...you don't know about."

"I know some of it," I tell him.

He looks at me. "You do?"

I come closer and stop beside him. "Yeah. I knew you were into drugs and stuff in high school. I'd hear you arguing with dad a lot when you were a teenager. I just never knew why."

His expression is pained.

"I've always wanted to ask you. Is there another reason you never call or...come around anymore? Because to me, Mom and Dad are pretty great. I'm just wondering..." I let out a small breath and then finally gather the courage to say what I actually want to say. "Is it really...me? I mean, am I the reason you don't come home?"

When Will looks into my eyes, I see some sort of brokenness there, or guilt or something, but then he looks away and it's gone.

"There's some stuff that goes way back between me and Mom and Dad, Lyla. It's got nothing to do with you."

I don't fully believe him, but I say that's good and then he says, "It's probably time for dinner."

We turn to head back to the car, and I drop the ball back into the trunk before we both get into the car to leave, although it's too early for dinner.

That didn't turn out at all like I wanted it to. I wanted to play football with him to change things between us. It backfired, but that's okay. I'm going to be awake now, so I have time to get close to him. At least I think I do. I hope.

Krista Andrews
The Pier Restaurant

My stomach is clenched tight and my heart is pounding. I wish I could duck down and hide behind the podium I'm standing at. That guy was such a jerk. I feel like crying but I can't because I'm in the middle of my first day of work as a hostess at the Pier Restaurant.

Apparently, he knows who I am. He knows my reputation.

"What kind of a place is this?" he joked with his friends when he saw I'm the new hostess. "Do they sell extra favors on the side?"

His friends busted up laughing.

My face turned hot pink. The old me would've said something back to him and not worried about what he thought for even a second.

But I've changed. A month ago, everything changed.

My throat grows tight, thinking of it. *Okay, I can do this. I can do this.* It's my first day on the job as a hostess. I glance back at my dad, who's been the bartender here forever. He happens to see me looking and he gives me a reassuring wave. I wave back, trying to smile. If only he knew. If only he knew what I'm going through.

If only I had the guts to tell him.

I watch as the woman in a black dress and green heels I just spoke to sits down at the bar. Samantha, table for three, I remember, and she told me they'll be celebrating a birthday tonight. She's very pretty with her dark skin and straight black hair, and I've never seen her around before. I wonder if my dad will talk to her. I wish he wouldn't, but he's kind of a ladies' man now. It's been that way ever since my mom left. He's also been drinking a little more than usual, which scares me. Not that I can judge him. I drink, too.

I turn around just as someone else steps up to put in their name for a table. I find out that there are seven people in their party, and I do the math nervously. I tell them how long the wait will take for a party this large. "Thirty minutes right now. I'm sorry."

Surprisingly, they say that it isn't too bad, and I breathe a sigh of relief.

When I'm done penciling them into the chart, I take another breath and look back at that guy who knows me, although I don't know him. I wonder what rumors he's heard. None of them are probably good.

Then I hear a voice again in my head. Remmi Tyler's voice. I painted her full name – Remembrance – on a fence near her house, so no one will forget her.

I tell myself I can get through one more night. Or one more hour, at least. For her.

Lyla

The restaurant is so fun and pretty, with tables set out over the pier and twinkle lights that are already on although the sun is still setting. They crisscross over everybody's heads as people stand and talk or sit at tables on the pier. I wonder if Will knows any of these people.

"Table for two?" the hostess asks us.

She has her straight blonde hair pulled back tightly, and she looks to be about my age. Her nametag says Krista.

"Three," Will says, annoyed.

"It'll be about ten minutes. I'm sorry about that."

My brother is silent.

"That's okay," I say for him.

"Can I put your name down?" she asks.

Will speaks up. "Put it under Will Brooks."

She pauses and looks up at him, blinking a lot. She looks at me next. She studies me for a second, and then she seems to snap out of it. She writes Will's name down on her clipboard.

I notice her hands are shaking. She drops the pencil and makes an embarrassed sound as she quickly picks it up and finishes writing. I feel bad for her. I know what it's like to be scared. And I wonder what she's afraid of. Is it my brother?

"How long have you worked here, Krista?" I ask her.

She looks up at me, thrown-off by the fact that I'm talking to her and that I read her nametag. "This is my first day."

"Oh, that's exciting! Do you like it?"

"Um, it's okay. I'm not very good with talking to people that I don't know." She looks behind her, and her face goes pink.

"Me neither," I laugh. "I get kind of awkward."

She doesn't respond. I notice she's looking at a group of guys not far off. It looks like they're saying things about her and laughing at her.

"Today, I met this guy," I tell her, "and his dog scared me so bad that I jumped into the lake and tried to swim away."

Krista looks back at me, her brow creasing. "Really?"

Will is staring at me, and I realize I forgot to tell him about that little adventure.

"I'm serious," I say to her. "I think you're doing great compared to that."

Her face relaxes and she laughs.

"Thanks." She looks down over me. "I like your dress," she says.

"Thank you!"

Will sighs and slides his hands into his pockets. I wonder if he ever simply strikes up a conversation with someone just because he can. I doubt it. Doesn't he realize how special it is just to be awake right now?

Someone steps up behind us to put their name in for a table, and I tell Krista I'll talk to her later. Her eyes seem to be shining and she tells me she'll let us know when the table's ready.

 Will and I walk over to the edge of the dock, and I look out over the harbor that's dotted with boats of different sizes. There are a few massive boathouses way out towards the end of the walking path.

"Do you think we could look at the boats while we wait?" I ask.

"No," Will says quickly.

"Oh…"

He clears his throat. "You can't get very far unless you own one of them."

I think of the boat magazines at his house. "So, you don't have one?"

"No."

"That would be cool one day, wouldn't it?" I say, trying to ignore his bad mood. "I've always wanted a little sailboat."

He looks at me. "You have?"

I smile. "Yeah. Nothing too fancy or anything. But I'd like to save up for one. Mom and Dad always say that if I work hard enough, I could get one."

Will laughs harshly. "Sounds like something they would say."

I am sorry I brought them up again, because his eyes have hardened. I try to think of something to recover the mood, but I can't. I awkwardly tuck my hair behind my ears and touch my scar, thinking of Justin without meaning to.

Glancing around, anywhere but at my brother, that's when I see her. Samantha's here. She's sitting at the bar. I'm surprised, because we still have about twenty minutes before we're supposed to meet up with her. She changed into a black dress with green heels, and she looks stunning. Nervous too. But she always looks nervous.

I sigh inwardly. I should have thought to have my brother change clothes.

"She's here," I say to Will, and he follows my gaze over to her. I watch his expression carefully, but it doesn't give anything away. That is, not until we both see that the bartender is talking to Samantha. He's leaning over to her as he says something. And that's when Will's eyes change slightly.

"We'll meet you at the table," he says.

My heart speeds up and I smile excitedly as I watch him make a beeline towards Samantha through the crowd.

Samantha

I am extremely nervous, and this bartender isn't helping. He won't stop talking to me. He's got to be at least late forties, so maybe he's just being friendly. I'm not sure. But I really don't want to talk right now. I have way too much to worry about.

I have decided to give Will a hint as to why I'm here. Tonight. Just to test his reaction.

It was Nell's idea.

"Just tell him you're a writer!" she said. "If he reacts at all, then you'll know he's a Bailey."

She also told me to go buy a dress. "You should look good when you tell him."

But now I'm regretting wearing this. I would be a lot more comfortable in the jeans and *I Heart Good Hart* T-shirt that are currently crammed in my purse. To top it off, the bartender has definitely taken notice of my dress. It makes me squirm.

I don't like the taste of alcohol, but I thought getting a glass of wine might help me relax. It didn't work. I down the rest of it and ask for my bill, hoping that'll get the bartender to walk away. Thankfully, he leaves me for a minute, putting my empty wine glass in a tub, and goes to his computer in the corner to print out my check.

I let out my breath.

"Okay, okay," I say quietly to myself.

I tap my fingers on the bar. *You are a confident woman. You look pretty good too. You can do this.* I think of what Lyla told me on the plane.

"Everything's fine," I mutter. "Everything's going to be just fine."

"Yes, it is," someone says beside me.

I turn sharply and see Will standing right next to me. I gasp, almost falling off the barstool. He grabs my arm and I try to get my balance, straightening my dress.

"You startled me," I say, breathless.

He apologizes with a slight grin on his ridiculously handsome face. He is still holding me, and his eyes drift down over me for a second. I'm suddenly very embarrassed that I changed, because he didn't.

I move away from his touch, tucking some hair behind my ears.

"Where's Lyla?" I ask.

"I told her we'd meet her at the table."

"Oh…" It makes me nervous to not have her around.

Will looks over at the bartender. I think maybe he's going to order a drink, but then he says to me, "Should we go?"

"I have to pay for my wine," I tell him.

He quickly slides his wallet out of his pocket and sets a twenty-dollar bill right where I was sitting. Then he takes my arm and starts leading me away from the bar before I can protest.

"Well, well, well. How are you, Mr. *Brooks*?" the bartender says.

I wonder if the emphasis he put on Will's last name is just my imagination.

Will sighs quietly and turns back to him. "I'm good, Bruce."

"Oh, well that's good," Bruce says with an unkind grin. He's holding my receipt, and he takes up the twenty-dollar bill without even looking at it. "I'm glad *you're* good because some people just…aren't, you know?"

"Okay." Will takes my arm again. "Let's go."

"I heard you stopped in and talked to Tricia," Bruce says. "That's real interesting."

Will stops, keeping his hand on my arm. "And?"

Bruce shrugs. "Just reminding you I'm here, is all."

Will gives a sarcastic smile. "Trust me, I'm aware."

Bruce's eyes flash. Then there's silence as they stare at each other. I watch them, heart thrumming with nerves. What's going on here?

After a couple more seconds, Bruce slides his eyes over to me again.

"Good luck with this one," he says. He gives a fake smile to both of us. "Enjoy your night."

Bruce Andrews

I slide my phone out of my pocket, watching Will and that woman walk away. I know I pushed it too far with him. I've signed multiple gag orders over the years that prevent me from saying anything about the Baileys, just like the rest of the staff has. Most of the old Carson Manor staff are extremely loyal to Will's parents and wouldn't talk anyway, but there are a few that would spread the word about Will being back in town in a heartbeat if not for the threat of a multi-million-dollar lawsuit hanging over their head.

Like me.

I hear the line pick up. "It's me," I say. "I just talked to Bailey."

"And?"

"Tricia's right. He got control of the Manor." I let that sink in for a second. "What do you need me to do?" I ask.

He gives me instructions and I listen, staring over at them as they walk through the crowd. This is the first time Will's been out in public like this, because he knows a lot of us in town loved working at the Carson Manor that his parents shut down. He hasn't lifted a finger to re-open it.

Until now. And apparently, he isn't hiring me back.

Samantha

I follow Will to our table at the edge of the pier, glancing back at the bartender. He's on his phone, staring at us. I wonder what that was about.

Lyla is laughing about something with the hostess when we approach. She stands when she sees me and gives me a hug.

"I'm so glad you're here," she says.

"Me too."

I close my eyes as Lyla hugs me. It's one of those long, meaningful hugs. It calms me a little. I forget about Bruce and whatever that was at the bar. I forget about Will and what I'm planning to do tonight…but only for a second until she lets go of me. Will is watching me with an expression on his face that I can't read.

We sit down, and the hostess lays out our menus for us. "Your server will be right with you."

She looks at Will for a second like she knows him. He doesn't even acknowledge her.

"It was good talking to you," she says to Lyla.

"You too," Lyla says. "Good luck tonight!"

"Thanks."

Lyla doesn't notice, but the girl looks back at her thoughtfully as she walks away.

Will meets my eyes and then picks up his menu. I look down at myself to smooth my dress again, then I glance around nervously. Usually I would enjoy a place like this – with the twinkle lights overhead, the friendly locals, the stage that is set up to host a band sometime soon. But I'm too scared to be enjoying this.

That's when I realize that people are looking at us. Will ignores them or doesn't notice them as he studies his menu. Dorothy said people talk about him – the young attractive man who doesn't socialize. I wonder if that's why they're looking. Will doesn't seem too concerned about it.

Lyla's attention is on the lights above our heads.

"I love twinkle lights," she says.

Will looks at her. "I'm pretty sure you love everything today."

"I do," she says happily, and I wonder what they're talking about, but they don't explain.

I glance at Will and I get to study him for a second while he decides what to order. His dark hair is slightly curly like his sister's, and dark stubble lines his jaw. His eyes are so blue and distant. He looks up at me, holds my gaze for a second, and surprises me by giving a faint smile. It's nice to see him smile, even just slightly. I look down at my menu without smiling back. I try to focus, but there is nothing I can order that I could actually manage to keep in my stomach right now with how nervous I am.

Lyla sets her menu down. "I'm getting a burger." She looks around happily. "So, what should we do tomorrow?"

He doesn't look up from his menu. "Nothing's open on Sundays around here."

She seems disappointed for a second. "I was hoping we could meet a bunch of people."

Will looks like he's just barely keeping himself from rolling his eyes.

Lyla's thinking. "A church would be open," she says suddenly.

Will shifts in his seat, already shaking his head. "I don't go to church."

"So? It's a great way to meet people! I saw one when we were driving around today."

Will ignores her.

"Let's just go," she says. "Don't think about it too much."

I can see how it would be hard to say no to a girl like Lyla. Will seems to know this because he's avoiding her eyes.

"I can't," he says. "I have work to do on the house."

Lyla is undaunted. "Oh, come on. It'll be fun."

Will looks around, then quickly waves at a waiter, who doesn't notice him. "We're ready to order, aren't we?"

Lyla rolls her eyes playfully. "Please? Don't you want to make some friends?"

He looks down at his menu again.

I am really amused by this. I watch the two of them, analyzing the fact that Lyla is so carefree, and Will is not. She wants to go to church and meet people, he doesn't.

Will finally meets her eyes. He presses his menu to the table. "How do you even know you'll be able to go in the morning?"

Confused, I look at Lyla. She only shrugs.

"I'm just...hoping," she says softly.

Will stares at her for a few long seconds, his mouth flat. Finally, he sighs loudly. "Fine. I'll go."

Lyla claps her hands and then looks at me. "What about you? Wanna come with us?"

"Oh," I say. "I...sure, I guess."

Lyla says, "Yay," and it is settled. The two people who are probably the Bailey siblings and I are going to church tomorrow, to "meet people." It'll be the first time I've gone since I was a little girl. This was not part of the plan, but then, I never really had a plan to begin with.

I can't wait to write about this.

A waiter takes our order and our food arrives rather quickly. Just as we begin to eat, a man steps up onto the stage close by and slings a guitar strap over his shoulder. Four other band members join him. The front man speaks into the microphone and introduces the band.

"We're here to make sure you people have a fine time tonight," he says.

Everyone cheers, Lyla especially. She claps and stares at the man with a big, open-mouthed smile. The music starts, and I find myself very relieved that it is too loud to carry on a conversation for the rest of the meal. My nerves are stretched tight and I know it probably shows.

Once we finish eating, dessert arrives – a big piece of carrot cake with candles. Three waiters gather around and sing Happy Birthday to Lyla. She's laughing and clapping. Her face is a little pink, but she's thrilled. It makes me feel good that she's enjoying such a small thing so much. I told the hostess when I arrived that it was Lyla's birthday yesterday.

"Thanks, Will!" Lyla says. "That was so special."

She leans over and gives him a side hug.

He opens his mouth to say it wasn't him, but I interrupt.

"Cheers," I say, holding up my water glass.

Will looks at me, his eyes searching my face. Lyla raises her glass, smiling big, and Will finally does too.

"To Lyla turning eighteen," I say.

"Thank you!" Lyla says, clinking my glass and then Will's.

"And to new friends," Will says roughly, his eyes holding mine as we touch our glasses together.

"New friends," I say nervously in agreement. Lyla is looking between us and biting her lip.

When the bill arrives, I take it so I can pay.

"I'll get it," Will says, taking out his wallet.

"But I said I would treat you."

He shakes his head. "I don't feel right about it." He meets my eyes. "Thanks, though." Again, a faint smile, and I know he's thanking me for the birthday thing.

I nod dumbly, my stomach twisting. "You're welcome."

The band continues to play, and people stand up to dance. Lyla watches them all. I can tell she wants to dance too. She glances at her brother and it seems like she's about to ask him, but she changes her mind.

Without giving myself time for second thoughts, I hold my hand out to her.

"Wanna dance with me, Lyla?"

Her face lights up. Will looks at me, surprised.

"Sure," she says.

She takes my hand and squeezes it. It reminds me of being on the plane with her. I feel a special connection with her. I want to thank her for comforting me on the plane. It meant more to me than she knows.

I can feel Will's eyes on me as we stand up and walk onto the packed dance floor, but I don't look back at him. I haven't danced in a while, and I have no clue if I'm any good.

Thankfully Lyla and I do silly dances together at first, spinning around and laughing. After a while I realize that Lyla wasn't just starting off with silly moves – this is how she dances. She is completely carefree, happy just to be dancing. Her orange dress whips around, the pattern of butterflies on it flocking around her. I look over at Will at one point. He's glaring at two teenaged boys a few tables over, both of whom are watching Lyla as she dances wildly. When they notice Will, their eyes widen, and they look away. It makes me grin. He is protective of his little sister. I like that.

We dance to two songs, and then a slower song starts so we make our way back to the table, both of us breathless and laughing. I sit down, but Lyla doesn't. She stands there looking at her brother. I know what she is about to do, and I open my mouth to stop her, but it's too late.

"Why don't you dance with Samantha, Will?" Lyla asks.

He goes absolutely still, and so do I. He doesn't want to do it. That much is clear. I don't want to, either, because the thought terrifies me. I would be alone with him, and there would be no more excuses not to talk to him.

I wave it off. "That's okay. I need to catch my breath."

Lyla doesn't budge. She's drilling Will with her eyes.

Will lets out a breath and looks at me. He holds his hand out to me on the table, and I feel like I am in high school again.

"I'll go easy on you," he says.

I blink at him, then down at his hand. "You don't have to do this," I say.

Will glances up at Lyla. "I think I do."

I laugh softly, and then I take his hand and stand up. He leads me out to the dance floor, holding my hand behind his back. Then, the man who is possibly Malcolm Willard Bailey the Fourth pulls me close, puts his other hand on the small of my back, and begins slowly dancing with me.

Emil

I watch Sienna as she quickly scans the menu for something to eat. She decides on a burger. Gluten-free bun. No onions. Ketchup and mustard on the side. Salad instead of fries. You can learn a lot about a person by the way they order their food. I ask for the steak, medium-rare. Mashed potatoes. No vegetables.

I nod towards the dance floor when our waiter's gone.

"Let's go," I tell Sienna. "Let's dance."

She looks at me sharply. "They would see us."

"They're bound to see us around if we keep on following them like this. So, let's dance. Let's act like normal people."

She hesitates and looks over at Lyla, who's alone at their table only twenty feet from here. There's another table with a few teenaged boys at it, and they've noticed her. I doubt they'll talk to her, though. They've seen that she's here with Will.

I stretch my hand towards Sienna. "She's fine. Come on. Let's go."

She finally takes my hand and we stand. We end up being just a few couples away from Will and Samantha. Too far from them to hear anything, but close enough to Lyla for Sienna to be within reach and feel comfortable, in case something happens.

Sienna stays twelve inches away from me. I want to ask her what the heck she has against men, but I already know the answer to that, at least part of it. Still, it doesn't make it any less mystifying to me. I've never been treated like this by a woman. Ever. I see it as a challenge.

Thinking of something I read in a book once, I say, "What if we act like we're together?"

She looks up at me. "Together? What do you mean?"

"You know what I mean. We live in the same house."

She shakes her head. "I'm not okay with that. I would never live with you."

I give her a look.

She blinks and her face blushes. "That's not what I meant. I meant I wouldn't live with a man outside of marriage."

I grin. "So, let's put a ring on it."

She doesn't laugh like I was hoping. In fact, I think she's severely uncomfortable and trying not to show it.

I sigh inwardly and turn us slowly to the song. "Never mind. Forget I said anything."

Guess I forgot reality is never as thrilling as fiction.

Will

I wouldn't normally be doing this. It's another thing that wouldn't be happening if not for my sister and my parents and this whole ordeal. I know Bruce is watching from behind the bar, wondering who this woman is and if she knows who I really am. I wonder who else at this restaurant used to work for my parents and holds a grudge against me even when they are fiercely loyal to my parents. There are a lot of bridges to mend, and people to hire back.

It hits me suddenly that it was smart for my parents to send Lyla here. Even if the story gets out, no one here could talk about me or Lyla to the press because of the gag orders. This is very safe place for Lyla to lay low for a while, until we see if the story gets out.

I'm drawn back to reality by the silky feel of Samantha's dress against me. She's looking up at me. I can't help but think her eyes are gorgeous.

"Where'd you learn to dance like this?" she asks me.

I sigh inwardly, tired of all the lying I've had to do over the years. My mom used to make me take private lessons from a world-famous instructor when I was young, but I obviously can't tell Samantha that.

"Guess I'm just a natural," I say.

I groan inwardly. That came out wrong – all cocky. But thankfully Samantha just smiles. It's beautiful.

We are silent now as we spin slowly to the song. Lyla comes into my view. She is resting her chin on her hand and looking out at the sun setting over the smooth water like she doesn't have a care in the world. If the nightmares don't come back, I wonder if my parents will talk to her about everything. She can handle it. I know she can.

I move us to the right, out of the way of another couple. Samantha smells nice, like strawberries or flowers. She's looking at our table where Lyla is too.

"She's something else," she says quietly.

I give a slow nod. "I'm starting to see that."

She looks up at me. "Are you two...close?"

"We used to be."

Her brow creases slightly. "When?"

For a fleeting second, I want to talk to her about it. I want to tell her that we were really close when my sister was little, but we've grown apart since.

"A while back," I tell her vaguely.

"She said she's never visited you."

"Nope."

"And she's never been on a plane before?"

I wonder why she would ask that. It's random. I dodge the question because again, I can't tell her the truth – that Lyla went on private jets all the time, and even a couple helicopters when she was little.

"She's pretty sheltered," I say.

"Because of your parents?"

I sigh. "That, and..." I debate telling her this. But I don't think my sister would mind. "She's been homeschooled for all of high school."

I don't need to go into the details as to why. That's Lyla's secret to tell.

Samantha blinks, thinking. She's nervous again, looking at me strangely. I'm amazed at how light her eyes are compared to her skin. They're a light brown while her skin is a darker shade. It's smooth and flawless.

I look away when I realize I'm staring. I find Lyla again. Her lips are turned in a small smile. I don't like everything I'm feeling with her around. I'm protective. I'm remembering the past. I'm yearning for a relationship with her again. I'm ready to drop everything and tell her *"Your last name is Bailey! Not Brooks!"*

But I can't, not until the story breaks, or doesn't. I don't know how much more of this I can take. I keep imagining the story coming up on a screen somewhere and people looking over. I'd have to take Lyla and duck out of here, tell her everything.

Maybe I *want* this journalist to leak a story about us. Maybe I would thank the person.

Samantha is reading my expression. I try to relax as I move her in another small circle. I can't think of a single thing to talk about. Nothing that means anything, anyway. Nothing that's the truth. How long is this song?

"What was that about back there?" she asks me carefully. "At the bar?"

My jaw tightens because I know I have to give her some sort of answer or else she'll think everyone in town hates me, which isn't entirely untrue. But I don't want her thinking anything bad of me. For some reason, I care about that.

I decide I can be partially truthful.

"He used to work for my family. He's mad that they let him go."

I clear my throat. I don't tell her that he was part of the security detail at the Manor. He knows everything about it, the ins and outs. Everything. I hate to admit that I might need him. I've never liked him.

"How long ago?" Samantha asks me.

"What?" I look at her again. I swear she's dancing closer to me now.

She blushes. "How long ago did they fire him?"

Wondering why she cares, I shrug, as if I don't know. "A long time ago."

She gives a small nod. "What did he do for them?"

What can I say now? I'm frustrated at myself for opening a can of worms.

"It's a long story," I say shortly.

She looks a little hurt by my tone. "Sorry. It's none of my business."

It *isn't* any of her business, but I didn't have to make her feel bad about it. Now I don't know what to say. I wonder if she can tell that I'm out of practice with women. That is not something I ever expected to be. My life should've been much different than this.

But it isn't.

We do a few slow turns quietly.

"What do you do for a living?" I ask, trying to recover the conversation.

She hesitates, looking up at me nervously. "My sister owns a coffee shop. My mom and I help her run it."

"Does it do well?"

I feel her left foot touch mine lightly as we turn.

"We have a little profit after we pay our employees and our bills," she says.

I nod. "That's good. That's all you need."

She suddenly has a curious look in her eyes that I wonder about.

"Is that what you want to do for a career?" I ask.

"I don't know. I'm sure my sister would love it if I did. But she also wants me to settle down with someone and give her lots of nieces and nephews." She blushes, embarrassed that she revealed so much.

I feel a stirring within me at her words and find myself inadvertently moving closer to her.

"You aren't...with anyone?" I ask carefully.

She blinks and shakes her head. "No."

This surprises me. I wonder why she isn't. She seems to be the last person on the earth to be single, but I push the thought from my mind and step back just slightly as we turn. The music swells. The song is almost done.

"What about you?" Samantha asks nervously.

I say no and leave it at that. I haven't had a serious girlfriend since Nikki. Since then, the few people I've dated haven't interested me enough to be honest with. Even Nikki didn't know I'm a Bailey. Alexandra did, of course, but I usually try not to think about her.

My parents always say that when the time comes and I meet someone I want to be with, I can tell her who I am and our family's situation as long as I trust her. Mom worries that someone will go after me for my family's money. She has the same worry for Lyla, if everything comes out someday and people find out who she is.

Besides Alex, who already knew who I was, my relationships with women have never gotten far enough for me to want to tell any of them who I really am.

But then tonight, with Samantha...I wonder. What if I told her? What would she think of me? What would she think about my plans for the Manor? It is the first time I've ever wondered that about a woman.

"So, which do you want?" I hear myself ask. "To settle down with someone? Or run the shop?"

"Neither, right now," she says quietly.

"Then what do you want?"

She lets out a breath and takes her hand from mine to tuck some hair behind her ear, then slips it back where it was. I hold it a little tighter this time, wanting to put her at ease for some reason. She meets my eyes, and she seems determined.

"I want to be a writer," she says.

My steps stall, only for a moment, and Samantha notices. She glances down at our feet.

"What kind of a writer?" I ask. My heart is starting to thrum in warning.

She closes her eyes, flustered again. I can feel she's shaking.

"Will," she says quietly.

I am suddenly thinking about the fact that she was on our plane. That she "bumped" into us at the festival and invited herself to dinner with us and asked a little too much about my family and my sister.

She's the journalist.

"What are you telling me?" I say in a low voice.

She opens her eyes again, and we hold each other's gaze. We aren't moving to the music anymore. We're just standing here, her hand in mine and my other hand at the small of her back, tucking her body close to mine.

Do you know who I am? Are you the one? I realize too late that if there was any question in her mind about who we really are, it's gone now. I have made it abundantly clear that she's right about me being a Bailey. But I can't help it. I was almost tempted to open up to *her*, of all people. The person digging into our lives for a story. I can't believe it.

The song ends, and I let go of her. We back away from each other.

Lyla walks up to us happily when a faster song starts. "Do you guys want to dance some more?"

"I don't think so," Samantha says quickly. "I think I'll head back."

Lyla is disappointed. "But we'll see you in the morning?"

I should stop this. I should tell her that we can't go to church anymore.

Samantha glances at me for only a second. I can't bring myself to say anything. "What time?" she asks.

"The sign said the service is at ten," Lyla says excitedly. "You can come over first and we'll all ride together."

"Great. That...sounds good."

Everything in me tells me to say no to this. Put a stop to it.

126

But for some reason – maybe my sister's feelings, or maybe something deeper than that – I can't bring myself to say anything.

Samantha's flustered. She starts to turn away.

"Do you need directions?" Lyla asks.

She stops. Her face is pink again. "Right. Of course, I do."

I study her. She's lying.

"Will?" Lyla says after a few silent seconds. "Maybe you could get her number?

I am silent.

"And then text her your address?" she prompts.

I bite the inside of my cheek. Samantha is avoiding my eyes. I bet she got my address a long time ago. Maybe she's already been there. Reluctantly, I take my phone out of my pocket and she gives me her number. I text her my address. Lyla watches me strangely for a second, but then she gives Samantha a hug. My jaw clenches. It's one thing for someone to break a story about us. Part of me wants it so we can come out of hiding.

But this woman got into our lives. She's befriending my naïve sister.

I watch as Samantha closes her eyes while she hugs her, like she cares about her. Right. Then she opens them and holds my gaze for a few long seconds.

She lets go of Lyla and backs up.

"Thanks for the dance," she says to me, making my stomach knot.

She says goodbye to us and walks away through the crowd.

Samantha

I am shaking as I stride through the parking lot in my painful green heels towards my car. I call my mom.

"How did it go?" she says immediately.

"I messed it all up!" I say loudly and miserably. "In less than 24 hours!"

I start to pace beside my car, then I bend to take the heels off. They dangle from my hand as I fish through my purse for my keys.

"This was stupid to come here. So stupid!" One of the heels drops to the ground.

"Honey, calm down. I'm sure you didn't mess it up. Tell me what happened."

"I told him that I want to be a writer! And then he freaked out and asked me what kind of writer and...I didn't know what to say!"

There's a long pause. "Oh my goodness," she says slowly. "It's them. They're the Baileys."

"Yes! But I ruined everything!"

Noticing two people who are walking to their car near me, I dig for my keys again and find them. Then I snatch my shoe up from the ground and get into my car, looking through the window. It's not Will and Lyla.

"No, you didn't," Mom says. "It's all going to be fine."

"No, it's not." Miserably, I tell her what all was said between Will and I as we danced.

"Wait a second," my sister says. I guess she's listening now, too.

I sigh. "Hey, Nell." I close eyes, my aching feet wriggling on the dirty pedals.

"He *danced* with you?"

"It was nothing." I should've left that part out. "Lyla made him do it."

"Did he hold you close?" she asks. "Or at a distance?"

I shake my head. "Close, I guess."

"Then it *was* something!"

"Nell!"

My mom cuts in. "Let's think for a second."

I can picture her pacing on the black and white linoleum floor of her kitchen, and Nell trying to contain her excitement as she watches.

"Did you make any plans to see them again?" Mom asks.

"We're going to church in the morning."

"That's good!" she exclaims. "See? You didn't ruin anything. He didn't make you leave."

"Not yet at least." I gasp, picturing a thousand scenarios in my mind as my imagination runs wild. "Oh my gosh…What if Will shows up at my house later tonight? To pay me off with a briefcase full of money? Like in the movies!"

Nell laughs. "Then you won't answer the door. He can't make you."

I rub my forehead. "I'm coming home. This is crazy. I should've never done this."

"Samantha Marie," Mom says firmly. "Listen to your mother, for just one second."

I pause, my throat growing tight at the sound of my name. "I'm listening."

"You can't come home yet."

"Why not?"

"Your whole life, you thought you knew who you were, and you didn't. Not really…. Just like Lyla."

"Mom – I *really* don't want to go into all this right now – "

"Just listen to me, Samantha. This happened to you – of all people – for a reason. I just know it."

I sit back and look up at the ceiling of the rental car, cringing as I remember the frozen look on Will's face and the feeling of his hand stiffening around mine. Then Lyla's total obliviousness to it all.

I got too involved. Way too involved.

And yet, I still feel strangely giddy about it. And I don't want to leave.

"You're the one to write this," Mom says.

I agree with her, but I'm afraid to say it out loud.

"So, what do I do?" I ask quietly.

"He didn't make you leave," Nell says, "so just see what happens tomorrow. Try to extend your time with them past church and get to know him."

I let out a breath and press my forehead to the steering wheel. "Easier said than done. Talking to him is like talking to a wall. And now it'll be worse after what I said tonight."

"You never know," she says. "Nothing can get a guy to open up like a beautiful woman."

I roll my eyes. "Nell…"

"What? I'm just saying. He probably likes you and that's why he doesn't want you to leave."

"But I followed them here like a stalker, just because we recognized his mom."

She's unconcerned. "We'll laugh about it at your wedding."

Lyla

My brother is mad. I couldn't figure out why for the longest time, until I called Mom from Will's cell phone to tell her about our fun day. He didn't want to talk to her. Then, he seemed to tense up when I mentioned Samantha. That's when I realized what it is. He's mad that I made him dance with her. And, probably, that we're going to church with her in the morning...And that I practically forced him to get her number.

It's past ten now, and I'm making tea. Will said he didn't want any. He's just sitting in the living room, staring at the black TV, deep in thought. The new blue tea kettle I bought earlier whistles, and Will finally looks over like it snapped him out of whatever angry daze he's been in. I turn off the burner and pour the boiling water over the little vanilla tea bag in my mug. I don't know why I buy any other flavors. I always go for vanilla.

"You sure you don't want any?" I ask Will.

"I'm good."

"Tea makes everybody happy," I tell him, holding up my mug I bought today that says those exact words on it.

He frowns and glances over, then rolls his eyes when he sees my mug and my big smile. He sighs and rubs his neck, going back to thinking.

I lean against the counter and dunk the tea bag up and down in the steamy water, glancing at my brother. I think back to when he was in high school and I was in elementary school. My life was normal then. I had friends. I slept eight hours every night without nightmares. But my brother and I never talked much back then, either, even though we lived in the same house. He scared me, honestly. He got in with a bad crowd and sort of spiraled downward into drugs until he was almost kicked off the football team. Dad forced him to do work on the house the summer before his junior year, and his life finally started changing after that – once he really focused on football.

But his relationship with me never changed. I can never tell what he's thinking. Maybe if we ever talked on the phone over the years or saw each other more than just a few days at Christmas, maybe things wouldn't be this way. But they are. Things are quiet and awkward, and I don't see that ever changing, unless Will puts some effort into this too.

Just when my tea is finished steeping, he stands up and says he's going to shower and go to bed.

"Thanks for the fun day," I tell him. "And thanks for the birthday thing at dinner."

He slides his hands into his pockets and looks down at the floor, silent.

"I'm excited to meet some people at church tomorrow," I tell him.

Will finally meets my eyes, and I can tell what he's thinking for once: I'll probably wake up screaming all night long and we won't be going to church at all. It looks like he wants to say it, but he doesn't. He turns towards the staircase.

"I'm sorry I made you dance with her," I blurt.

Will stops and looks back at me. "Samantha?"

"Yeah. I'm sorry...I just thought..."

He sighs. "I know what you thought." His mouth flattens. "I'm not going to ask her out."

I shrug. "Why not?"

He shakes his head, glancing away. "I'm just not, okay? She's not even going to be here very long."

"But maybe she'd stay longer if – "

He interrupts me. "I'm tired. I'm going to bed."

I am a little hurt, but I nod and try to smile. "Okay, yeah. Me too. I'll just...finish my tea."

But I don't want to go to bed. I don't want this day to end, not like this because as much as I'm trying to believe that my nightmares won't come back, I'm afraid they will. I don't want my brother to hear me screaming in the middle of the night. It's personal and it's embarrassing, and my brother is not the comforting type.

"Get your earplugs ready," I say, hating that I said that out loud because I feel like I'm jinxing it.

"I've got them."

We say goodnight to each other, and he leaves me in the kitchen.

I stand here for a few minutes and drink my tea, reluctant to go upstairs. I hear the shower start, the water rushing through the pipes in the wall. It is a few minutes before I put my empty mug in the dishwasher and realize there is nothing more for me to do, and I am pretty tired, to be honest. I haven't done this much in a single day in a long time.

As my last act of the day, I go to the back door and unlock it, stepping out onto the deck. I wrap my arms around my torso, looking out at the moon over the lake. I think of dancing out on the beach this morning. I think of meeting Samantha and Krista. And I think of Christian especially. I wonder if I'll see him around again. I think of being nearly attacked by his dog. What was his name? I shiver and wrap my arms tighter around myself, touching my scar. This was the best day I've ever had. And I'm grateful. I guess that's all I wanted to do before going to bed and probably going back to my old life. I wanted to think back over it and be grateful. And I am.

"Everything will be okay," I whisper to the dark air around me.

I go back inside and lock the door, then I turn off all the lights, grab my gray blanket from the couch, and head upstairs. I get ready for bed slowly, changing into my pajamas that are worn from so much use. And then I crawl into my bed and try to get comfortable. It's my first time sleeping in this bed because I slept on the couch last night. It feels strange, foreign. The sheets are cold and very different than my sheets at home, silkier or something.

I blink up at the ceiling for a while, thinking of my yellow ceiling back home and the pretty decorations my mom and I put up to try to keep my spirits up, the smiley-faces we painted all over my dresser. Should I turn the light back on? No one would know. But I decide not to. I am eighteen years old now. I don't need to be afraid of the dark anymore. I can be brave.

But I picture my nightmare, and I dread going to sleep.

"Everything will be okay. Everything will be okay."

But I miss my parents all of a sudden and this mattress feels too soft and I have a lump in my throat because…what if it's all over? The fun? The freedom and energy I felt?

I groan and pull the sheet over my face. *Please, Will, put in your earplugs.* I don't want to be embarrassed. And I don't want to go to sleep.

But I know I have to because I'm exhausted. It's like trying *not* to fall asleep makes you even sleepier. I've always thought that…

I hum my mom's favorite song. That's the last thing I do.

Sienna Rodriguez

I rub my face. It is only 11:30 and already I'm fighting to keep my eyes open. I keep waiting for screams to come over the sound system. Carlos reminded me of her nightmares, that they might come back. I'm not looking forward to it. Hearing her scream on the beach earlier sent me back in time, to the day I came back from college and ran into my parents' house after hearing my sister's screams. I found her in her own...

I hear the basement door open and I jump.

Emil sighs heavily when he comes down here and sees me sitting in my chair again. I look back at him. His hair is tousled, eyes groggy. He went to bed right when we got home from the restaurant earlier.

"You don't have to watch them like this," he says to me.

I don't answer. It's supposed to be his night to watch them, but I know he won't. I turn to the screens again.

"Why don't you get some rest," he says. "You were up for hours last night."

"I don't know what Will's going to do if her nightmares come back."

"He'll leave her be. There's nothing you can do anyway."

"He might go to the Manor."

"And again. There's nothing you can do."

I come up with something else. "I have to follow Lyla if she goes anywhere."

"She won't."

"She's eighteen and it's Saturday night. She could sneak out, meet up with that guy from this morning. We don't know what all they said."

I can hear a smile in his voice. "I have a feeling she'll stay put."

"Why?"

"From what I've seen of her, she's different than Tessa Lands. Or anyone you or I have ever guarded."

I sit silently with my arms crossed. I agree with him. Of course, I do. But I don't want to give him the satisfaction of saying it.

He's the first one to talk, still behind me. "I wanted to say I'm sorry for earlier."

I frown. I can't think of the last time I heard a man apologize. I never heard my dad apologize to my mom. And then there was my sister's toxic relationship with her boyfriend her junior year of high school. He turned out to be a murderer. I close my eyes for a second, swallowing, still not looking at Emil. Part of me thinks I should be the one to apologize, but I can't bring myself to.

"And we don't have to act like we're married," Emil adds. "I didn't mean to make you uncomfortable."

I sigh.

"It's not a bad idea, actually. I got that ring out of my bag," I say, nodding at it on the desk. It was my sister's.

Emil doesn't say anything or come and sit. I almost look back at him because I don't like him just standing there behind me like this. Instead I stare quietly at the paperback book he's currently reading, sitting on the desk. A Clancy novel. It looks like it's been read ten times.

Emil finally says, "I can see why this case would be harder for you than with Tessa. It was that way for me, too, in the beginning. Less control, you know?"

I slowly turn to him, curiosity overriding everything else. "What sort of jobs did you do before you started guarding Will?"

He crosses his arms and leans against the wall, yawns. "Actors, actresses, some rappers."

"Any incidents?"

"A couple shootings at clubs." He rubs his neck and looks away. I wonder about that scar I saw on his bicep, the one that looks like a bullet wound.

"What made you get into this?" I ask him.

"Watching the Baileys? I told you, the paycheck."

I shake my head. "I mean guarding in general."

He shrugs one shoulder. "After a couple tours in Iraq, I met a buddy who did it. When he heard I had a degree in Homeland Security, he got me signed with a company. I guarded low key celebrities at first, then word got around or something and I started guarding higher profile people. I met Carlos at a hotel in Chicago. I was guarding Gus Kyle at the time. He was shooting a movie in the area."

I raise my eyebrows at the name.

"Carlos talked to me in the hotel lobby and asked me if I wanted to join his company."

I nod, translating that all to mean that Carlos researched him, and then sought him out. Carlos Sanchez never asks anyone to join his company without doing his homework first. And he especially wouldn't entrust the Bailey clients with anyone but the best of the best.

I feel like Emil is leaving something out. He's not looking into my eyes in that intense way he usually does. He's avoiding them. He's leaving me in the dark about something, but I can understand it. I'm leaving him in the dark, too.

He changes the subject. "I heard you're trying to start your own company," he says.

"Yes, that's right." I don't tell him that he is a huge disappointment in that department, since I can tell already that there's nothing he can teach me.

"Is Carlos going to help you get started?" he asks.

I nod. "He said he knows of a couple of women who are interested. They've heard about me."

"I can tell why. You're good at what you do."

The compliment surprises me. "Thank you."

He grins. "Maybe a little too good."

I roll my eyes but can't help but smile slightly.

He watches me for a second. "I've noticed the way you are with Lyla," he says quietly. "If any teenaged guy comes within ten feet of her, you're on edge. Is that how you were with Tessa?"

I shake my head. "No." I swallow. "I think Lyla reminds me of…her."

He nods and looks down at the floor. He knows who I mean. My sister.

"What was she like?" he asks quietly.

I look at the screens, seeing the quiet house, the little flowers Lyla left around, the tea kettle she bought for Will, the magnet on the fridge in the living room. She put it up right when they got home. *"See?"* she said, clapping a little. *"It makes it happier."*

I think through my answer before speaking. "She was…good."

Emil is suddenly sitting down next to me. He keeps his eyes on the screens.

"I'll stay up and watch her," he says. "I'll follow if she goes anywhere."

I smile a little. "Thank you."

"You're welcome."

He meets my eyes. It makes my heart race, and I'm afraid he knows it. I wonder if he's thought about us dancing together tonight. I have.

Trying to act relaxed, I stretch and stand up slowly to leave, but Emil stops me by taking my wrist. I reflexively start to twist out of his grasp, but his grip is too tight.

"Hold on," he says, and he gently puts the ring on my left ring finger.

I try to ignore the warm flutter in my stomach, but it's getting harder and harder.

Emil looks up at me, acting nervous. "Marry me, Rodriguez."

For the first time, we laugh together. He tells me to go get some rest, and he waves me off.

I go upstairs to do just that, a small smile lingering on my face.

Part III
28 Days and counting…

There's a rustling through the trees. Scrambling to my feet, I stand protectively over her bleeding body.

"Thatcher?" I call. He just came over the radio and said he was close to my location. I can't move her anymore. She's bleeding too much.

There's no answer.

"Thatcher!" I yell. "Over here!"

Suddenly, someone steps out from behind a tree. It's not Thatcher, I can tell that already from his build. I swing the beam of my flashlight over there, and then everything happens very fast. Simultaneously, I process a few things. First: it's the guy who did this to her. Second: he has a gun pointed at me. Third: he's crying and mumbling and shaking…

All of this goes through my brain in the same second that the shot rings out.

Lyla

The next thing I know, I am waking up to the distant sound of a bell ringing. I rub my eyes, confused by how bright it is. And I'm really hot. I kick the sheet off me and roll over, looking at the clock on my nightstand. Wait. That can't be right. It says it's nine-fifteen. My mouth falls open. I look around at my room that is so bright because the sun is blaring through the naked window.

If it's nine-fifteen, that means I got over ten hours of sleep last night.

The bell sounds again, the one that woke me up, and I realize it's the doorbell. I practically fall out of bed and run over to the window. There's a car out there. Samantha is here for church.

I start laughing. Hysterically. I feel a little emotional too. I run to my door and open it.

"Will!" I shout, hurrying across the hall. I fling his door open. "Samantha's here!"

Will startles awake, and I realize too late that I should have knocked. He's in his boxers, and that's it.

He pulls his earplugs out. "Lyla, what the – "

Blushing, I shield my eyes. "Sorry! But we slept in. You have to get up. I'll stall her."

He groans and I hear him shifting around. Still shielding my eyes, I carefully back out of the room, saying sorry again.

I am breathless with excitement by the time I answer the front door. Samantha is relieved that somebody finally answered, but she looks down at my shorts and flannel shirt and big knitted socks. "Ready to go?" she says, confused.

I explain to her that we accidentally slept in and she'll have to wait for a few minutes. I lead her into the kitchen, smiling brightly. Ten hours. I can't believe it.

Samantha looks around nervously at everything.

"Sorry it's a mess," I tell her. "Get something to eat if you're hungry. Will has some fancy food."

"Okay…sure," she says, eyes wide as she looks around.

I hurry up the stairs to get dressed. I brush my teeth quickly and put on some pretty-smelling lotion and even some mascara. I decide to arrange a few braids in my hair, leaving it down to cover my scar of course. I'll wear another sundress today, and my thin gold necklace my mom got me that says *cheery,* with a tiny cherry on it. I look in the bathroom mirror, smiling at myself because I think I've already gained a couple pounds and some more color has come into my cheeks. I head down the hall to pick out a dress in my room – the blue one, I decide. There's a bounce in my step.

I love my new life.

Samantha

I am standing inside his house. The home of a Bailey.

Glancing at the staircase, I start to carefully and quietly look around. I wish I could take pictures. Palms sweaty, I take a few slow steps past the counter with tools on it and look around the corner, seeing that there's a small dining room with a circular table and wooden chairs. Is this where he eats in the morning? It's strange, seeing into his home like this. And very, very exciting. I try to think of how I'll describe it later. It's very...*him*. Sparse, masculine, secluded. Needs a lot of work.

I smile to myself.

The fridge is in the living room, making me wonder if Will is planning to tear down the wall in the kitchen that has no cabinets. I nervously walk over to it and open it. It's full of fresh produce and what looks to be homemade pasta and jars of things that look expensive. This surprises me, but maybe I should've expected it, considering who he is.

I close the fridge quietly, seeing a smiley-faced magnet on the door that's out of character for Will to have. Lyla's? I slowly walk through the living room to the backscreen door, looking out. There's a gorgeous view of the lake, and a wooden path that leads all the way down to the beach, where a fire pit sits surrounded by four chairs.

Hearing movement upstairs, I turn quickly. No one comes down yet, and I realize it was noise from a running shower I heard.

The couches are real leather. They look old. Are they from his past? I wait another minute or so, then decide to carefully make my way down the hallway. There's an office with bookshelves lining the walls and a big wooden desk. If I could just spend ten minutes in there, what would I find out about him? Across the hall, there's a bathroom and a laundry room. Curious, I look inside the laundry room to see if he's organized and clean, or if he's messy. There are two piles of clothes on the floor, sorted into

145

darks and lights. The door behind them must lead to the garage, and it's strange to me that he has clothes piled in front of it, like he hardly ever goes in there.

When I hear footsteps on the stairs, I quickly move back and turn in the doorway of the laundry room. Will is coming down and when he sees me, his steps slow. He's not in church clothes but just a white t-shirt and workout shorts.

"Morning," I say, unable to stop thinking about what it felt like for him to hold me close last night. My entire body was tingling the whole time. Did he feel that too?

He slowly walks up to me stops in front me at the laundry room door. His hair is wet, and he smells good, fresh out of a shower. The fact that he shaved makes me wonder about what Nell said last night. Does he find me attractive?

What a stupid thought. He definitely wants me gone. I can see it in the way he's looking at me – without even a hint of feeling. My heart is pounding. His jaw works and he glances past me into the laundry room, then back at me.

"Looking for something?" he asks flatly.

"Um, I was just…I was looking for the bathroom." I hope he can't sense me shrinking under his stare and his close proximity.

He searches my face. "Sure you were."

He knows I'm lying. I've been doing that a lot lately, and I hate it.

"Sorry, I'll just…" I trail off and start to move past him, but he leans over and grabs a pair of pants from the top of the dryer, inches from me. He seems both angry and amused at whatever look he sees on my face. Then he nods towards the door next to the laundry room.

"That's the bathroom."

"Right," I say nervously. "Thanks."

I clutch my purse, feeling like it's red hot right now because of the journal I have in it with all my notes about them. I picture pulling it out and handing it to him bravely and saying, *"Read what I've written so far. Let me write this."*

But in reality, I lock eyes with him for just a second and feel like I'm going to throw up. I can't tell what he's thinking.

Finally, he says, "We'll be down in a minute."

146

"Sure. Okay, yeah," I say before I close the bathroom door and lock it. I spin around and go to the sink, looking at my frantic self in the mirror.

Touching my fingers to my temples, I give a silent giggle.

This is the craziest, most fun and possibly wrong thing I have ever done.

Lyla

Samantha and I do all the talking on the way to church. Will is silent, brooding about something. I have decided that I will *not* let him ruin the second day of my new life. Nothing can bring me down.

I feel a little bit of hope when I notice that he checks her out a few times. I made her sit in the front seat for that very reason. I try to think of a way to find things in common between them.

"So, where did you go to high school?" I ask Samantha. She told me a second ago that she is originally from Chicago, like Will and I both are. She works at her sister's coffee shop that's close to our house, like this was all meant to be.

"Crestview," she says.

I laugh. "Will went to Piedmont. You were rivals. Maybe you went to his games and didn't even know it."

Samantha looks away, out the window. It looks like maybe she's covering a smile. That's a good thing.

"What hospital were you born in?" I ask her.

She hesitates, and then looks back at me. "Um…actually…I don't know where exactly I was born. Somewhere in Chicago, probably."

"You don't know for sure?" I ask.

"Lyla," Will says, and I realize I'm asking too many questions.

"It's okay," Samantha says. She looks at me, and then at Will, and seems to be gathering her courage. Then she says, slowly, "I was abandoned at a Chicago fire department as an infant. They found me in a bag by the main entrance."

Her words seem to suck all the air out of the car.

"In a bag?" I ask quietly.

Samantha shrugs, smiling bravely. "It was a brown paper bag. It had a blanket in it, so somebody was trying to keep me warm."

148

I don't know what to say. Apparently, Will doesn't either because he glances at her only once without a word.

After a few silent seconds, I quietly ask, "Were you adopted after that?"

"Yeah." She smiles at me. "You would love my mom. You remind me of her."

"And your dad? Your adoptive one, I mean."

"He passed away."

"I'm sorry," Will says finally.

"It's okay." She studies the side of Will's face for a second. "The crazy part is that my mom didn't tell me I was adopted until I was in my twenties."

I gasp. "Your mom waited *that* long to tell you?"

"Yeah," she says, still looking at Will. "A lot of people choose not to tell their kids, which I can understand, I guess. But my story's a little different."

I notice that Will's eyes have changed in the rearview mirror.

She goes on. "My dad was part Pakistani, so I always thought that I took more after him with my darker skin and hair. But I did a DNA test after my mom told me and I found out that I'm mostly Indian and partly Swiss." Even with the brave front she is putting on, casually telling us the story, I wonder if she still hasn't gotten over it.

"All those years," she says softly, "I thought I knew who I was. But I had no clue."

Will changes lanes too sharply. I have to balance myself with my hand on the seat. He glances at me in the mirror and I give him a look.

"What was it like?" I ask Samantha. "Finding out."

"It sucked." She laughs lightly. "It really sucked." She brushes hair out of her eyes. "But now that I know," she says, "I'm closer to my mom than I ever was before." She looks at Will. "There are no more secrets between us."

For some reason, that makes Will finally look at her. He meets her eyes for a few long seconds, and then focuses on the road again. I wonder, for the millionth time, what my brother is thinking. Samantha seems to be wondering that too.

Christian Freeman

This is the first time I've been seen in public in over a month, and people notice. Since I decided to stop going to Remmi's neighborhood because of that new girl, I needed something else to do. Something within my control, because everything else is so out of control.

Maybe I should've shaved. Maybe I should've gone to Grant's house instead of coming to church to talk to him, so it wouldn't cause such a scene. But maybe I *want* a scene. If he's enough of a hypocrite to show up to church after everything, then I want to embarrass him. My ex-best friend.

We used to do everything together. We were both accepted to Michigan State on full-ride football scholarships at the same time. Almost unheard of for two friends from the same high school. There were some articles written about us. Remmi taped them to my wall for me. Back when things like that used to matter.

Is Grant still going to college? That's all I want to ask. Forget everything else.

Right. I wish I could forget, instead of having it all come up in me every day like murky backed-up water from a clogged drain.

Estes is in the truck. I wish he was next to me right now because I hear Remmi's voice in my head, like usual. The voicemail she left me that night is burned into my memory. I listened to it way too many times in the first few days after she died. She didn't sound like herself. She was worried.

Hey, she said quickly, sounding out of breath. *Hey, I've been trying to call you and text you.* She sighed. *I didn't want to say this on the phone, but Grant kissed me tonight. I wanted you to hear it from me first, in case he tells anyone. I pushed him away, and he admitted it was to try to get back at you and Audree, but I didn't know what he was talking about. Where are you?*

My teeth clench as I remember everything.

Anyway, she said. *Meet me at our spot in thirty minutes.*

I didn't check my phone in time. And she didn't get back to shore in time before the storm came in.

I watch for Grant in the crowd of churchgoers heading up to the front doors. Some of them glance over at me, probably surprised to see me here, especially if they witnessed what I did after the funeral.

A lot of people were there. A lot of people loved her. So, a lot of people watched as I grabbed Grant by his collar that day, yelling, "You killed her, you know that?" right in his face.

I remember he was crying. He tried to shove me off of him. "Me? *Me?!*"

By that time, three men, including Coach Lamar, were pulling at us, trying to break us up before we throttled each other. Best friends. I haven't seen him since that day.

I'm determined to just talk to him today. Get some answers. Just talk. I can do that.

Even as I tell myself that, my hand curls into a fist.

Will

Samantha knows exactly who we are. I'm sure of it now. After a story like that? How could she not? I bet the whole thing was made up just so she could judge my reaction. Maybe she's still trying to figure out if it's us – if we're the Bailey kids. It's probably pretty clear to her now, considering the way I reacted last night and today. I'm such an idiot. I've been wondering why the story hasn't leaked yet. It's because the reporter is right under our noses, gathering more information directly from the Bailey heirs themselves. I wonder what newspaper or tabloid she works for.

I pull the car into a parking space too quickly. The tires screech. Samantha has to grab the handle above the door and Lyla looks at me again in the rearview mirror like I'm crazy.

"Ready?" I say shortly.

Neither of them answers me. We just get out of the car and quietly walk across the parking lot towards the church. I glance at Samantha beside me and the anger bubbles up again. Was she trying to make me feel guilty with that story? What my family chooses to share with Lyla or not is none of her business. Who does she think she is?

I was hoping to be late so we wouldn't have too much of a sermon to sit through, but we're early. I must have been driving faster than I thought. People trail up to the church in jeans and casual collared shirts, and I realize I'm overdressed. I unbutton my suit jacket and take it off as we walk.

Samantha leans towards me. "Don't worry. You look nice."

I glance at her and she gives a soft smile. I don't say anything because I don't know what to think. Her words made something twist in my stomach.

Lyla stops suddenly.

"Christian's here," she says, surprised.

I follow her gaze to find an athletic-looking blonde kid who needs a shave and is standing beside a storage shed by the church. He doesn't see us and seems tense as he looks around.

"How do you know him?" I ask Lyla, feeling strangely alarmed that my sister knows a boy already.

"He came over yesterday morning."

"When?" I say, confused.

"Yesterday morning," she says again, laughing like it's no big deal. "You were right there when I told Krista about it last night. Remember?"

I vaguely remember that now. I was too nervous about having dinner with Samantha to ask Lyla any questions about it. I'm about to do so now, but she's already walking over to him.

Samantha and I are left standing beside each other on the sidewalk. I stare after my sister as she calls out to the kid. I study everything about him. The kid's shoulders sink, and he looks down at the ground when he sees Lyla. He rubs his neck and it almost looks like he wants to leave.

Who is this guy? Was he hanging out with my sister behind my back? This is seriously the last thing I need right now.

"She makes friends quickly," Samantha says.

I glance at her. "Too quickly."

At my tone, Samantha meets my eyes. She swallows. *Yeah, you should be nervous.* I look back at my sister. She's saying something to the kid. He nods vaguely and glances around. Is he looking for an escape? People are watching him, I notice. They pass by and glance at him, whispering things.

I walk over there, very interested in whoever this kid is.

"This is my brother, Will," Lyla says happily when I come up to them.

He shakes my hand firmly, looking away. "Good to meet you."

"You too." I give him a nice little warning squeeze, and he looks at my face, expression unreadable. I drop his hand.

"Are you with anybody?" Lyla asks him. "Your parents?"

His jaw flexes as he looks up at the church. "I'm not staying."

He's wearing a collared shirt. I wonder if he was planning on staying, but now, something about my sister has made him change his mind.

Lyla laughs. "But you came all this way."

"It's five minutes from my house."

"Oh, come on. Maybe we'll even let you sit with us."

This isn't much different than how I got roped into this last night. Christian notices that people are still looking at him.

"I don't think so," he says shortly.

"It'll be fun," Lyla says.

As if she already knows he's going to give in, she starts walking back towards the sidewalk where Samantha is waiting. Lyla glances back at us over her shoulder.

"Come on," she says. "I want to meet people before the service starts and see if Krista's here."

Christian frowns. "Krista Andrews?"

She stops and shrugs. "I don't know her last name."

Something about this Krista Andrews makes Christian suddenly change his mind. He follows Lyla towards the church and I follow behind the two of them, watching him closely. He's too on-edge, too uptight.

Or maybe I just think that because *I'm* uptight right now.

A man and a woman stand at the entrance of the church, greeting everyone who walks in. Lyla shakes their hands and then hugs them with the excitement of a little girl being welcomed to the North Pole by elves. Christian watches her curiously, and Samantha is smiling a little, amused. It almost seems sincere.

"This is my brother, Will!" Lyla says.

I barely shake the man's hand and move on before he can strike up a conversation with me.

Inside, people are standing around and talking in the foyer. Someone hands us programs, looking surprised when they see Christian, and I take Lyla's arm and walk her into the sanctuary before she tries to introduce me to more people. Samantha and Christian follow behind us. I can't believe I'm doing this. I'm attending church with a woman who might be after us for a story and a kid who is attracting attention to us. Not to mention my sister who shouldn't even be awake right now and seems determined to introduce me to all of Northern Michigan.

When she doesn't find her new friend Krista out in the foyer, Lyla takes the lead and brings us all the way to the very front row. She lets Samantha go first, then waits for me to go next. I hesitate, looking down at her.

"Go," Lyla whispers.

I roll my eyes and step past her. Samantha doesn't look at me as I come to a stop beside her. Lyla comes to stand beside me and then Christian is last. The music is already going and Lyla is excited about it. She actually *wants* to be here. She's probably the only one out of the four of us. Watching her, I'm reminded of what her life has been like for years now. Mom and Dad said her friends stopped talking to her. She doesn't even own a phone. She's missed out on a lot, and she knows it. The nightmares will probably come back, and she probably knows that too.

I let out a quiet breath, deciding that I should try to act normal today for my sister's sake. I tell myself that maybe I'm wrong about Samantha. Maybe it's all in my head and she doesn't know anything. Maybe she isn't the one looking into us, which is what forced me to go to Chicago to get my sister and bring her back here and now my quiet life is in shambles. But if Samantha *is* the one, then this whole mess is her fault.

As the pastor starts his sermon, that's what my thoughts mainly consist of – all of this being Samantha's fault. She is completely motionless beside me, her hands clasped in her lap. I try to read her posture, but it doesn't give much away. She moves her hair and I smell her sweet smell again. I try not to think about what it felt like to have her in my arms last night. It's been so long since I let myself get close to anyone. The fact that I let it happen with this woman in particular is what bothers me the most.

I look down at the program in my lap, trying to distract myself. It doesn't work. I glance at Lyla. She seems to be listening to every word the pastor says. So does everyone else.

Except for Christian. Christian looks like he's about to be sick. I watch him for a second. He tugs at the collar of his shirt and rubs his neck. He's sweating. Lyla looks at him nervously. She whispers something to him. He nods.

"I'm fine," he whispers back.

He doesn't look fine. He sits forward with his elbows on his knees, and then sits back and grabs at his collar again.

The pastor is talking about forgiveness. I wonder if that's what's making him so uncomfortable.

"Is there someone in your life you need to forgive?" he asks the congregation.

I think of my parents for a second, Juanita, Alex, and I shift uneasily.

"Is there something in the past that you haven't let go of?"

Suddenly, Christian is on his feet. He steps out into the aisle and walks all the way out of the sanctuary. Lyla stares after him. There is an awkward pause in the sermon, a few murmurs and a lot of glances. And then, my sister stands up too. I try to stop her but it's too late. She follows him out.

And so, it's just me and Samantha left sitting next to each other in the front row. I can't leave now. It would be too disruptive because the pastor saw the whole thing and looks slightly troubled about it. Samantha seems to realize this too. We're stuck.

Sienna

My whole body is stiff as I try to sit still in the back row of the church. The echo from that kid slamming out the door and Lyla following is the only sound for a second. Then some whispers, a couple stumbling words from the pastor as he tries to ignore what just happened.

That kid is a ticking time bomb. I don't want him anywhere near Lyla.

If Emil were here, he would probably tell me to remain calm. It's okay, he'd say. He's just a kid. But a guy who was "just a kid" got into an argument with his girlfriend eight years ago, my sister, and in his rage he stabbed her, then tried to run after he panicked. It was too late for her when I pulled up to the house. Her boyfriend was caught four blocks away, then sentenced to life in prison.

It can happen to anyone, at any time.

My palms are wet. I never had such strong reactions to guys being around Tessa. It's what makes me realize that I didn't really care about her like I thought I did. It also makes me realize that maybe I'm not cut out to do any of this at all – guard Lyla well, run my own company after this…none of it. Not if I'm going to be like this.

For now, I am still on the job with Lyla. I will wait another minute or so. Then I'll follow them outside and watch from somewhere close by.

If he tries to drive her somewhere in the state of mind he's in, I don't know what I'll do.

Christian Freeman

I unbutton the first two buttons of my shirt and yank it away from my throat, trying to breathe as I reach the far end of the parking lot. Sweat is beading on my face. My mouth is watering like it does when I'm gonna hurl.

I'm almost to my truck. Estes is in there. Just the thought of seeing him begins to calm my nerves slightly. I walk faster, almost running. Finally, I get to my truck and yank the driver's side door open. Estes is in my seat, happy to see me. I move him aside and get in and close the door. He whimpers and nudges me with his nose, and I pet him roughly behind his ears with one hand, using the other hand to wipe the sweat from my eyes.

I saw Grant's parents in there, towards the back. Grant wasn't with them.

I look down at my hands. I'm shaking, bad. My chest is heaving. It feels like something is swimming laps inside my stomach. Is this a panic attack? I curl forward and press my head against the steering wheel as Estes rests his head on my leg. He's total calmness right now because he's trained to be. It's supposed to help, but it isn't doing much.

I try to relax. Why am I here again? I can't think clearly. All I can hear are the pastor's words about forgiving and moving on. I could feel everyone's eyes on me.

"Is there someone in your life you need to forgive?"

Anger grips my stomach. I can't forgive. I can't.

"Is there something in the past that you haven't let go of?"

Someone knocks on the window and I jump and look over. It's Lyla, smiling at first, but it disappears instantly when she sees me hunched over like this and breathing like I just ran a mile. I sit back, shaking my head, annoyed. I didn't want anyone seeing me like this, especially her. I should've known she would follow me.

158

She opens the door because she's all worried and I grab it to stop her. "Lyla, wait."

Estes sits up and when Lyla sees him, terror fills her eyes and she backs up from the door, her hand going up to the back of her neck.

"Stay," I tell Estes and I open the door to get out.

Lyla backs up further, checking to make sure Estes doesn't follow me out. He tries to, which is surprising. I have to shut the door quickly before he jumps out. What is it with him and this girl?

She relaxes a little once the door is closed, and her hand slowly drops to her side. She looks me over because I am still sweating and breathing hard. I swallow and bend over, spitting on the ground. Lyla steps forward and touches my back.

"What's wrong with you?" she says frantically. "What's going on?"

"It'll pass. I just need a minute."

"What will pass?" she says, flustered. "What's happening to you?"

I look up at her and move away from her touch. "I need you to not ask questions right now, can you do that?"

She opens her mouth like she's about to ask another one, but she forces herself not to with some effort. I look down at the pavement again, my hands on my knees. I wish she would just leave me alone. I don't want anyone seeing me like this.

This isn't normal. What would my dad say about this? Throughout this whole process, this hasn't happened. Then again, I haven't made myself go back to this church. I screamed in my best friend's face just a few yards from where I'm standing now, while Audree watched in horror with her hands up over her mouth. It was the last day I saw her too.

"Let's sit down by that tree," Lyla says.

I shake my head and take a breath. Then I reluctantly look around for this tree and notice that someone has come out of the church. It's a short Hispanic woman I don't recognize. She looks over at us and hesitates, like she's checking on me, and then she pulls out her phone and casually makes a phone call. I'm glad she didn't come over here.

I follow Lyla as she takes me into the cool shade of the tree by the edge of the parking lot, and we sit down together. I rest my forearms on my knees and lean my head back against the rough bark. Lyla take her shoes off and scrunches her toes in the grass, then sits cross-legged, looking out

159

at the manicured lawn. I can see the harbor in the distance, the water crystal blue today like Lyla's dress. I try to focus on the water instead of the sickness in my stomach.

I don't know how long we sit like that. A while. And I don't know why I'm not getting into my truck and leaving this place.

At one point Lyla picks some of the grass and starts a little pile of it on her dress. I close my eyes, breathing deeply.

Finally, Lyla breaks the silence.

"So," she says casually. "That was crazy."

I look up at the branches above us. "Yep."

"Wanna talk about it?"

"Nope."

She nods, picking more grass. "Then we won't."

I find myself staring at her. I'm able to because she's sitting forward and can't see that I'm watching her. It's nice, distracting, looking at her. Her dark curly hair is like a blanket over her back. Some of it is in loose braids. A cool breeze rises up and Lyla holds her hair down with one hand until it's gone, then she focuses again on the small pile of grass in her lap and adds more to it. She turns her head towards me, and she smiles peacefully over her shoulder. Her nose crinkles. I've never seen blue eyes like hers with dark hair. It's like they're sparkling right now, with her blue dress and the water behind her.

I wish I could deny the fact that I've thought about her a few times since yesterday. But I can't.

I wet my lips, deciding I want to talk.

"You asked me about my friends," I say.

Lyla's smile falters a little. "Yeah."

I swallow and look away. "My best friend and I were accepted to Michigan State with scholarships for football, but I'm not going anymore. We're not friends anymore. And I don't talk to my other friends, either."

Lyla stays silent for a second, probably not knowing what to say. I don't know why I told her that. It's more than I've opened up to anyone recently. My dad wants me to see a counselor, but I refuse. I hear enough from my dad as it is. He's a therapist. Besides, I don't need to share my "feelings" with some stranger who's going to judge me.

160

But then again, Lyla's practically a stranger to me, and I'm telling her some of it.

"My brother did the same thing," she says, looking at me.

"Did what?"

"He gave up a full-ride scholarship to the University of Michigan. For football."

I wonder who in their right mind would do that. "Why?"

"I don't know. But I think he regrets it."

I look away, jaw flexing.

"Do you want to talk about…why you're not going?" she asks carefully.

I consider it. I consider telling her everything. But then I change my mind and shake my head. It's a relief having at least one person in town not know what happened. It's only a matter of time before she finds out. I wonder what she'll think of me when she does. I wonder why I care.

We go back to being silent for a while. Lyla looks out over the parking lot.

"I thought Krista was going to be here today. I haven't seen her."

I tense up, remembering only now that Lyla mentioned her. It's the only reason I walked into the church. Krista Andrews would corrupt someone like Lyla, just like she corrupts everyone else around her. Even Remmi. Almost.

"Don't talk to Krista Andrews," I say in a low voice.

Lyla frowns. "Why not?"

"Just don't."

Lyla smiles. "She seems really nice to me."

My jaw flexes. "Probably a different Krista then."

"Maybe. She works at that restaurant on the Pier. I invited her to church last night."

"The Krista I know couldn't hold a job for a day in her life. And she would never step foot inside a church."

"That's kind of mean," Lyla points out.

"Yeah, well…it's true."

Maybe that's my queue to go. But instead, I find myself tearing some grass and adding it to her pile.

"Thanks," she says, happy again.

161

We do this silently for who knows how long, tearing off grass together and making a mound of it like we're five years old. I toss some at her face and she laughs, brushing it away.

Am I flirting? Lyla seems to have no idea about it. When I realize that I definitely *am* flirting with this girl, I stop tearing off grass and giving it to her. I almost get up to leave, but Lyla says, "How old is Estes?"

I'm surprised she's asking about him since she's afraid of him. "He's four."

She nods, using the tip of her finger to round off the edges of our pile of grass on her knee. "Did you train him?"

I shift. "No."

"That's good." She laughs. "He doesn't really listen to you."

I study her, finding that I'm grinning. "Usually he does. You do something weird to him. I don't know what it is."

"Is that why he attacked me?"

I roll my eyes. "He didn't attack you."

She nods adamantly. "Yes, he did."

"Whatever."

"Is he a therapy dog?" she asks.

I look at her sharply. "How did you know that?"

She shrugs. "I guessed."

She tears off more grass and adds it to the pile and I study her.

"How long have you had him?"

"A while," I say a little too shortly. She glances at me, and I look out at the harbor, avoiding her eyes. "His favorite thing is the water. It's weird because German shepherds aren't known for being that way, not like retrievers are. But he likes going out on my dad's boat."

"Your family has a boat?" she asks, as dreamily as she did about my friends yesterday.

"Yeah."

"I've never been out on a boat before."

I frown at her. "But you live in Chicago."

"I know." She blushes. "I want a sailboat someday. Wouldn't that be fun?"

I shake my head. "Too slow. I need more speed than that."

She smiles towards the harbor. "Well I want a nice, smooth ride over the water," she says, making the motion with her hand slowly cutting through the air.

I find myself studying the back of her again. I think of the few girls I've dated, and all the times they would pretend to be into whatever I'm into and go along with whatever I want. Except for Remmi, of course.

I think Lyla's more like her. She knows what she wants. She wants a slow sailboat, she wants to wear dresses and go to church and dance on the beach and dig her toes into the grass, no matter what anyone might think of it. What else does she want? I swallow. I almost offer to take her out on my dad's boat while she's here, especially to show her how much better it is to go fast. But I keep my mouth shut. And the urge to even offer that to her surprises me. I haven't been out on it since the day Remmi died. Haven't even wanted to see it since then.

"I don't have friends, either," Lyla says suddenly.

I squint at her. I don't believe it. "What?"

"I said I don't have friends, either." Her face is red. "I don't even have a phone."

I stare. "You don't have a phone."

"No."

"Why not?"

She shakes her head. "Just one."

"Just one what?"

"Secret. If you give me one of yours, I'll give you one of mine."

I frown thoughtfully. "A secret for a secret," I say.

"Yeah. I guess so."

I add one last bunch of grass to our pile and then dust my hands off. People are starting to leave the church because the service is over. That went by really fast. I notice that my hands aren't shaking anymore and the sickness in my stomach has passed.

"You're not as pale now," Lyla says.

I nod. "My stomach's better."

"And you're not all gross and sweaty."

I laugh. "Yeah, thanks."

Lyla smiles. "You have a good laugh," she says. "You should use it more."

"How do you know I don't?"

She shrugs. "I just know."

"Yeah, well." I get to my feet. "I can tell you don't laugh much, either."

This, of course, makes her laugh. I grin down at her and take her hand and pull her up. It's an easy movement, like it's natural for us. Lyla dumps all the grass off her dress and shakes it around and dusts it off.

"Did I get it all?"

My gaze goes down over her, and I clear my throat. "Yeah."

I meet her eyes, seeing that the faint shadows under them are still there, but they aren't as pronounced as they were yesterday. She's pretty to me, but I realize it's not just because of her looks. It's because she's so happy. She doesn't have any friends or even a phone and yet she's the happiest person I've ever met. And I want to tell her that I don't want her to ever leave. I want to tell her that I'm glad she was here today.

But I shouldn't be feeling this. I shouldn't.

Lyla has no idea what I'm thinking. She's smiling again about something. "I'm glad you feel better."

"Me too," I say roughly. "Thanks for distracting me."

"Of course," she says. She claps her hands lightly. "Yay."

This makes me roll my eyes because she is so ridiculously happy all the time. Should I hug her or something? I want to, but no I shouldn't. I definitely shouldn't. I glance over at the church. Her brother hasn't come out yet. How much does he know about me?

Lyla is about to leave, but she stops.

"Guess what," she says.

"What?"

"You have a friend now."

We stare at each other for a second. I feel this warmth spread through me. I slowly smile. "So do you."

She smirks. "Maybe I should get a phone and we can call each other."

We laugh. I haven't felt like this since Remmi died. My laugh sounds like someone else's in my ears.

Lyla starts to walk backwards. "Everything will be okay, Christian," she says.

I almost believe it this time, simply because I know she wants me to.

"Thanks," I tell her quietly.

She walks away, and I can't take my eyes off her. Her dress moves like water in the breeze. She holds her hair down over her shoulder again, glancing back at me. She smiles, and I swallow. I didn't think I would ever feel this way again. And I definitely didn't think it would happen so soon.

I shake my head, staring after her. It's way *too* soon. I would hurt her. And I hate it.

Estes barks from inside the cab of my truck. He sees her walking away and he's not happy about it. *Neither am I, buddy.* I let out a long breath, frustrated at myself for staying here and talking with her for so long. I walk back to my truck, looking over at her one more time. And I tell her I'm sorry in my mind.

I'm putting a stop to this before it's even begun.

Will

Lyla is outside waiting for us when we walk out of the church. To everyone else, it probably looks like Samantha and I are together because Lyla left us alone, when she was the one who wanted to come to church in the first place.

I should've cancelled this whole thing last night.

"Is he okay?" Samantha asks Lyla.

Lyla looks behind her at what must be Christian's red truck backing out of a spot.

"Yeah, he is now," she says. "I think he went through something recently." She looks at me. "Did you recognize him?"

"No."

"Your house used to be his grandma's house."

"Huh," I say quickly. I start walking over to where my car is parked, wanting to get out of here. Now I know who the kid is. Christian Freeman. His dad knew our parents years ago. He's a counselor in town and has offered to talk to me if I ever need it. Twice, I've actually considered it – when the bitterness against my parents was eating me alive. But in the end, I decided not to because I realized I wouldn't even know where to start or what to say.

Lyla looks sideways at me.

"Christian was planning on going to Michigan State for football in the fall," she says. "He decided not to. I don't know why."

I glance over at his truck as he drives out of the parking lot, thinking about my own decisions when I was his age. I wonder why he gave it up. Probably not because he inherited a ton of money like I did.

I don't want to think about my parents' disappointment in me, and what happened with Alexandra when I gave it all up. I've got enough to think about right now. I push the memories away.

166

To my severe displeasure, Samantha asks if we want to grab lunch together after church, and of course, Lyla is all for it. They even decide to go swimming at my house afterwards, and they buy Samantha a bathing suit at the only store in town that's open on a Sunday – Tricia's store. Tricia raises an eyebrow when she sees Samantha, and she grins at me. I ignore her.

What game is Samantha playing? And why haven't I put a stop to it yet?

I study her in the rearview mirror once we're back in the car. She told Lyla to take the front seat this time, and Lyla reluctantly agreed. I catch Samantha's eyes in the reflection. She holds my gaze for a second, and then she's the first one to look away.

When I pull the car back into the driveway at home, Lyla takes something out of the bag from the store they stopped at. It's a pink sort of fabric. She hands it to Samantha.

"I secretly bought this for you, from the store we went to."

Samantha takes it from her. "That's so sweet of you." She smiles and unfolds it. "It's beautiful. Is it a scarf?"

Lyla shrugs happily. "I think it could be a sari. I was thinking maybe you'd like it, since you found out you're partly Indian."

Samantha swallows, going quiet. She looks touched.

I almost roll my eyes.

"Thank you, Lyla," she says. "That's so thoughtful."

"You're welcome," Lyla says, looking pleased.

I study Samantha. Is she starting to regret the lies she's been feeding to my sister?

Lyla claps lightly. "Ready to go swimming?"

"Sure," Samantha says, avoiding my eyes.

"What about you, Will?" Lyla asks.

"No," I say shortly. I clear my throat. "I've got work to do."

"Are you sure?"

I give her a look that says, *"Stop trying to get us together."* She has no idea what's really going on here.

"I'm sure."

167

Lyla seems unaware of my irritation. She gets out of the car, but Samantha doesn't move yet. She holds the scarf in her lap, looking down at it.

"I hope this is okay," she says. "Your sister and I hanging out, I mean." She looks at me.

I don't need to say it. I know she can read my expression. *I don't want you here.* My eyes inadvertently move down over her. She looks good for a reason, like she did last night in that black dress. Is she trying to seduce me, so she can get information out of me? I've heard of people doing worse for a story. And ours would make her famous.

I let out a long breath through my nose and look out the windshield, jaw flexed.

Samantha hesitates again, like maybe she wants to say more. She doesn't. From the corner of my eye I watch her put the scarf into her big purse. I suddenly wonder if she'll leave her purse inside the house, so I can take a look through it. Maybe there's something in there about us. I could see how much she knows.

"Are you coming?" Lyla asks through the window.

Avoiding my eyes, Samantha gets out of the car. They go into the house together, and I sit in silence. I know I should call my parents to tell them that I'm suspicious of this woman. They'll probably be able to find out within minutes if it's her or not, given their connections. They would make her leave, probably have her sign a gag order, like usual.

And then Lyla can go back home, and things will go back to normal. I'll get the Manor.

I pull my phone out of my pocket and stare down at it. *Just call them.* What's stopping me?

Nostrils flared, I shove the phone back in my pocket and get out of the car, slamming the door behind me.

They are already down at the beach by the time I get inside. I look around for her purse, but it's not in here. Frustrated, I go directly upstairs and take my suit off, changing into jeans and a casual shirt. I check myself in the mirror for longer than usual, then curse myself because I realize why I'm doing it, and I head downstairs. I'm *going* to call my parents.

I pick up the house phone off the kitchen counter and dial my dad's cell phone. I walk over to the window while I wait for him to answer.

"Will?"

"Hey, Dad."

"What's wrong?" He doesn't normally get calls from me unless something's wrong.

"Nothing. I was just..." I look out the window.

Lyla's laughing with Samantha down at the beach. She runs out into the water and dives in. Samantha follows, caught up in the excitement of the moment because my sister has that sort of effect on people.

"Will?"

I blink. "I was just...wondering if you'd heard anything about the story leaking."

He clears his throat.

"Not yet," he says. "But it's still just the weekend."

"Yeah, good," I say absently. What is wrong with me? Do I *want* this woman leaking personal details about our lives if I'm right about her?

"How's it going?" he asks.

"It's fine," I say tightly. I try to loosen up. "Lyla's happy she's awake." I back away from the window. "We went to church this morning."

A few awkward seconds pass. He's probably surprised I would go.

"That's...great," he says.

Tell him Samantha's the journalist. Just tell him.

"Will," he says. "Thanks for doing this. I know things haven't been easy between us for the last few years."

I roll my eyes. Last few years? Does he mean the last twenty-seven years? Because that's the way I see it. My parents were never around back when they were too busy to raise a family. I was raised entirely by a nanny who was practically a mother to me, and then she was taken away suddenly when I was twelve, along with everything else I knew and loved. After that, my parents changed our last name and tried to be actual parents and give us a "normal" life. It was too late for that, at least, for me it was.

"I have to go," I say quietly.

There's a pause. "We'll let you know if anything changes."

We say goodbye and end the call. I pace around in the living room after that because I don't know what else to do. I'm such an idiot. What will my parents do if they find out I suspected Samantha and didn't do anything about it? Would they keep the Manor from me?

I try to get some work done on the house, deciding that now would be a perfect time to rip out the tile in the bathroom. I hammer away, breaking up the old black and white squares, shards flying. I jam the chisel into the grout, thinking, what is *wrong* with me? I should've told Dad everything.

I drop the chisel and go out into the living room, looking out the back door. Lyla and Samantha are standing in the water together, talking. Whatever my sister is telling her could be released to the public. We've given Samantha enough to write an entire book on us.

I dust myself off, then look around frantically in the living room. Grabbing a magazine off the coffee table, I head down to the beach.

"Will!" Lyla says. "Yay! Come swimming with us! The water feels great!"

"No, it doesn't," Samantha says, a few feet away from her. "It's freezing."

"I'm good," I tell them.

I sit down in a lawn chair and open the magazine. Samantha's purse is sitting beside the chair next to me. There's a notebook sticking out a little. If I could just look through it for one second, I could see what she's writing about us. I glance over at her as she laughs with Lyla about something. She's too close. She'd see me. I flip through a few pages of the magazine, then realize it's upside down. I quickly turn it and act like I'm reading it.

Lyla disappears under the water for a few seconds. I find myself thinking of playing in our family's pool with her when we were younger. It was the Olympic-sized pool at the Manor. Juanita would always watch over us as we played. I would dunk Lyla in the shallow end of the pool because she was adventurous even at the age of two. She'd laugh and laugh, clinging to me with her little fists. She'd look into my eyes, completely trusting me as she squealed, *"Again?"*

I suck in a breath as Lyla's laughter brings me back to reality. I haven't thought about that in years. I shift in the lawn chair, annoyed at the strange emptiness the memory left behind.

I sit out here for a long time while Samantha and Lyla laugh and talk like there's nothing in the world to worry about. I keep glancing at Samantha's bag, but I can't risk looking through it. But she left it right here, open.

Lyla wipes the water off her face and wrings out her hair. She turns and looks out over the lake. My muscles tense up when I realize she isn't covering her scar. I glance over at Samantha. It's too late. She's seen it.

"Lyla," she says. She comes closer, concerned as she looks at her neck and back.

I sit up, my heart starting to pound. I do *not* want this woman knowing something so personal about my sister. What if she somehow gets a picture of it and publishes that too?

"What happened to you?" she asks.

I get to my feet. "You should get out now, Lyla, before you get too cold."

Neither of them responds. "That's just my scar," Lyla tells her, touching it nervously. "I was attacked by a dog."

Samantha examines it in a motherly way. "I'm sorry," she says. "How old were you?"

Don't tell her anything, Lyla. Keep your mouth shut.

"I'm going to build a fire if you want to come out now," I say loudly.

Without looking at me, they start walking through the water towards shore. Lyla's still talking.

"I was three," she says.

"That's terrible."

Lyla shrugs. "It's no big deal. But I try to cover it, so people don't have to see it. And I've always been afraid of dogs."

They reach the shore together and to my surprise, Samantha grabs her arm to stop her and she gives her a long hug.

"You're beautiful," she says. She glances at me as she lets go of her. "And you're worth more than you know."

My mouth opens slightly. I can't believe she had the guts to say that.

"Really?" Lyla says. "Thank you." She's blinking a lot and swallowing, like she can't believe a woman like Samantha would say that to her. She's clueless as to what she really meant.

Don't get attached to this woman, Lyla.

Samantha smiles. "Now where did I put my towel? I'm freezing."

"It's on the chair behind Will," Lyla says, and I'm forced to grab it off the back of the lawn chair.

Samantha locks eyes with me when she takes it from my hand. There's a hidden message in her expression.

"Thanks," she says.

It's only then that I notice her beautiful skin and body in her orange bathing suit. She wraps the towel around herself and I force myself to look away. She might be beautiful, but she's also manipulative. She dug into my family's company, my family's life, all to try to find us and write a story.

"We'll go change and grab some stuff to make dinner over the fire," Lyla says.

Dinner? "Wait," I say.

She ignores me. "Do you like bratwursts, Samantha?"

"Yeah. That sounds great."

She picks up her purse, looking at me with a nervous, hidden message as she pulls it over her arm. It is such an obvious move that I'm starting to wonder if she actually *wants* me to see something in there. I think about dancing with her last night. If we'd had a longer time to talk, what else would she have said?

They walk back to the house together, talking about something else now. I groan and rub my neck. My sister is an open book.

I don't know what else to do except to make a fire because they're expecting it. I go to the wood pile in the trees and start gathering what I need, finding some release of my frustration by snapping branches with more force than necessary. I dump the wood into the fire pit and start arranging it into a teepee. I don't know what to do now. I'll have to see how this plays out tonight. If they make more plans to see each other, I'll have to try to stop it from happening. And I'll have to figure out how to get rid of her.

Lyla

Samantha changes in my bathroom upstairs, and I change in my room. We meet up again in the kitchen, me in my casual blue dress and Samantha in her perfectly fitted jeans and flow-y white shirt. Samantha is one of the most beautiful people I've ever seen in real life. It's no wonder Will was checking her out all day, especially when he saw her emerge from the water in her bathing suit. The orange flecks in it made her dark skin look stunning. And yet, she seems even more insecure than I am sometimes. She'll blush and look away or seem even scared at my brother's perusal.

"Are you single?" I ask her as I gather plates for dinner.

She laughs and blushes again. "Wow, Lyla."

"What? I'm just curious."

She rolls her eyes. "You remind me of my sister."

"That's fun," I tell her. "I didn't know you had a sister."

"Yeah. She's three years younger than me."

"So are you?" I ask, not letting her change the subject. "Single?"

"Yes," she says reluctantly. "I'm single." She thinks about something for a second, then says, "But I *was* engaged."

I gasp and push the plates aside. "Tell me every detail."

She laughs again, sitting down on a bar stool across the counter from me.

"We were going to get married a few months ago." She brushes some hair out of her eyes. "It was weird," she says quietly, "when the day passed with no wedding."

"That would be sad. Were your friends and family disappointed?"

She shakes her head. "It was going to be a small wedding at a park by my mom's house. I don't have much family in Chicago." She studies me. "What about you?" she says. "What about your family?"

"It's just the four of us – me and Will and our parents."

Something close to anger flashes in Samantha's eyes for some reason, but after a second, it's gone.

"Not even grandparents? Aunts or uncles?" she asks.

"My grandma and grandpa on my dad's side died before I was born, and he's an only child. So is my mom. Well…now, she is, I guess. Her parents and sister died in a car accident when she was in her twenties. Before I was born."

Samantha seems to be thinking of other things. I hope I'm not boring her with my family history.

"And…she was already with your dad?" she asks.

"Yeah. She met him when she was eighteen. They got married when she was twenty."

"You don't have any cousins, or anyone else in your family?"

I wonder why she's still asking about that. "Nope. Just us."

She seems to be deep in thought. "Huh. That's pretty rare."

"I know," I say, "and we only see Will at Christmas. For the past few years, he hasn't even come home for that." There's a sadness in my voice that I can't mask.

Samantha smiles thoughtfully. "I think he has a hard time getting close to people," she says.

"Even his own family?"

"*Especially* his own family. You're the biggest threat to the wall around his heart."

I have never thought about it that way. Not once in my life. It's like a light has suddenly come on inside me. Maybe that's what keeps him from coming home.

Samantha is watching me with a gentle expression.

"I've never thought of it like that," I tell her.

She shrugs. "Sometimes the people who matter most to us are the ones we're afraid of getting close to."

I swallow, looking at her. "Is that how it is with you?" I ask.

Her eyes narrow, but she's smiling. "Very perceptive, Lyla Brooks."

I laugh. "You should give him a chance. I know he seems like an old grumpy man sometimes, but he likes you. I can tell."

"Because he's being a complete jerk?"

"Yes. Exactly."

We laugh together, and I try to remember the last time I had a conversation with someone like this who wasn't my mom or my dad. It was with my friend Emma in the eighth grade during a sleepover. We were talking about boys who we thought maybe liked us.

"What about you?" she asks me.

"What do you mean?"

"What was his name? Christian? At church today?"

My face heats up immediately. "He's a friend."

She grins. "Have you ever had a boyfriend?"

"No," I say honestly. "I...don't get out much."

She frowns slightly, and I decide it's okay to tell her about my nightmares. Since she's been honest with me about her struggles and her past, I feel like it's time for me to be honest with her about mine. In fact, I decide that I can tell Samantha absolutely everything about me. I love her like a sister, already. After just one weekend.

And so, I do. I tell her more about myself than I've told anyone else in the world.

Emil

I quickly open the basement door to the smell of homemade tortillas. Sienna must've started dinner.

Heading down the hall, I find her at the stove in the kitchen. "We need to talk," I tell her quickly.

She pauses and turns to look at me. "What is it?"

"Come downstairs."

She turns off the burner and slides the tortilla off the pan and onto a plate before following me. We stop at the desk and I sit down.

"Lyla's doing way too much talking," I tell her.

Sienna leans over with her palms flat on the desk, watching the screen that shows Samantha sitting with Lyla in Will's kitchen.

"What's she saying?"

"Her entire life's story."

Sienna sighs, more annoyed than worried.

"But that's not the thing," I tell her.

On another screen I rewind the recording of their conversation and play it back for her. We both hear Samantha say, "I don't have much family in Chicago…"

Sienna looks at me. "She's from Chicago?"

"Listen," I tell her.

"What about you?" Samantha asks Lyla. "What about your family?"

"It's just the four of us," Lyla says innocently. "Me, Will, and our parents."

As Samantha proceeds to dig more into this with prying questions, Sienna sits down and pulls up an internet screen.

"What's her last name?"

"Foster. She told me she's from Phoenix."

She sighs and runs a search on Samantha Foster from Chicago instead.

Eyes trained on the screen, she says, "I noticed she was acting a little strange when she first walked into Will's house this morning. She was looking around a lot. I should've realized."

She clicks through a few things that come up on the search.

"Nothing," she says. "No social media accounts. Nothing." She sits back. I can tell her mind is reeling. "If she lied about where she's from..." She looks at me. "Maybe she lied about her name."

I look back at the screen. "She has her purse with her, but I could check her car. See if I could get a name off something."

Sienna nods. "Where's Will?"

"I think he's still down at the fire."

"Be careful."

I stride up the stairs and out the front door, looking around for Will as I head next door, making sure I'm not seen. I stop beside Samantha's car, glancing around. I'm glad people feel safe in small towns. It means her car is unlocked. I get in and shut the door, so the light goes out, and start to rummage through the glove compartment and the center console. But there's nothing. No receipt for the rental with her name on it, like I was hoping. I get out and quietly close the car door, heading back through the trees towards my house without using a light so I won't be noticed.

I think through everything. I know she didn't follow them after I talked to her Saturday morning, because Sienna and I would've noticed. Samantha seemed like she knew Lyla already that day when Lyla approached her at the festival. Then they went to dinner, church, shopping, now dinner again at Will's. Their fire down at the beach right now glows like a signal flare.

After listening to their conversation, it sure doesn't seem like they knew each other from before in Chicago. It sounds like Samantha is trying very hard to get to know her now. Too hard.

My mind works through everything quickly, growing more uneasy as I remember all that Lyla said to her earlier. Headlines flash through my head: `Bailey Heiress Found. Lillianna Bailey Living as Lyla Brooks for 15 Years`. The articles would go into her night terrors she told Samantha about, her scar. It would be devastating for her. And people would know where she is. The girl who's worth eighty-million dollars.

If Samantha is a reporter, she's getting more information on the Baileys every second that passes. I have to do something.

I remember she told me where she's staying. She knows Dorothy Freeman, and I know exactly where Dorothy's rental cottage is. It's just a few minutes from here.

Instead of going inside the house to talk to Sienna, I get into my car and start backing out of the driveway.

I call Sienna. "I'm going to check out where she's staying."

"Don't do anything crazy," she says.

Samantha

I've always hated the taste of wine, but as I sit across the fire from a real live Bailey with a glass full of it in my hand, I want to down the whole thing. But I can't do that without showing him how nervous I am. And frustrated. I'm a mix of emotions. There is a great big Bailey family out there, and Lyla knows nothing about them. Plus, she's been having night terrors about the dog attack that happened to her fifteen years ago. When she was still a Bailey.

I used to have night terrors occasionally before I knew everything. Something was off-balance in my life. I didn't even know what it was.

I sit here silently in a green lawn chair across the fire from Will, clutching the stem of the wineglass he handed me a little while ago, swirling the red liquid and taking sips every so often like I know something about how to drink wine. But really, I'm trying not to wince every time. You'd think that wine that costs over two-thousand dollars a bottle would taste better than most. It doesn't. It tastes worse.

And what game is he playing by giving this to me anyway? He probably knows I looked it up. There's no internet at his house, so I called my sister from the bathroom earlier and whispered for her to look it up.

"It usually costs over two-thousand dollars at auction!" she said, and we giggled together.

"Tell him the rest, Sam," she said, getting serious. *"Get him to let you write this."*

Right. She doesn't know how intimidating he is.

Will's grim face glows orange from the fire. He stares into the flames silently. He's leaning back in the lawn chair, his elbows on the armrests, hands clasped together over his stomach. His wineglass rests on the sand beside his chair, empty. He's had three glasses of it already, and we haven't even eaten. Even though his body is relaxed, I can feel his tension. I keep

179

glancing at him, but I finally force myself to stop. I look out at the black water. There's a storm developing far off. I can only see it when the lightning makes the mountainous cloud glow. I watch it for a while, trying to calm my churning stomach.

Lyla went into the house a few minutes ago to find longer skewers because the shorter ones were causing us to burn our hands as we tried to roast bratwursts over the fire. Will and I have been left alone, and we haven't said a word to each other yet.

The truth is out, I'm pretty sure, considering the way Will's treating me. And he can't say anything about it because he can't give too much away about himself. This is complicated. I have dug myself into a hole that's way too deep to crawl out of with any sort of dignity now. I recognize the hole wouldn't be so deep if I'd just had the guts to tell him everything while we were dancing last night. I tried. But I should have said more. And now, we've been to church together and Lyla has revealed intimate things about herself because she trusts me.

Lyla is taking a long time, even though Will told her which drawer the skewers are in. My guess is she's purposely leaving us alone, so we can get to know each other. We haven't. The fire cracks, offering at least a little fill to the silence. Distant thunder rumbles. I glance at Will again and I find that he's looking at me now. My mouth goes dry. I don't speak. I take a sip of wine and choke it down.

Will suddenly speaks. "Why did you really come to Good Hart?"

Wow. Okay…so this is happening. I take a gulp of too much wine on accident and wince.

"Is it the wine or the topic of conversation you don't like?" he asks quietly.

Both. "The wine is…okay." I clear my throat. "Tastes expensive."

He doesn't respond, just picks up the bottle and pours some more into his glass. It makes me nervous. He's scary enough as it is when he's sober. He looks down at his glass cryptically, drinks.

"You do pretty well for yourself," I say, testing him. "Flipping houses?" I add nervously.

He takes another drink.

"How many…have you done?"

He tilts his glass, staring at it. "A lot."

180

I don't believe him, but at least he finally answered me. "Is that what you want to do with your life?" I hate that my voice is shaking.

He just looks at me.

I don't know what to think of him. I can't figure him out. He lives in a relatively modest house but buys two-thousand-dollar bottles of wine. Or maybe he kept it from the past. He got this bottle out of the garage earlier, then locked the door when he was done. I wonder what else he keeps in there.

I take another sip and can't help but make a face.

Will grins dryly, amused. "You don't have to drink it."

"It's fine," I say.

"You don't like wine?"

I decide to be honest. "Any alcohol, really. I don't like the taste."

He shrugs. "Dump it out if you want."

Is he trying to say he doesn't care how wasteful that would be? Is he trying to show me how much money he's worth? Slowly, I tilt the glass over the side of my chair. Will looks down at the red stain in the sand. That's probably the equivalent of four-hundred and fifty bucks in that little puddle. I immediately regret it.

"I'm sorry," I say in a whisper. "That was wasteful."

His eyes narrow slightly as he studies me. He sits forward, and some of the anger he has worked to hide all this time comes to the surface. "Who do you work for, Samantha."

My heart jumps into my throat. "What do you mean?"

"You know exactly what I mean. Some tabloid?"

"What are you talking about? I told you, I work at my family's coffee shop."

"Don't give me that. It's too late."

"I'm serious. Will – "

He cuts me off. "If I see *anything* about my sister's scar –"

"Will, I'm not a journalist. I'm *not*. I promise you. I would never do that to you. Or Lyla. I swear."

He searches my face, trying to discern if I'm telling the truth. "You're telling me you did all that research and yet you're not a journalist."

My face blushes. I don't know how he knows about the research I did on them at the library. I think of all the papers in my car at the airport in

181

Chicago, things I printed off about them, books I checked out. Did someone see it?

"I...yes. I guess so," I say.

"And then you followed us here."

"I had to see if it was you. Anyone would *have* to see if it was you, Will."

He laughs humorlessly. "I can't believe this. This is all because of you."

"What is?"

He chugs the last half-glass of his wine and pours what little is left from the bottle.

"My sister being here. All of this. My parents think some story is getting out, so they sent her away from them so she won't find any of it out." He downs the wine and sets the glass in the sand. "And now," he says cryptically, "you're telling me there *is* no story."

He sounds almost angry about that. And is he...disappointed?

My mouth opens slightly. I stare at him, watching as the flames spin in his eyes. Something shifts inside me – my perspective of him.

"You don't agree with them," I say, stunned.

He lets out a long breath and reaches down to the fire, not answering as he grabs a stick and turns it. It crackles, sending more smoke up as the branch burns.

His lack of an answer is enough for me. "Why haven't you come out with the story yourself?"

Still nothing from him.

"I would write it for you," I blurt. There, I said it.

He laughs humorlessly. "Of course, you would."

I keep going. "But it's not just about the story, now."

"Uh-huh," he says without inflection. He doesn't believe me.

"It's more than that, Will. Do you really think it's a coincidence that I'm the one who found you guys? Me? Of all people?"

He looks at me, eyes blazing from the fire, or anger. I can't tell.

"The truth will come out someday, Will. I could make it happen the right way. If you helped me."

He shakes his head once. "I can't."

"Why not?"

182

His jaw flexes. "You don't understand."

"I understand she has this whole family out there she doesn't even *know* about."

The thunder against the silence is like an echo. Will is watching, waiting.

"After we changed inside," I go on, "Lyla said it's just the four of you. That's what she thinks. Four family members. She deserves to know the rest. Like your aunt Marjorie, who runs everything now. She has what, six children, who all have kids? Family for Lyla. Friends. She deserves to know them. And *you*." I pause. "She deserves to know you. She deserves to know *herself*."

Silence hangs.

"I used to have night terrors too," I admit to him. "Before I even knew anything was missing from my life."

He watches me, then picks up his wineglass, remembers that it's empty and so is the bottle, and sets it back down. "So, it's true then," he says.

"What's true?"

"That story you told us in the car."

"Yes. Of course." I feel the familiar sinking in my chest. "I wish it wasn't."

He stares at the empty wineglass in my hands.

"The part about me being closer to my mom now is true too," I tell him quietly.

He looks up at me. A full silent minute passes. And then, I can't believe it, but his eyes suddenly don't look so much like a wall anymore. They are more like a door, cracked just slightly. Maybe he's about to let me in.

But then, we both hear Lyla.

"Found them!" she calls to us as the screen door slaps closed.

Will and I quickly sit back and look away from each other. Within a few short seconds, Lyla appears through the darkness. She smiles at us and sits down in her lawn chair, handing us skewers.

"What'd I miss? Anything?"

"Nope," Will says. "Nothing."

His expression is still slightly different than it normally is. He looks down over his sister, maybe because she's wearing one of his jackets over her dress now.

Lyla glances between the two of us, then goes to work roasting a bratwurst. Will and I follow suit. We eat in almost complete silence, and I can tell Lyla is worried about it. She keeps looking at her brother expectantly, probably hoping he'll say something for once and try to make polite conversation. But he doesn't. He has a lot on his mind.

"Can we hang out again tomorrow?" Lyla asks me. "I wanted to go to this coffee place I saw in town, and maybe do some shopping."

I hesitate, glancing at Will. He's still watching me, but he doesn't stop me from saying anything.

"It's up to you," I tell her.

Will's eyes flicker because he knows I'm talking to him.

This is it. If he wants me to stay away from them, he'll make up some excuse as to why I can't come over ever again. I picture him standing up and pointing his finger in my face and yelling, *"Get out of our lives, you liar!"*

He is silent for a few seconds. Then, looking at Lyla now, he says, "I thought we'd hang out tomorrow. Just the two of us."

I stare at him, my heart sinking.

Lyla is a mixture of joy over that, and awkwardness because I'm being left out.

"That's fine," I say quickly. "I just remembered something I wanted to do anyway."

Will's avoiding my eyes.

"Then we'll do it the next day," Lyla says. "You can have dinner here again."

I'm proud of her because her tone doesn't leave room for discussion with her brother. In her mind, Will can't force us to not see each other.

In my mind, considering the circumstances, I know he can.

"We'll see," he says.

I still don't know what to think. Maybe he just needs time. Maybe there's still hope. Or maybe I'm going home.

We finish our food, watching the lightning and hearing the distant thunder from the storm that probably won't reach shore. And then eventually the night draws to a close.

We stand up and I lean over to pick up my wineglass, but Will says, "Leave it. I'll get it later." He rubs his neck, looking at me. "I'll walk you to your car."

Both Lyla and I are dumbfounded. My heart is pounding.

"Um...sure. Yeah." Lyla hugs me goodbye, and I squeeze her tightly. Maybe her brother is about to send me home.

"Give him a chance," she whispers. "He's not so bad. Remember what you told me earlier about the wall around his heart."

I swallow, feeling a stirring in me...and a sickness.

Lyla lets me go and starts gathering our paper plates with a barely masked smile on her face.

Will uses his cell phone as a light as we walk on a path around the side of his house to the front yard. I trip twice just slightly because I'm so nervous, and he slows down for me. I feel his hand at the small of my back, guiding me, and the touch surprises me. I try to look over at him but can barely see his somber, handsome face in the darkness.

It's brighter in the front yard because of the light from his porch. He puts his cell phone away as we come to a stop beside my car in the driveway. I pause for a second, wondering why he walked me here. He doesn't say anything. Neither do I.

Not knowing what else to do, I open the car door. Will stops me, grabbing the door from me and curling his fingers over the top of it.

"My sister trusts you," he says quietly, staring at me intently. The blue light from my car glows up the side of his face.

My breathing stops. "I know."

"I hope you don't betray that trust."

I stare at him, then put my hand over his on the car door. "I wouldn't do that. Will. I swear. I would never do that."

His eyes search my face. Then he nods, slipping his hand out from under mine. "Then have a nice life."

He backs up and opens the door wider for me to get in.

My mouth opens slightly. "That's...that's *it*?"

He shrugs, his expression like a wall again. "Did you expect something more?"

I look away. Yes, I expected something more. Because I'm an idiot. I should've never come here.

"I…" My words trail off because I don't know what to say. My face is burning.

Will doesn't move, and I look up at him again. His throat works in a swallow, the only evidence that he might actually feel something right now.

"Can I say goodbye to Lyla?" I ask him, probably sounding pathetic.

His jaw flexes and he looks off at the trees where we just came from.

"Never mind," I say quietly. "It's fine."

My throat closes as shame rises up inside me. What kind of a person does this? Follows someone like this to a whole different state? And then admits everything to the very person she followed. I am so embarrassed.

"I'm sorry," I say lamely. "I'm…sorry for all of this."

I start to get into the car, but Will closes the door suddenly. I look up at him as he steps closer to me. "Samantha…"

I wait, holding my breath, trying not to hope…and trying to ignore whatever this is that I feel for him while he stands so closely to me.

He seems to be debating something. "I want to tell her," he says, looking into my eyes. He scratches his head roughly. "But I can't."

I shake my head. "Why not? Are you afraid?"

"No – I…"

"I could help you tell her."

He shakes his head. "We can't." He presses his lips together, looking guilty.

Studying him, blinking, something slowly occurs to me.

"Inheritance," I say under my breath.

When his nostrils flare and he avoids my eyes, I know.

"Oh my gosh."

He looks at me sharply. "You don't know the whole story."

"Then tell me."

"I can't."

I nod angrily, backing away from him. "Yeah. Okay."

I have a thousand things I want to say to him about my own hurts, my own story. But it's all jumbled so all I can do is stare at him, my mouth turned in disgust. What do you do when you thought there was more depth to someone, and you discover they're as shallow as sink water?

You say goodbye, and you don't look back. And you definitely question your judgment. Especially of someone you were beginning to let yourself have feelings for.

Will doesn't defend himself, just stands there with a stiff jaw. I open the car door and get inside, closing myself in and wishing I was home already. Curled in bed at home. Able to cry.

I start the car and pull quickly out of the driveway. I look back at him once. He stands there like a shadow, feet spread and hands in his pockets. He bows his head for a second, then kicks at something and turns for the house.

I don't want to cry. I swallow it back. He's not worth it. I take some deep breaths, and I catch the light scent of cologne. It must be left over from Will standing at the open door, only it doesn't smell like him.

I can't call my mom, or Nell. I don't want to talk to them right now, although they are probably dying to know what happened. I'm going home, back to Chicago empty-handed. That's what happened. And I don't want to talk about it.

When I get back to the cottage, I fumble to unlock the door because my hands are shaking. I finally get it unlocked and I hurry inside, shutting the door behind me, locking it again and then pressing my back against it. I couldn't even say goodbye to Lyla. I probably won't see her ever again. She'll never know who she really is.

I go into my bedroom at the back of the cottage. I swear I catch the scent of cologne again, which is strange because it didn't smell this way at all before. But I don't think about it too much because now I am crying. I toss my purse and keys onto the table beneath the window, then I curl onto my side on the quilted bears and trees of the lumpy, foreign bed. I give in to a grief that must go way deeper than this whole thing. It's older grief than that. Too big, too hurtful for it to be about Will and Lyla and this whole adventure that's now over.

I sob harder and harder, thinking there is something very wrong with me.

Emil

I can hear Samantha crying from where I stand behind the bathroom door. It's cracked open. If she comes in here, I'll have to subdue her somehow before she sees my face. Great. This is just *great*.

My adrenaline spiked the second I saw headlights swoop across the interior walls of the cottage. I only had time to make my way down the stairs from the loft, and then I nearly got caught as I stepped into the bathroom as the front door swung open.

Sweat drips down my back. I can smell myself. I try to stay calm.

This was so stupid. I am such an idiot. I could lose my job for this. Go to jail, actually. I started out by just looking into the back window with my flashlight. I thought I'd see pictures of the Baileys or notes about them or a laptop. But then, I noticed that the latch of the bedroom window could easily be opened. I was right, and I have to admit, I was thinking of one of my favorite Clancy novels as I opened the window and climbed through, just for a quick look around. I didn't find anything. Not a single hint that she knows about the Baileys at all. I checked the desk in the loft upstairs and every drawer in the kitchen, even under her mattress. Nothing. Not even a laptop.

And then she came home.

Sienna is on her way here. I texted her to come knock on the door, then disappear. It should buy me enough time to slip back out the window.

Samantha suddenly shifts on the bed, rustling. I can hear that she's trying to stop crying. Then I hear her feet on the floor, getting closer. She stops at the bathroom door. My breath silently catches in my throat and I brace myself. I swallow, hands out, ready to…what? Knock her out?

But instead, I hear her soft footfalls heading out of the room. I wait. I hear the sound of the kitchen faucet, so I open the door and head straight for the back window that I left open.

There's a knock at the front door. Sienna. Soft footsteps sound as Samantha heads over to the door and opens it.

"Hello?" she says, pausing. "Will?"

I'm starting to heft myself up onto the window ledge, but I pause, seeing Samantha's purse on the table under the window. I quickly riffle through it. I go right for her purple wallet, but the front door closes. I panic, unzipping the wallet quickly. First thing I see is a small ticket stub for a flight. I study it, blinking, heart pounding.

I can't believe it. We were right.

Hearing that she's coming back, I shove the wallet into her purse and grab onto the window ledge to pull myself up. I vault over the table and out the window, shutting it behind me, and then duck down when I see her come back into the room. Her shadow stops for a second. Maybe she heard something. Maybe she's heading over here to look out the window.

Crawling now, feeling stupid and reckless, I scramble off the back deck and out into the dark woods. I swear under my breath as I straighten and trample through the bushes to make my way to the hidden spot where I left the car. Sienna will meet me there. The ticket stub is clenched tightly in my sweaty hand.

She was on their same flight. And that's not even the most condemning part about what I found.

Within seconds I see the car. Sienna leans against it. She pushes off from it when she hears my approach.

"I told you not to do anything crazy!" she whispers harshly.

I shake my head, heart still thrumming as I stop in front of her. "I had to do what I had to do."

"You crossed a line, Emil."

I know she's right, but I'll never admit it.

"It was worth the risk." I hold the ticket stub out to her.

"What's this?" she asks quickly, taking it from me and shining her phone light on it.

I let her find out for herself. Even in the darkness I can see her eyes get bigger as she studies it.

"Time to call the boss," I tell her.

She blinks up at me. She knows I'm right.

189

Samantha

My feet come to a stop in the bedroom when I smell the cologne again. A minute ago, I thought I heard something by the back window. This is all very strange – the knock at the door, then the sound in here, and the scent of cologne. When I answered the door, I hoped it was Will. I hoped he'd followed me, even though I wouldn't know what to say to him if he did. The jerk. I never want to see him again.

But no one was there.

Shuddering, I go to the back window and look out. I can't see much, just the trees that are like a dark crowd of people, staring in. I gasp when I notice the window isn't locked. It probably hasn't been locked this entire time, and I didn't know it. I push the lock down and close the blinds, stepping back.

Okay, okay. You're being paranoid. Maybe the knock on the door was the wind.

But it's not windy right now.

I decide to sleep with the lights on, if I can even sleep at all.

Part IV
27 Days and counting…

The echo of the gunshot rings in my ears. The guy drops when my bullet hits him. It takes me three seconds to snap out of it. I look down, my breath puffing in short spurts. She's still bleeding. I check her pulse. Still alive.

Flashes stripe through the trees. The ambulance. I haul her up into my arms again, pain licking up my side because of my bad knee. There's no time to check the pulse of the man. My legs are starting to fail me, both of them. Shock, maybe? I am practically dragging myself through the vines and roots. Her warm blood drips down the front of me.

"Everything's going to be okay. You're all right. You're okay."

Christian

I'm watching Lyla from the trees. She's dancing on the beach, in a dress that shines brighter than the sun. I reach out to her, but she runs out into the water.

"Come out here!" she yells happily. "Come swimming, Christian!"

I want to, but I can't. I shouldn't. "I'm not ready!" I call to her.

And then she goes under. She comes back up, only she has red hair now.

She is Remmi. Alive. Laughing.

I suck in a breath and snap awake.

Breathing hard, panicked, I look around and see my room in the morning light. My mind starts to clear and I curse under my breath, swallowing bile and running my hands through my hair.

Estes gets up from his bed and comes over to me, licking my elbow while I try to slow my breathing. I turn onto my side and scratch him under his chin, trying not to think about the image of Remmi standing there in the water. It's much better to think about Lyla dancing.

In fact, since Saturday, I haven't been able to *stop* thinking about her.

"Go eat," I tell Estes, and he saunters out of my room to go to the kitchen, where my mom will feed him.

I lay back and stare at the ceiling, knowing I have another long day ahead of me filled with not much of anything. I'll work out until I puke or almost puke. I'll do some chores for my mom, like fixing the handle of the sliding glass door in the kitchen. I'll play video games for a while.

It all sounds so incredibly lame. Maybe I should go back to Remmi's house just one more time. I don't want any teddy bears or cards to get lost if they blow away.

Or maybe I should try to find Grant.

My door creaks, and I expect to see Estes when I look over at it. But it's my cousin, Ben. He's five, and he's been staying with us for a while now. His mom isn't the best person in the world. We don't know where she is right now.

Ben hesitates at the door, his fingers curled in front of his mouth. He's looking at me cautiously because he knows I've changed in the last month. I don't wrestle with him like I used to. I don't play with him at all anymore.

I eye him with a pretend angry stare and then scoot over on my bed and pat it.

He laughs and runs over, climbing up. He lays back and we both look around at the bare walls together. I used to have posters up of my favorite football players. And the articles about me and Grant, and pictures of friends. I tore them all down in a rage a few weeks ago. Probably won't put them back.

I glance at Ben. He has his whole life ahead of him. And what do I have?

Nothing.

"I have a crush on a girl," Ben says suddenly.

I try not to grin. "Yeah? What's her name?"

"Emma."

I nod slowly, acting like this is big news. Ben has a new crush every week.

"What are you going to do about it?"

He rubs his nose real hard, making his eyes water. "I'm going to ask her to play. We can play with Estes. Think she'll like him?"

"Yeah."

We lay here for a while. Then I say, "I think I have a crush on a girl too."

Ben laughs, like a real belly laugh. "I know! Rem Rem!"

My throat goes tight. We haven't told him what happened to Remmi yet, which isn't good, but we're waiting for things in his life to get more stable first. My aunt needs to get her act together, or else we're going to end up adopting him.

I swallow hard. "I'm not with Rem Rem anymore," I say.

He nods, like this is no big deal. "Okay. Someone else?"

I sigh heavily. "Guess so."

"What are you going to do about it?"

I almost laugh because he's repeating my own question back to me. He's always been too smart for his own good.

"I don't know."

"Ask her to play. With Estes."

I shake my head. "She doesn't like him."

He laughs way too loudly in my ear. "Then *get* her to like him, silly goose!"

That's what my mom calls him sometimes. I nudge him. "What do you suggest I do, bud?"

He nods decisively. "Play fetch."

I'm amused just thinking of what Lyla's reaction would be to that. But there's part of me that wonders if it's actually possible.

Ben can't sit still for very long, being five, so he barrel-rolls off my bed and lands hard on his stomach. Then he runs to the door and stops.

"Where's Rem Rem?" he asks, because she used to be over here all the time.

I scramble for an answer, but then he says, "And Grant. And Audree."

I sigh. "They've been...busy."

"You need friends!" he laughs.

Sometimes, like now, he's really annoying. He sticks his tongue out at me and shakes his butt before he runs off.

I roll my eyes and rub my face with both hands. He's right. I do need friends. But not the old ones. New ones.

Lyla comes to my mind again. Maybe it doesn't have to be anything more than that. She would be perfect to hang out with. She doesn't know anything about what happened. Doesn't know anyone else here. And she's only going to be here for the summer.

I sit up slowly, thinking. Maybe that's all this has to be right now. Friendship.

And maybe Ben's idea about Estes isn't so bad.

Will

For some reason, I care what Samantha thinks of us. Of me, particularly. So, there's something I'm going to do before I get her sign a gag order and leave. It might be reckless, but after a night of no sleep – just tossing and turning and picturing her judgmental, ashamed expression – I don't *care* if it's reckless. My parents will never know. Lyla thinks I'm running errands in town because I left a note on the counter. She won't know either.

Last night, I did a check on Samantha Foster from Chicago, Illinois, just to see if she works for some tabloid or gossip column. I couldn't find anything. Not even a blog. It made me feel slightly better, like maybe she isn't lying completely.

Still, though, I have my family's standard gag order ready for her electronic signature on my phone. I'll have her sign it today, then I'll buy her a ticket home. Then I'll call my dad and tell him I took care of the reporter, and Lyla will leave too. I'll get the Manor.

My grip tightens on the steering wheel when I think of my sister. I shake off the thoughts of her leaving as I pull up to Dorothy's cottage. I honk the horn and rub my neck while I wait, feeling like a rock is lodged at the base of my skull. Too much wine last night. I honk again, wondering if Dorothy has another rental house I don't know about, but then I finally see Samantha open the front door. She's in a robe and big knitted socks that make me think of my sister.

I roll down the passenger side window, leaning over.

"Get dressed, then get in," I say loudly.

Samantha processes the sight of me and tucks her hair, that's in all sorts of odd angles, behind her ears. "What are you doing here?"

"It has to do with that inheritance of mine that you're so judgmental about. I'm going to show it to you."

She stares at me. "Why?"

I look straight ahead out the windshield. "Does it matter?"

When she doesn't answer, I look over at her again. She's torn, I can tell. And then, she just can't help her intrusive and meddling self. There's a tiny sense of excitement in her as she quickly shuts the door. She's dressed and ready to go within ten minutes. She shuts and locks the front door, then turns towards me and pauses for a second. I grudgingly admit that she looks good after such a short amount of time to get ready. She looked good even before she got ready. That was something else I couldn't get out of my mind last night. The fact that I am attracted to this woman who followed us. I'm an idiot.

I let my eyes trail down over her as she nervously makes her way down the front porch steps and the driveway, then I look straight ahead as she gets in my car.

"I don't want to talk," she says immediately as she buckles her seatbelt. "Just drive."

Gritting my teeth, I pull out into the road, knowing it'll be a long twenty minutes to the Manor.

Emil

I groan when I realize where Will is going. He's taking her to the Manor. Either he's giving her a big send-off – which is my guess after hearing her crying last night – or, worse, he's going to pour his heart out to her.

I am waiting to hear from Mark Bailey. He'll tell me what he wants me to do. He doesn't want me to interfere and blow my cover unless I absolutely have to. I pull over and park beneath some trees, waiting reluctantly. Mark is trying to call his son right now to warn him not to tell this woman anything.

Because Samantha Foster is not who Will thinks she is.

She's been lying about her name this entire time.

Samantha

The inheritance that Will was talking about...I don't know what to do, or what to say. I started to have an idea of what it was when we turned off a secluded road and onto an even more secluded road. He stopped at a massive gate, at least fifteen feet high, and got out of the car and unlocked it. When we drove through, I stared out at the gorgeous land around us. The trees seemed excitedly green. The sloping hills of the long driveway brought us to a big bend around a cove of the lake.

I gasped quietly when I saw what was sitting, waiting for us, on the other side of that cove.

A massive, decadent, ridiculously huge mansion.

My heart is pounding. It feels like it's another country we've driven to, as ancient as royal properties in France or England or Spain. Except this is more like ruins, mere memories of a grander time. Bricks are disintegrating. Tall grasses grow untamed. Grout cracks between stones. It seems like an injustice because this place is so beautiful, like it deserves more than just sitting, rotting away.

I'm starting to understand things now.

"This is yours," I say, my hands over my mouth as Will stops the car in front of the rock steps that lead up to the front door. "This house," I say in disbelief. "It's yours?"

"Technically, it's a mansion," Will says, cynically joking but also correcting me. Then his voice drops to a deeper tone. "And technically, it's not mine. Not until this is all over."

I shake my head slowly, eyes wide as I take it all in.

"Why would they leave this all behind?" I ask him.

He sighs deeply, and I guess that's his only answer. We silently stare through the windows.

"When it was up and running," Will tells me quietly, "it was a complete village. Over eighty people lived and worked here with their families." There's a new emotion in his voice, something other than anger and annoyance. It's a tone that's gentle, and maybe even caring.

"They bought their groceries from a little market on the property," he adds, "and fresh produce from the massive vegetable garden on the north end."

I'm looking at him now, watching his throat convulse in a swallow and his eyes comb the place over with sentiment.

"I don't understand," I almost whisper.

Will turns the car off and looks at me. "You don't understand what?" he asks softly.

"Why did you bring me here?" I hold my breath, waiting for an answer.

He opens his mouth to say something, but his phone vibrates. I hear the thrum of it. He pulls it out of his pocket and I can see that his dad is calling him. Will turns it off and slides it back into his pocket, looking over at the lake.

"Are you up for a walk?" he asks me.

I swallow. "Yeah. Sure."

He gets out, and I follow him. I walk slowly, stepping with care, staring back and forth between Will and the extravagance around us.

Our footsteps echo on the uneven brick beneath us. Green grass is like fingers stretching up the lowest story of the house. Vines like volcanoes climb green out of the ground, all the way up and over the tiled, uneven rooftops. There is so much work that needs to be done that the expenses would be in the tens of millions. Even just the upkeep would be in the tens of millions.

I walk behind the man who can afford all of it, and I am perplexed by him.

I'm hoping he takes me inside the house and gives me a tour, but instead he turns towards the lake. He glances back at me.

"It's because of what happened to Lyla," he says quietly.

"What is?"

"You asked why my parents would give all of this up. It's because they don't want anything to do with the past anymore, because of Lyla being attacked by the dog and almost dying. It changed everything for them."

I think of her scar. The image of it twists through my memory. It's like nothing I've ever seen before. I remember that her bathing suit strap was cutting into it and wondered if she could feel it. It started from her jagged hairline and fell like a dead tree branch down the right side of her back. It was blue in places – probably veins – and chunky in spots and smooth in others. I can't imagine having a scar like that at eighteen years old. And I can't imagine having to hide it. She must be an expert at it. I never saw it Saturday, even though she was wearing an orange sundress. I didn't even see it while we danced wildly Saturday night. It's probably two feet long.

My arms are cold, and I rub them, like it's not summer but winter. I look back at the house as we walk.

"So, your parents don't want to face the past," I say.

It's all making sense to me now. After all the articles I've read of theories other people had, all the rumors circulating and books written…

"They don't want her knowing about any of it," Will says. He stops and turns in a circle, gesturing dramatically up at the expanse of brick and stone and beautifully painted trim. "Or any of this."

He looks at me, and I hold his gaze. *Why are you showing it to me?* I want to ask again. Is he going to let me write about all of this?

He clears his throat, and then we continue towards the blue cove. We make our way into the overgrown grass, sand starting to take over the ground beneath our feet. When we get to the beach, we follow the turns of the shoreline together.

"Have you ever thought there was something more to the story?" I ask. "Some deeper reason they gave it all up?"

"Of course, I have," he says grimly. "But when I ask my dad about it, he just says that their eyes were opened after the attack. They suddenly saw it all for what it really was."

"And what was that?" I ask him.

He shrugs. "Nothing, if you lose your kids because of it."

I nod. "And you? What do you see it as?"

He stops and looks back at it, sliding his hands into his pockets. "My life's purpose."

When I find myself admiring him, I slowly start walking again. He does too, right beside me.

"My dad told me he started seeing his friends and their families in a different light too," he tells me. "Their kids were spoiled and didn't have to work a day in their lives. My parents wanted more for me and Lyla."

"So, they gave up everything and tried to raise you like you were normal kids?"

"They tried, but it was too late for me," he says.

"And they withheld your inheritance?"

He looks at the house, then away. "Part of it."

"There was more?"

He sighs and rubs his neck. "It's all from my grandfather, obviously, because my parents are still alive. I doubt they'll leave us a dime anyway," he mutters under his breath. "But yeah. There was more. When my grandfather died, he left eighty million for me to inherit on my eighteenth birthday. Plus, the Manor."

My mouth is hanging open. "Eighty million *dollars*?"

Despite himself, he smirks at my stupid question. "Yes, dollars."

"And you inherited that at eighteen?"

He shakes his head. "I didn't know it was going to be eighty million. The conditions of his will were different than normal. I inherited just ten million at first, along with a few other things, and I wasn't told about the rest of the money yet, or the Manor. My grandfather was a smart man, and he wanted to test me – see how I would handle a smaller amount first."

"And what happened?"

"I failed," he says flatly. "I gave up my football scholarship to the University of Michigan, and instead I traveled the world. I went through three million of it in three years. My parents lost all respect for me after that."

His throat works. I suddenly want to reach over to take his hand. The impulse surprises me so much that I blush. Still, I try to offer him some understanding.

"I've disappointed some people in my life too," I tell him.

He looks at me and lets me go on.

Because he's opening up to me, I can do no less. Something has changed today, obviously. Things are very different than they were last night. I'm not going home yet, that's clear. I haven't even had a chance to process that.

I take a quiet breath, and I tell him my secret.

"My name isn't Samantha Foster," I tell him.

He stops and turns to me, accusation in his eyes. "You've been lying to us?"

"No, no…" I go on quickly. "I've been going by Samantha for a long time now, but my legal name is Alyssa Riley."

He blinks at me, brow furrowing. "Why did you change it?"

"Because I found out about a note that was left with me in the bag I was found in as an infant. It said my name was Samantha Marie. I found out about it after my mom finally told me I was adopted."

Silence hangs between us.

"I just…I needed to be the real me, as much as I could. You know?"

He stays silent. Maybe he's wondering if I'm telling the truth. Or judging me.

"You have to understand," I say. "Around that time, I found out about my half-sister. Nell and I have the same birth mom, but different dads. She doesn't know who my dad is." I swallow, looking away. "When she told me that my birth mom had died, I didn't handle it very well. My parents had kept the truth from me, and so I never got to meet her. She even put out a post through social media when she knew she had stage four cancer, looking for a Samantha Marie who'd been left at a Chicago fire department. She wanted to meet me before she died, and she never got the chance."

As usual, I hate the lack of emotion I feel over the whole thing. I wish I was choked up or something, but all I feel is…confusion about what to feel.

I start walking again, finding it easier to talk about this when Will's not staring directly at me.

"So, when I found all of that out from Nell," I say, "and that my birth mom's last name was Foster, I started going by Samantha Marie Foster. Not many people in my life understood, not even my fiancé, Brian."

Will lifts an eyebrow at me.

"Especially not my fiancé, actually. He said it was a complete slap in the face to my parents who'd actually raised me. But he didn't get it. I needed…roots or something. I don't know."

"You needed to honor your old life. Your birth mom."

We both stop and I turn to him. "Yeah. Exactly."

He searches my face with his eyes and this look that makes my throat grow tight.

"I get it," he says roughly.

Everything on the beach seems to go completely still. Even the waves pause for us. We are staring at each other in complete understanding. I didn't know how much it would mean to have someone like Will say that to me – that he understands. But if anyone would, it's this man right here. This man I suddenly realize I am completely falling for. Or maybe already have. After just one weekend.

He clears his throat and breaks our gaze, and he starts walking again. "What happened after that?"

I shrug. "My mom and my sister and I got really close after that. We healed. We focused on running the coffee shop and sort of starting over, I guess. My mom took my sister under her wing, and it's been really great seeing them bond. I moved into her apartment above the coffee shop so we could get to know each other more."

We walk quietly for about twenty feet, then Will speaks again. "Did your mom understand you changing your name?"

"Not really," I say honestly, "but she was supportive. I think she was so scared to lose me after she told me the truth that she supported almost everything I chose to do at that time. Like dropping out of college before getting my journalism degree. And breaking up with Brian."

I don't tell him that Brian has been trying to contact me again.

He nods slowly, and I notice he's getting a little closer to me on the narrow beach we're walking.

"So that's it," I tell him. "I guess you know my secret. I have an alias."

He smiles a little. "Get in line," he says.

My heart feels lifted. "Do you ever want to be a Bailey again?"

He laughs softly. "It'd be nice." He gets serious and looks straight ahead. "But...that part of me has been gone so long I wouldn't even recognize him. But yeah."

"What made you start living like you are now, after you traveled the world?"

He rubs his neck, wincing. "I woke up one morning, hungover and unable to remember what city I was in, and I realized I had become my father – the way he used to be. So, I spent some of my inheritance on the house I'm in now, plus a small house that needed remodeling in Harbor Springs. I fixed it up and sold it, and I've done the same with a few other houses. I haven't touched the rest of the money since."

There is this weird, warm stirring in me at his words. He is so not what I judged him to be.

"And why Michigan?" I ask. "You could live anywhere in the world."

He grins slightly. "My grandfather always loved Northern Michigan. He made me promise, just before he died, that I would end up here, running the Manor. He knew it was my dream." He shrugs. "Good Hart is as close as I could get to all the people who used to run it. A lot of them still work in town, and they think I could've gotten them their jobs back in a heartbeat all this time and yet I haven't. Not until this weekend."

I suddenly understand a lot more about this strange weekend.

"The bartender," I say.

He nods.

"But you've had no authority to get them their jobs back. Don't they know that?"

"People can think what they want to think about me."

"Like me," I say unexpectedly.

He glances over.

"Last night," I explain, "I thought you weren't telling Lyla the truth because of money." I look over at the impossibly beautiful but neglected house behind us. "But this would be a lot to give up. And it's been your dream. So...I guess, I can understand that. Sort of." I grin. "Just a little."

Especially because it's obvious now that he wants me to write this, or else why would he bring me here?

When Will looks at me, I can see that he's relieved. He was probably worried about what I would think of him. But all of a sudden, there is something else in his eyes, like a secret, maybe. But that seems to always be there with this man. And maybe with me, too. He looks away and starts walking again. The calm waves are like a song to our silence.

I have so much more I want to ask him. Maybe there's time to. For now, there's only one question that really matters.

"I guess..." I say slowly, "I guess, I don't really understand why you're telling me all of this." I look back at the house, then at Will beside me, the blue cove against him in the background making his eyes seem almost fake. "Why did you bring me here today?"

I hope he says it's because he trusts me, and maybe even likes having me here knowing everything. Or because he's so excited he can finally be open with someone. Or because he's wanted to take someone here and show them this for years, and I'm the one who gets to experience it. Then I'll get to write about the Baileys. Dog attack or not, Lyla deserves to know everything, to see all of this grandeur that was her life. I want to go inside the main house, but I've refrained from asking. I also want to video call my mom and my sister to show them all of this…

Will finally answers. "Because I wanted you to see that we're not who everyone thinks we are." He comes to a stop again, moving a rock by his foot. "Samantha…"

He takes a breath, lets it out. "My parents – as much as I want Lyla to know everything – they do have their reasons for not telling her. And I do too." He turns to me, but he doesn't look into my eyes. "I just…I wanted you to know that…" He swallows. "…before you leave."

I stare at him. I don't understand, not at first because I am still distracted by the beauty of this man, the unexpected depths of him. But then, my heart slowly moves its way down to my stomach as I realize what he means.

He's sending me home.

I feel sick all of a sudden. I watch him take his phone out of his pocket. He turns it back on, pulls up a screen. He hands it to me.

"I need you to sign this," he says.

I shakily look down at it. I can't speak or think.

"It's a gag order," he explains quietly. "If you publish anything, you'll be sued for three million dollars."

I cough out some sort of sound and then step back from him, handing his phone back before I drop it, or throw it. "Are you…Are you serious right now?"

His eyes have morphed back into being distant. "This is how it works with my family."

"I thought…" I shake my head, starting to cry to my horror and embarrassment. "I thought we were just…talking. I was getting to *know* you. You showed me all of this. Told me things…and I told you *everything* about me. And now you're just having me sign a *gag order?* And sending me home?"

Rage starts to bubble up inside me, old and threatening. Again, I can tell it's deeper than whatever this is, but I don't care. I hate being strung along.

His jaw flexes. "Yes."

"You could've just let me leave after last night."

He groans. "Samantha, I told you because I –"

"Do you feel *anything* for me?" I suddenly say.

I immediately wish I could put the words back into my head, but they're out there now.

Something flickers in his eyes.

"I'm not going to let *feelings* get in the way of this," he says, gesturing at the ridiculously massive Manor.

"I don't understand." I sound small and pathetic.

"I'm sorry it has to be like this," he says quietly. "You'll be on the morning flight out tomorrow. We'll buy your ticket."

Now I'm just angry.

"Oh my gosh." I laugh and swipe tears off my cheeks. "I don't want your freaking charity." I shake my head. "You're just like your parents. But worse."

That breaks through the thin crust of control he had over his temper. "What are you talking about."

"They're not telling Lyla the truth because they're protecting her, and why aren't *you* telling her? Because of a stupid huge mansion!"

"You said you understood."

"Yeah, well, I decided *not* to understand anymore. After you strung me along and then told me good riddance! *Again!*"

He stares at me, blinking angrily.

"Don't you know that it won't last?" I ask him.

"What won't last?"

"This!" I say, throwing both of my arms out at everything, remembering every tear I cried over being lied to, the betrayal I felt with Brian.

This betrayal – though Will and I are the farthest thing possible from being engaged – is somehow worse.

"Everything you're putting between your sister and the truth!" I yell. "You can't let a little thing like telling her who she actually is get in the way of your stupid dreams, right?"

His nostrils flare. "My parents will tell her at some point. They've asked me to respect their timing. And all I'm doing is sticking to that."

"Right. Of course, they will." I have never wanted to slap someone so much in my entire life. The anger inside me right now is scaring me. "Let me sign your stupid gag order."

I rip the phone from his hand and sign it, handing it back to him.

He sighs as he looks down at it, then slides it back into his pocket. "I'm sorry."

My throat tightens, and I close my eyes.

"Samantha – "

I look at him sharply. "Don't." I try to control myself. "Tell Lyla I said we'll talk when she gets back to Chicago. I'm guessing you're sending her home too?"

I can tell I'm right and he doesn't want to admit it.

"You can't have contact with her anymore," he says.

My chin quivers and I swallow the burning in my throat. "Fine. Just...tell her I'm sorry."

"Samantha..."

"What, Will? What is it?" I yell. "Are we going back to your house right now and telling her everything? Is that what you're about to tell me? Forget your inheritance? Nothing else matters? Is that what you're going to say right now?"

He lets out a deep breath and rubs both of his hands down his face. Then he drops them to his sides and stands there, just watching me. There's regret in his eyes.

"You're putting wealth before your sister. Things like this!" I yell, pointing at the main house. "This stupid mansion! It's all worth more to you than Lyla is."

And me, I mentally add. I back away from him.

"It's all stuff that's going to burn up someday, and rust, and rot. All of it."

He presses his lips together, silent.

210

"There's nothing more to say here." I turn from him and start off into the trees.

"Where are you going?"

"Back to my cottage."

"It's twenty miles from here."

"I don't care! I'll go back to the highway and hitchhike."

"Don't be ridiculous."

I ignore him, stomping away and wanting as much space between us as geographically possible.

"The highway's the other way," he calls out to me.

Feeling so stupid, I turn and start in another direction. When I am far enough away, I start to sob. Will catches up with me easily and puts his hands on my shoulders. I rip away from him.

"Stop it! Just…" I turn to him, tears streaming down to my neck. "I told your sister yesterday that you have a heart somewhere behind a wall inside you. Do you know that? I can't believe I told her that! Because you *don't*! Stop acting like you do!"

It works. My words cut him. Good.

"Just…take me home," I cry. "Take me home."

Lyla

Even though Will said he wanted to hang out with me today, he's not here. He left me a note this morning on the kitchen counter saying that he went into town to run some errands and he'd be back in a little while. That was hours ago.

I've decided that I won't get down about it. If we can't hang out today, then I'll do something special for dinner tonight with him. I've been cleaning all morning, dusting and vacuuming up every speck of sawdust in the house. I even ran three loads of laundry. After I find a recipe for a steak dinner in one of Will's cookbooks, I start looking for the ingredients.

When I'm poking through the fridge in the living room, the doorbell rings. I close the fridge door and head down the hall to answer it, excited that maybe it's Samantha. Maybe she decided to come over no matter what my brother said about it.

But I'm surprised when I open the door, because it's not Samantha standing there.

It's Christian.

I feel my face light up. "Hi, Christian!"

He smiles. "Hey, Lyla."

He's in jeans and a t-shirt with a light jacket over it. He looks nice, like he showered and shaved a little and did something to his hair. He slides his hands into his pockets and his gaze trails down over me for a second, stopping on my feet. I'm in big knitted socks again. I can never find the matching ones when I need them. Life's too short to waste time matching socks.

I curl one foot over the other, embarrassed. "My feet got cold."

He meets my eyes and I see his jaw flex.

"You wear a lot of dresses," he says.

"Yeah, I know."

I look down at the one I'm wearing today. It's hunter green with little black birds on it. I don't tell Christian that my mom and I have hoarded them over the years, waiting for the day when I don't have nightmares and don't have to wear pajamas all the time anymore. Like now.

I smile about that, and Christian's eyes go to my lips. He doesn't say anything. I clear my throat, forcing myself to not touch my scar beneath my hair.

"What are you doing here?" I ask.

He swallows and looks down the hallway behind me. "I um...I thought I'd stop by to see you."

I smile. Christian is my friend. My first real friend since my new life started. It makes my stomach do a little flip.

"Do you want something to eat?" I step to the side so he can come in.

Christian's eyes change, but I'm not sure how. He doesn't move.

"Wanna...come in?" I say awkwardly.

"Umm," he says. Once again, I can tell that he doesn't want to step foot inside this house for some reason. Is it because of my brother?

Christian squints back at his truck. Is he leaving already? He meets my eyes again.

"Actually, meet me out back," he says.

I try to read his expression. "Okay."

"I had an idea this morning. I want to try it."

"What is it?"

"It's a surprise. You should put some shoes on."

He turns away and heads back to his truck without saying anything else. I close the door and go to the closet in the hallway, pulling off my socks. I decide I don't want to wear shoes, so I go barefoot out the back door and down the steps of the deck.

Christian isn't out here yet, so I walk through the tall sandy grass, touching the tops of the blades. They're wet from dew, lightly dampening my dress. I stop and look up through the trees for a second, the sand and leaves beneath my feet making me feel alive. I close my eyes, smiling. Life is so great. I would normally be asleep right now. But I'm awake. And I have a new friend who has a surprise for me.

I hear something in front of me and I open my eyes, still smiling and expecting Christian...

But my smile dies away immediately, and all the air goes out of my chest.

Christian's dog is standing right in front me.

His mouth hangs open, tongue and teeth exposed as he pants. There's no leash tying him to anything. He whimpers a little, looking behind me. I whip around to run back to the house, but I slam into something. There's a loud grunt. It's Christian. He catches me by the arms.

"Lyla, relax."

"Relax?"

"Just wait. Don't freak out."

"What are you *doing*?" I struggle to get past. "Let me go!"

He's too strong. "I just want to try something. Would you calm down a minute?"

The dog's probably charging at me, ready to grab me by the neck and shake me around like a rag doll. That's what happens in my nightmares.

"Please let me go!" I yell. "What are you doing?"

"He won't hurt you."

"He *attacked* me that morning."

Christian laughs. "He didn't attack you."

"Yes, he did! Is he coming at me?"

"No. I told him to stay."

I close my eyes. I can't even look. I start singing under my breath. "When peace like a river…"

"Are you…singing?" Christian asks me.

"Yes."

He scoffs. "Why?"

"Because that's what I do when I'm scared." I try to move again but his grip tightens on my elbows and he pulls me closer.

"Hey," he says roughly. "Shh. Just stop a second, okay?"

I look up at him. His face is only an inch or so from mine. My hand is clutching my scar beneath my hair because I'm thinking of what happened to me when I was three, but I'm also thinking I don't want Christian to see it. I take a few short breaths and almost tell him that a dog nearly killed me once, but then I think better of it. He might ask if I have a scar from it.

"You don't understand," I say, shaking. "This isn't something you can just fix."

214

"Lyla – "

"Christian! Please let me go. I'm not doing this – whatever it is you're doing."

"Relax, okay? Breathe." His voice is low and calming, his mouth so close, just above my eye level. He smirks a little. "Pick up that stick by your foot."

I pause. "What?"

"That stick right there. Pick it up."

I force myself to look down at this random stick by my foot.

"Pick it up."

"Why?"

"Because you trust me. I know you do."

Slowly, he lets me go, looking deep in my eyes. He backs away with his hand out, like I'm a spooked kitten.

"Pick it up," he says confidently.

I'm grabbing the back of my neck so hard it's getting numb. I look over at the dog, swallow hard, and then slowly, very *very* slowly because I don't want the dog to think I'm making any sudden movements, I bend and pick up the stick.

"Good," Christian says. He goes over by Estes. "Now throw it out towards the water."

"What? Why?"

"Just do it. He won't move. I promise. I've got his collar."

I bite my lip, indecisive and terrified. Christian nods at me confidently, and something in his eyes makes me want to for some reason. I want to throw the stick. I turn slightly, and when I am pretty sure the dog isn't going to attack, I chuck the stick as far as I possibly can.

Christian's eyebrows rise. "Good arm."

I stare at him, confused and waiting.

"Okay, ready?" he says.

"Umm…"

He lets go of Estes' collar and I gasp and back up because I think he's going to charge at me. But the dog bounds off towards the beach. I watch with my mouth open and my hand still up at the back of my neck. He splashes into the water and paddles off towards the stick, grabbing it easily and doing a wide turn back to shore. He comes out of the water, shakes his whole body violently, and then he heads right at me in a full-out sprint.

A small scream escapes my mouth. I step backwards but Christian suddenly yells, "Come!"

The dog pauses, looks at Christian like he's confused, and reluctantly changes direction towards him. Christian takes the stick from his mouth and pets him affectionately. I watch, noticing even in my terror how Christian seems more at ease with Estes around. He tells Estes to sit, gets a good grip on his collar, and he tosses the stick back to me. I catch it without thinking.

"Throw it again," he says.

I hesitate, but then I throw it hard and it splashes in the same area.

The dog takes off again like it's racing ten others. I stare after him, realizing that my heart isn't pounding quite as hard now. He emerges from the water, shakes himself off, then starts towards me again. But Christian says, "Come!" before I can panic. The dog doesn't even pause this time. He changes direction immediately.

"Good boy," he says. "Good dog."

He scratches him roughly behind his ears and I notice all the muscles tightening down Christian's arms.

He looks up at me again, and I blush because he caught me looking at him. He seems pleased and surprised that I was watching.

Then he says, "You're doing it."

"I'm doing what?"

"Playing fetch with a dog."

I blink at him. I'm playing fetch with a dog? I look at Estes. I *am* playing fetch with a dog, in a way. I was so scared I didn't even realize it. I cover my mouth with my hands and start laughing.

A big grin breaks out across Christian's face. "Congratulations."

"Gimme the stick," I say quickly, before I lose my nerve.

He laughs and tosses it to me, and we do the whole thing over again. Estes fetches the stick and comes immediately to Christian. He understands our strange game of fetch now. We do this again and again until I'm tired from laughing and my arm feels like it's going to fall off. I try to throw the stick left-handed a couple times but it's so bad that it goes into the trees, making both of us laugh. Estes still retrieves it and brings it to Christian, and I throw it one more time. It lands on the beach.

"You're tired," Christian says. "So is Estes. Let's stop."

I really don't want to, but I agree. He has Estes by the collar again.

He squints at me. "Wanna pet him?"

"Nope."

He smirks. "I'll put him back in the truck."

I give him a grateful smile. "Thanks," I say quietly, and we both know what I'm talking about. Christian nods and watches me for a second, then takes Estes around the side of the house.

I walk down to the beach, deciding to get the stick and keep it. I'll frame it. My first game of fetch with a dog. I can't wait to tell my parents. Will probably won't care, but I'll tell him, too.

Estes' tracks are all over the place down here. I shiver, looking down at the massive paw prints. They're probably the size of a rabid wolf's tracks. I find the stick by a big rock and pick it up and rinse it off in the water. As I'm kneeling down with my bare knees in the rocky sand, something catches my eye down the beach to my left. I look over and see a girl a few properties away. She's out there alone, looking out over the water. Her fiery-red hair blows around her in the breeze. I straighten, still watching. I can't tell how old she is from here, but something about her makes me unable to look away. I consider going over to talk to her because I want to meet all of Will's neighbors. She sees me looking, and I give a small wave. She stares. She doesn't wave back, just hurries into the trees and disappears.

I hear Christian coming up behind me and I turn to him. He gives a crooked smile.

"Are you gonna frame that or something?" he asks.

"That's exactly what I was going to do!"

Christian laughs softly and shakes his head, studying me.

"You make me laugh," he says. It sounds like he doesn't know how to feel about that.

"Isn't that a good thing?"

He nods, his face turning serious. "You have no idea."

He looks into my eyes…like he's hungry or something.

My heart flutters. I've never felt this way before. I wonder what he's feeling and thinking.

Slowly, Christian reaches out and touches my hair on my shoulder. I go totally still, wondering what he's doing and hoping he won't see my scar. I do *not* want Christian to see it. He takes one of my curls between his fingers. His eyes are on mine and then they move down to the curl he's holding. I am frozen, feeling a new kind of fear in my chest. We're only a foot away from each other. I wonder what it would be like to hug him. It wouldn't be like the normal hugs I give everyone else. It would be more than that. Him holding me – what would that be like?

There's a sudden gust of wind off the lake and I frantically reach up to hold my hair down. Christian drops the curl, misreading what just happened. I am afraid that I ruined everything.

Christian rubs his jaw, nervous.

"Would you…" He lets out a breath. "Would you want to go out on my dad's boat sometime?"

My eyes widen. I've always wanted to go out on a boat. And is he asking me because…maybe he likes me? Or is it just as friends?

I am about to say yes, but then something happens. I think of Justin, the last guy who liked me. Until he saw my scar.

How would I hide it if I'm out on a boat?

Christian waits, staring at me, breathing kind of hard. "It's just…as friends," he clarifies.

I nod slowly. Is it? I swallow, trying to think. My fingers are clutching my neck, still holding my hair down. "Um…when?"

"Today."

I shake my head. "I can't. I have plans with my brother."

"Then tomorrow."

I can't believe this is happening. My pulse is pounding, and I know that I'm blinking way too much, but I can't stop. "I…don't know. I might have plans with Samantha."

He frowns just slightly. "Then this weekend."

"I need to ask my brother."

"So, ask him."

"He's not here." My voice is shaking.

Christian studies me. "Are you saying no?"

I can't imagine any girl has ever said no to Christian. He is very attractive and very mysterious, and I don't know why I haven't realized it until now.

My words come out very quietly. "No, I'm not saying no."

"Then you're saying…?"

"Um…"

My mind is foggy and confused, my hand tired from holding my hair down over my scar. The wind dies off, so I slowly drop my hand and go back to clutching the stick instead. I pick at a little nub on it.

I know the real reason I'm stalling. It's not fair to Christian, the fact that he hasn't seen my scar. He thinks he likes me, but he wouldn't if he saw it. I can't hide it forever.

Then again, one summer isn't forever.

"Lyla. I just want to hang out," Christian says.

I hear a vulnerability in his voice that is very, very cute.

"Okay," I say quickly. I look up at him, trying to be more confident. "Yes."

His face lights up. "Yeah?"

"Yeah." I smile. "I'll ask Will, and I'll let you know."

He nods. "I'll call you tonight to see what he says."

"Okay, but a little later. Like nine."

For the first time since I've met him, Christian seems…free. He has this great big handsome smile now. And suddenly, he steps forward and he wraps his strong arms around me. I am so surprised that I drop the stick and almost lose my balance, but Christian is as sturdy as a rock. My hands eventually slide to his back beneath his jacket. Yes, this is definitely different. I am hugging a boy, being held by him. I like the warmth of his strong chest against my cold cheek.

A twig snaps somewhere close by and we quickly back up from each other, worried that it's Will. But when we both look over towards the trees where the sound came from, we don't see anything. We meet each other's eyes again and laugh awkwardly. Moment broken.

"I'll talk to you tonight," he says.

I smile and actually bite my lip. I've never bitten my lip because of a boy before.

"Yay," I say.

He smirks and rolls his eyes jokingly, then slides his hands into his pockets. He backs away from me.

"Bye, Lyla."

Him saying my name like that sends butterflies into my stomach. I've always wanted to know what that feels like. I didn't know it would feel this scary…and good.

"Bye, Christian."

He tilts a smile, and then turns and walks away. He looks back at me twice, and I wave nervously. He shakes his head, smiling, and then disappears around the corner of Will's house.

When he's gone, I turn around and do a little dance. I was just asked out by a boy for the first time…I think. I can't wait to tell my mom. And Samantha. Maybe she can help me find something to wear that'll help cover my scar.

Life is such an adventure.

Will

Samantha slams the door to my car and doesn't look back at me as she strides up to the front door of the cottage. She fumbles with her keys, still softly crying. I have pains in my stomach and chest as I watch.

This was my plan, I tell myself. It had to be this way.

But I didn't have to open up to her about anything. I didn't have to go for a walk with her. I didn't have to bring her to the Manor at all.

Why did I do it?

It's because I have feelings for her, and I wanted her to see who I really am. Even if a relationship could never work with her.

Knowing that makes me force my gaze forward and speed away from the house. *Being a true Bailey means you have to make hard decisions,* my grandpa warned me when I was young. I had no idea he was talking about my inheritance, or the people who might get hurt if they got in the way of it. *But you've got Bailey blood in your veins. You can handle it.*

I pull my cell phone out of my pocket and turn it on again to call my dad. I'm surprised when I see there are ten missed calls from him. I quickly press his name to call him, wondering what his urgency is about.

"Will," he says immediately.

"Is everything okay?"

"No," he says. "That woman you've been seeing. She knows who you are."

I squint out at the trees through the windshield. My heart is still pounding from the argument, from my shame and whatever else this is.

"How do you know about her?"

He pauses. "Lyla told us about Samantha hanging around. She likes her and trusts her. We started looking into her today."

I roll my eyes. "I was just calling you about it. I took care of it. It wasn't even what we thought. She's not a reporter. But I still had her sign

221

the gag order. I'll send it over to you. She'll be on the first flight tomorrow." I pop my aching neck, trying not to think. "Then Lyla can go home on a different flight, and you can transfer the deed to the Manor to me."

"That's what you want," he says tonelessly. "For your sister to come home as soon as possible?"

I swallow. "There's a lot to do, and she can't know about it."

"How are you going to get her to leave?"

I tighten my grip on the steering wheel. "Trust me, she won't want to stay when she finds out I sent Samantha away."

My dad doesn't speak for a while. Then he says, "So, you took care of it, huh?" with that fake-calm voice he uses when he's really angry.

Or disappointed in me. Which is nothing new.

"Yeah," I tell him.

"Before or after you showed her the Manor?"

I frown. I start to say, "How did you..." but then my voice dries out.

Slowly, the truth washes over me like a cold, unexpected flood. Of course.

I slam on the brakes in the middle of the Tunnel of Trees and yank the steering wheel to the right, my tires skidding on the graveled shoulder of the two-lane road. A truck honks loudly as it swerves by and I'm tempted to flip him the bird as I get out of my car, but I don't. I slam the door and start pacing around.

"Will?"

"Bodyguards, Dad?" I yell. "Really?"

He sighs. "Yes, you have an executive protection team. Don't sound so shocked. You're the son of a multi-billionaire."

"You're insane."

That sets him off. "Do you know how many officers they *wanted* me to hire? An entire five-person team! Or more!"

"Why would we need that? No one even knows who we are, Dad. You've made sure of that."

He sighs loudly. "We didn't know where you were for years, Will. Do you know what that does to parents?"

"Don't act like you care!"

"We *do* care. You know that! You also know I made a few enemies years ago."

"Oh, trust me, Dad," I say with feigned humor. "I'm well aware of the man you used to be."

Silence.

"How long have I had this one?"

He clears his throat and doesn't answer.

"How long, Dad?"

"Since you settled in Good Hart."

I can't believe this. "Who is he?"

"His name is Emil Alanovic."

I stop and stare. At what, I don't know. "My next door neighbor?" Rage blurs my vision as I realize something else. "There's a woman staying there now. I've seen them around town together a couple of times."

He sighs. "Sienna Rodriguez. Lyla's guard."

I start laughing crazily, pinching the bridge of my nose. My head is really pounding now.

"I can't do this anymore," I say. "They're going home tomorrow with Lyla. If not, I'm going to sue my own parents."

He's quiet.

"And I want the deed transferred to me tonight," I say in a low voice.

That makes him respond. "You think we're giving it over to you now? You showed it to that woman, when you knew she followed you for a story!"

"That doesn't matter," I yell back. "The deal was, I can't tell *Lyla* anything. And I haven't."

There's a long pause. "Have it your way, Will. I'm so glad it happened this way, aren't you?"

"Oh yeah, let's talk about being *glad* about how things have turned out, Dad," I say angrily. "I just sent away the woman I'm falling for all because my parents are crazy. And oh yeah, you already know about it because you have *bodyguards* following your kids everywhere, without telling them about it! To report back to you every move we make!"

"That's not why they're there, Will! What kind of father do you think I am?"

I stop. He shouldn't have asked that. He set himself up. I am about to say some things I probably shouldn't, but I don't care.

"You're the kind of father who wasn't around for the first twelve years of my life, Dad," I say quietly.

"Will, don't – "

"You're the kind of father who tried to make up for lost time by smothering me in middle school and high school after you *ripped* me from everything I knew and loved. You're the kind of father who continues to lie to his kids every day." I am breathing hard, my blood pounding in my ears.

"You're the kind of father I *never* want to be," I say, voice trembling.

There is absolute silence on my dad's end. A sudden pang of regret hits me.

"You'll have the Manor once Lyla comes home," he says. Then the line goes dead as he hangs up on me.

I drive around aimlessly after that, trying to cool down. For a while, I picture going to Emil's house next to mine and throttling the guy. But he is twice my size, and trained.

Then my thoughts shift into the conversation with my dad. I play it over and over again in my mind. When did it all come to this? How have we gotten this far wedged in a web of lies? I can't get Samantha out of my head either. Her tears, that look of betrayal…the feelings she knows I have for her. I can't grasp the fact that I'll never see her again, but it's true. I made sure of that. She's going home tomorrow.

It makes me sick.

I get halfway to Harbor Springs, thinking over things and buying myself some time. I'm not looking forward to the next thing I have to do: get my sister to leave. It'll crush her. This isn't how I wanted any of this to happen. But I can't back down now. Especially after what I just did. It's too late.

I turn the car around and grimly head home.

Lyla

There's nothing left for me to do. Everything is decorated. The food is ready to start cooking for our special dinner tonight.

I'm sitting on the couch waiting for Will. It's almost five o'clock now. I can't believe how long he's been gone today. I keep smoothing my green dress on my knees and straightening the forks and knives in front of me on the coffee table. I might have gone a little bit overboard with the decorating. I realized it right around the time I was hanging the curtains and twinkle lights I brought from home. The dried leaves are out on the table, a few pictures of our family on the mantle.

There's a part of me that did all of this so that I could butter him up before I ask him for permission to go out on a boat with Christian. But mostly, I just did it for…us. Because everything is better when you let someone get through that wall around your heart. I'm going to show Will that tonight.

I hear a car door shut outside. My heart jumps into my throat and I stand to my feet, straightening my dress. "I respect you," I practice under my breath, "and that's why I'm asking for your permission to hang out with Christian." I whisper it over again to myself, my heart pounding.

I hear Will push the front door open. The rhythm of his footsteps slows as he appears at the end of the hallway. His face still has that normal hardness, until he sees what all I did.

"Welcome home!" I say, clapping lightly.

He blinks at everything, absently hanging his keys on the hook on the wall.

"I cleaned! And I hung curtains! Yay!"

Will is stunned. This is exactly the reaction I was hoping for.

"And I put up all the twinkle lights, obviously. But you don't have to keep them up because I know they're kind of girly." I laugh. "I just thought it would be fun for tonight."

He looks like he's never been in his own house before. I wait for him to say something, anything. But he doesn't. He walks into the living room, then stares at the coffee table that's set for dinner. I have the movie ready to go – the football one we watched the night of my birthday. We can start over.

I nervously start rambling. "I thought I could tidy up and decorate a little, since Samantha's coming back over here tomorrow."

I realize I'm touching my scar, so I drop my hand to my side and instead fiddle with my dress. "We could start cooking, if you're hungry. And then I have something I need to ask you, but..." My face grows warm. I wish I didn't say that last part. "But anyway, I – "

"Lyla," he finally says. "Stop."

"What?" I say innocently, although I know exactly what it is. He's terrified to be feeling something. "Can you show me how to prepare the caviar? And the steaks have been sitting out for a while so we should probably start the grill..." My words trail off because I see some sort of deep sadness fill my brother's eyes.

"What, Will?" I say gently. Maybe this will be a breakthrough for us.

He blinks a few times, and then, after a second, his jaw muscles flex and his blue eyes go back to being distant again.

"Samantha's going back to Chicago in the morning."

I stand here, rooted, stunned.

"What?" I say quietly, feeling my smile melt away. I shake my head. "No. She can't be. She was coming over for dinner tomorrow. And she's going to be here all week – "

"I could tell she wanted something more than I could give," he says. "And I didn't want to lead her on." He swallows, then looks away. "So, I told her she should probably stop coming around. She decided to leave."

My mouth drops open. Anger suddenly boils up in my stomach.

"You *what*?" I say in shock.

"It was for the best."

I scoff at him. "For the *best*?" My voice rises. "Did you think about *me*? I loved being around her."

His eyes flash. "Of course, I thought about you. I *did* it for you. I didn't want you getting too close to her."

"Oh, because getting close to people is a terrible thing?"

"She was only going to be here for a week, Lyla."

"Not if you asked her to stay longer!"

He goes silent.

I back up. I can't believe this. I can't believe she's gone.

"She didn't even say goodbye to me," I whisper.

He closes his eyes. "Lyla…"

I realize suddenly that I really dislike my own brother. Not just for this, but for everything, for the way he's been treating me and Samantha and everyone else in his life.

"Why do you do this?" Tears sting the back of my throat. "Why do you push people away? You *always* push people away!"

"Don't say that."

"But you do!"

He doesn't respond. We just stand here quietly. I look around at the twinkle lights and the pillows I straightened on the couch, the stupid steaks out on the counter, ready to grill. I regret doing all of it. I'm embarrassed, angry, and hurt. My eyes stop on the laundry door, where the locked garage door is.

"What's in the garage?" I ask suddenly, looking back at him.

He blinks. "What does that have to do with anything?"

"What are you keeping from me?"

"Nothing."

My chin quivers. "Why do you have all these secrets and keep your distance from everyone?"

"I don't."

"So, tell me what's in your garage!"

His mouth flattens out. "That's *my* business," he says with measured calm. "But that doesn't mean I keep my distance from people."

I shake my head. "Then name one friend you have here."

He is silent because he can't name even one.

"You've lived in this area for five years, Will. Five years! Isn't that a little sad to you? Doesn't that worry you a little?"

"Lyla," he says, his eyes on fire. He's trying to control himself. "This is *not* my fault. Samantha leaving is *not my fault*."

"Really? How is it not?"

"You just have to trust me."

"How can I trust you if you never tell me anything? Tell me! Make me understand you. Please."

His hands clench into fists at his sides. He levels his gaze on me. "I can't," he says through his teeth. "But it kills me," he whispers.

I stare at him, my heart clenching and my head hurting from holding back tears.

This is so terrible and feels so wrong. I shouldn't have to beg my brother to open up to me. What is *wrong* with him? If it kills him to not be able to talk to me, then why doesn't he just *talk to me?* Aren't older brothers supposed to be different than this? Aren't they supposed to be loving and affectionate and protective? I've spent half my life being terrified of my brother, and the other half wondering why he doesn't call or hang out with our family.

Now, though, I'm just angry. I'm angry and I'm sick of him already. And it's only been a few days.

"Did you even want me to come here?" I say quietly.

He sighs. "Don't cry, Lyla."

"Answer my question!" I yell, angry tears streaming down my face.

He remains silent, closing his eyes and pinching the bridge of his nose like his life is just so difficult and he just can't take this anymore. That's answer enough for me.

"I want to go home," I say, wiping my face. I hiccup a little, trying to control myself.

He hasn't moved. "Lyla – "

"Just stop, Will. I want to go home as soon as possible. Can I leave tonight?"

"There are only two flights out every day. The last one left already."

"Then I'll be on the one tomorrow morning."

He lets out a long breath and runs his hand down his face, like he's tired of me. "Not the morning flight. Maybe the later one."

228

I am shocked. He wants to be rid of me that easily? Fine. That's just great. I grab the house phone off the kitchen counter and head upstairs, trying to hold in my sobs.

But Mom doesn't answer her phone. Neither does Dad. When I call the house, it goes to the answering machine and I hear my own voice, happy but tired. "You've reached the Brooks! Leave a..."

I hang up on myself.

I stand here in my room looking down at the phone in my hands – the phone that isn't even mine because I *have* no phone and no friends and no one I can even call right now.

I literally have no one.

Loneliness swallows me up, and I sink to the floor. It's not meant to be like this. I am so alone right now, as alone as my brother is, but for very different reasons. I close my eyes and curl up, still crying, and I hate it because things are so much better than they used to be, aren't they? At least I'm awake. At least I didn't wake my brother up a million times last night screaming.

But part of me honestly misses my old life now. It wasn't fun, but it was simple. I was miserable because of nightmares. Now I'm miserable because my brother is a terrible, selfish person. Samantha is gone and will probably never want to speak to me again even when I go back to Chicago.

I try to call my parents again. I will tell them I am coming home. They probably *made* Will take me back with him so that I could try to fix things with him. But I can't. Things with him are unfixable and awful and that will never change.

Still, though, they don't pick up.

And then I remember. Christian is going to call me at nine tonight, to see how it went, asking for permission to go out with him. I didn't even get to it.

What am I going to tell him when he calls?

Sienna

Mark and Kathy aren't answering the phone because I called them and warned them not to. Because obviously, Lyla can't go home yet. They want to give her the night to sleep on things and see if she still wants to leave in the morning. If she does, they'll have to figure out a plan B.

Nothing has changed. There was never a story getting out. Their daughter is still worth an insane amount of money, and they are still trying to figure out a way to change that. Samantha was just a complication.

I wish I could go next door and comfort Lyla. I wish I had actual contact with her. If she stays, and if she still has contact with Christian, maybe I could somehow start a friendship with her. That way I wouldn't have to deal with the stress of guarding her from a distance so much.

I look at the clock. It's almost nine. When I was hiding behind a tree earlier as Christian and Lyla played fetch with that dog, I overheard Christian tell her he'd call her tonight. I plan to listen to every word.

I hear Emil come down the stairs and I turn and look at him. We're both tired, stressed. He didn't want to watch Will and Lyla argue, so he went upstairs to heat up a frozen pizza for us. He hands me a plate with two slices on it.

"Thanks."

He nods and sits down and leans back. "They done?"

"Yeah. Lyla tried to call her parents to say she wants to go home. I told them not to answer. Hopefully she'll change her mind by morning."

He takes a bite of his pizza and wipes his mouth.

"You think Will's coming over here to fight me?" he says with a slightly cocky, tired grin.

I look at the screen, where Will can be seen sitting on the couch in the living room.

"Probably not. He's seen the size of you." I sigh. "He would, though, if he found out about the cameras. Thankfully he still doesn't know."

Emil finishes his pizza within a few minutes, then pushes his plate to the side. He pulls his phone out of his pocket.

"There's one more complication," he says, pulling up a screen.

"What is it?"

He hands me his phone, where I see the electronic signature for the gag order Samantha signed earlier.

"What about it?" I ask.

"Her name isn't Samantha, remember? Not legally."

I groan. "She'll have to sign it again."

He nods. "They want it done tonight." He looks at me. "Wanna come with? So I don't scare her half to death at her cottage?"

I shake my head. "I can't leave Lyla. Not like this."

I don't mention the phone call that's about to take place between her and Christian.

Emil takes in a breath through his nose and lets it out.

"I know what you're thinking," I say.

"No, you don't."

"You're thinking I'm crazy."

He leans over, clasping his hands between his knees. "No," he says adamantly. "I'm thinking Lyla's lucky to have you. I'm thinking I wish I could have half of your passion. You care about your clients."

I stare. *Not all of them*, I think. Not like this. Just Lyla. Which scares me.

He sits back again, and we go silent for a minute. I realize I'm not eating my pizza, but I'm not hungry. "When are you leaving?" I ask him. I didn't mean for my voice to sound so disappointed, but it did.

"As soon as I can pack things up. I'll get a moving truck tomorrow. Won't take long." A muscle jerks in his jaw.

"I still think they should just transfer you over to guarding Lyla with me. Will wouldn't have a choice but to let you stay."

He shakes his head. "His dad thinks he'll never talk to him again if he does that."

I laugh humorlessly. "I doubt they'll talk again anyway, as it is."

"Pretty messed up family."

"Yeah." I look at the screen. "At least Lyla hasn't been corrupted by it."

He sighs. "Not yet, anyway." He is looking down at my hands, which makes me realize I'm twisting my sister's ring on my finger. The one he put there. He sits forward again, and I find myself admiring the muscles in his arm. Then he stands up.

"I'll head over to her house in a little while, then I'm going straight to bed." He looks back at me, and I feel something in my stomach that I try to push back down. "See you in the morning, Rodriguez."

I nod slowly and watch him as he walks out.

Christian

I'll wait until three minutes after nine to call Lyla, because I don't want to seem like I've been waiting around for this, which I have. It is the longest three minutes of my life. I keep checking the time. Then, finally, it's 9:03 and I pick up my phone and call my grandma's old house line. It rings and rings, and now I know that Lyla wasn't waiting by the phone for me to call her. I picture her as the type of girl who would maybe even forget I was going to call.

It goes to Will's voicemail – "Yeah, leave a message," – and I hang up. Then I try back. I'm not giving up that easily. I'm about to hang up and call right back again after five rings, then there is a click sound, and silence.

"Hello?" I say.

I hear something. A sniff, maybe. "Christian?"

The heaviness in my chest lifts when I hear her voice.

"Hey," I say quietly.

There's a pause. "Hi."

She sounds choked up or something.

"How are you?" I ask.

"Um...I'm fine. I'm okay."

She sounds like she's crying. I sit up on my bed. "What's wrong?"

"Um..." She sniffles, cries.

"Hey, shhh. Lyla, what happened?"

"I had..." She coughs a little sob, and my heart wrenches. "I had a fight with my bother. And I'm going home tomorrow."

I shake my head, stomach sinking. *"What?"*

"I'm leaving. I'm sorry."

"You were going to be here the rest of the summer."

"I know."

"We can fix it. I'll come over there and talk to him."

"He's not going to change. Ever. I'm done trying to get him to be…better. I don't know."

She takes in a shaky breath, and I want to be there and hold her and tell her that everything's going to be okay. I find that I'm looking over at the top drawer of my desk, where the notes from Remmi are.

Sometimes, things aren't okay.

Suddenly, I am so mad at Lyla that I want to hang up on her. I don't know why. I'm twisting the bed sheet beneath me, ready to rip it to shreds.

"There's nothing I can do to change your mind?" I ask.

"Nothing could get me to stay here with him. Nothing. I'm sorry."

I nod, jaw flexing. "Yeah, I get it," I say angrily.

"Please don't be mad at me."

"I'm *not*," I yell.

There's a long pause. "Christian –"

"Nice knowing you, Lyla."

I end the call and throw my phone onto my bed, feeling like I just snuffed out the last little light in my life.

I stand up and go to the bottom drawer of my desk, where I keep a bottle of whiskey that hasn't been opened. I've never tasted hard alcohol in my life, because Coach doesn't allow it. The guys and I stick to beer at parties, and even that we don't have much of. Every time Coach got wind of a party, he would make sure practice was bright and early the next morning, and twice as hard.

But the day of the funeral, I snuck this bottle of whiskey in here and have kept it ever since, in case of emergencies. Like now.

It'll make me feel better, right? It'll drown out everything? I take the cap off, stare at the brown liquid. One smell of it tells me that this isn't going to be pleasant. I close my eyes, but all I can see is Lyla dancing on the beach that first morning. I open my eyes and blink, but then I hear her laughter.

"Everything's going to be okay, Christian. Everything will be okay."

"I could make my mom's raspberry pancakes, to celebrate!"

"Celebrate what?"

"Life."

"Get out of my head!" I yell through my teeth.

234

She left. Like Remmi. I'd started to picture this whole fun summer with her, just like I pictured with Remmi. Now, it's all gone. Again. That's just great. Fine by me. I don't need either of them. What I need is to get really drunk.

I take the first swig, then cough some of it back up into my mouth and swallow it down again. I've never felt burning in my throat like this before. I choke down some more. How much does it take to get drunk? A quarter of the bottle is probably good, but I keep going even past that. There is a tilt to the room now, a weight that's in my brain, pushing on my eyes. Half a bottle now, I think, but I'm not really sure because I drop it and it spills on the white carpet. When I quickly move to grab it, I feel insanely queasy and then I'm suddenly throwing up in the trashcan by my desk. I hurl until I can't breathe. Next thing I know, I'm ripping that top drawer out of my desk and Remmi's letters go flying everywhere. I don't care right now. I want to rip them up. I start to heave again and bend over the trashcan. I can't believe how much liquid is coming out of me.

"Dad!" I yell, not knowing what else to do. I sink to my knees, falling over until I'm partly underneath my desk. "Dad!"

He appears in the doorway, and then he says, "Aw, son," with this face that's so sad that it makes me start to cry my head off.

He comes to me and pulls me up into his chest. I feel like a weak little kid as I cry into his shirt.

Samantha

All of my meager things are laid out on my bed, but I can't bring myself to pack them yet. The pink scarf that Lyla gave me slips off the side of the bed, like it is just as depressed as I am.

That's what makes me start crying again.

I call Nell for the third time tonight.

"I just don't feel like it's over," she says.

"It is, Nell," I say brokenly. "I should've never come here. I wish I never met them."

"You don't mean that." She huffs out a sigh. "I've looked up the Manor. There are old pictures of it online. It's…pretty amazing."

I don't respond, just shake my head stubbornly. I don't care how amazing it is. Will is choosing it over his sister. And he's choosing it over me.

Not that he would ever feel anything for the woman who followed him here for a story.

"There was a ballroom," she says, and I can tell she's reading this online.

"Nell —"

"And weddings used to be hosted there. It brought a lot of revenue to the town. It was a tourist attraction."

"I know all of this already."

"I'm just saying. It would be a lot to give up."

I close my eyes. "I told him that, just before he told me I was going home."

"And he would be giving up a relationship with his parents, too, if he told her."

I swallow. I didn't think of that.

"I'm just…wondering…" she says.

"What?"

"Do you think there's a bigger reason they gave it all up?"

That's when I hear a loud knock on the front door. I gasp and spring to my feet, wrapping my robe around myself.

"What is it?"

"Someone's here."

"Who?"

"I don't know."

I tiptoe out of the room and carefully approach the door. Thankfully the lights are off in the living room, so the person won't see me through the window. There is a teeny part of me that hopes that it's Will.

"Keep me on the phone," she says. "Especially if it's Will. Just set it on a table or something, so I can listen."

I push back the curtain just slightly, trying to see out. Whoever it is, it isn't Will. This man is huge.

I gasp and back up.

"Who is it?"

"I don't know!" I whisper. "It's not Will."

He knocks loudly on the door again, and I almost scream.

"Hang up and call 911!" Nell says.

"Alyssa Riley?" the man calls.

I go absolutely still.

"Did he just call you Alyssa?" Nell asks.

"Ms. Riley, my name is Emil Alanovic. I'm sorry if I've scared you, but I need to speak with you."

I don't respond. My mind is whirling. Emil Alanovic. It sounds familiar, but I can't remember why, and I'm too afraid to let him know I'm home.

"What the heck…?" Nell says.

"We met Saturday morning," the man says, "outside of Will's house."

"What's he saying?" Nell asks.

My mouth falls open. It's the guy who came out to speak with me at my car. Military, definitely. The size of a large couch. But how does he know my real name?

I gather my courage.

"What are you doing here?" I ask loudly.

Nell gasps.

"Can you open the door, please?" the man asks.

"Um, no thank you," I say.

He pauses. "It's about the gag order you signed earlier. I need you to sign your legal name."

I don't respond. I'm trying to remember where I put the bear spray, but then I realize I never *bought* any bear spray.

"It's okay," he says. "I work for the Baileys."

Nell is frantic. "Oh my gosh. Oh my gosh."

"Why should I believe you?" I call to him.

"I'm part of their security team. I've lived next door to Malcolm Willard Bailey the Fourth for five years now."

"Oh my gosh, oh my gosh," Nell is still saying.

"I just need you to sign the gag order as Alyssa Riley, and I'll be on my way."

I am shaking. I cannot believe this is happening. Will and Lyla have a security team.

"Hand it through the mail slot," I tell him.

After a second, the old mail slot creaks open and his glowing phone slides through. He holds it there until I take it. It has the same white screen that was pulled up on Will's phone earlier, with a box for a signature.

"Wait!" Nell says. "Did you ever read what you were signing?"

"No," I whisper.

I scroll up on the screen and try to read through some of the extensive writing. The gist is that I'll be sued for millions of dollars if I breathe a word about the Baileys to anyone. I wonder if my sister and my mom count.

I sign it, and I slide it back out through the slot. He takes it.

"Thank you," he says. "That's all I needed."

I wait. I don't know what to say in this weird situation. Thanks? Goodbye?

"I'll see you in the morning," he says.

"In the morning?"

"I'll be at the airport tomorrow to make sure you make your flight."

"You don't have to do that," I say quickly.

"Actually," he says, "I do. Have a good night, Ms. Riley."

He walks away. I watch out the window as he goes back to his car, gets in, and drives away. I back up, heart pounding, phone pressed firmly to my ear.

"Sam," Nell says. "This is crazy! Lyla and Will have a bodyguard."

"I know," I say distractedly, fingers to my lips as I stand here still staring at the door.

"Do you think Will knows?"

"No," I tell her honestly. "I don't think he has any clue. But I guess I'll never find out."

"Sam," she says, determined. "There is something else going on here. Something more than just a dog attack they're trying to keep Lyla from knowing about. Don't you want to find out what it is?"

"Of course, I do. But I'm going home. You heard him. He'll be at the airport tomorrow to make sure of it."

"No," she says firmly. "We'll figure something out. You're not going anywhere."

Will

My fingers dig into my hair as I sit here on my couch and stare at the floor in my living room. I am trying to process everything. I have bodyguards. I took my anger out on my sister, who only wants what's best for me. For us. And before that, I heartlessly sent away the first woman I've had feelings for in years. The woman who knows the truth about me. And has feelings for me too.

But is it so wrong to want to get the Manor up and running again? To give people a purpose and a livelihood again, like they had fifteen years ago?

I know it's not wrong, but how I handled it was wrong. I could've stayed distant with Samantha and simply had her sign the gag order and leave. But no, I decided to let my guard down. Samantha already knows the truth about me, and she was leaving anyway, so I thought it was fine. In fact, I almost *needed* to tell her more about me. Like a release. But it sent the wrong message: Hope.

And now I've lost her. And Lyla. My parents, too, probably, after the conversation with my dad today. After everything that's happened, I am alone again.

Leaning back on the couch I look up at the ceiling now, reminding myself that tomorrow the Manor will be mine. Soon, it will be full of life and people. I used to pretend I ran it back when I was twelve, bossing around some of the workers. People laughed it off like I was just an entitled rich kid. But really, I was practicing. I would run that place someday with Alexandra. Just knew it. I lost part of the dream – Alex – but I'll get the rest of it tomorrow around six o'clock. The evening flight takes off around five. Lyla will be on it.

Thinking of her again, I clench my teeth together. We'll go back to the relationship we had before – never talking to each other. I'll go to Chicago for Christmases, maybe. If they want me there, that is.

I rub my face and lean over again, resting my elbows on my knees. This is all so complicated. I never expected bodyguards. I never expected to wish my sister wasn't leaving. I never expected to fall for the woman who set this whole fiasco into motion. And I never expected to have to make such a difficult decision.

But I did, didn't I? I chose the Manor. No going back now. Even if I tried to fix things, it's too late. They both hate me.

I reluctantly stand to my feet. Might as well move on, start this new life I asked for. After turning off all the lights, I stand at the back door for a second, looking out at the place on the beach where Lyla and I stood that first night. I wanted to hug her that night as we stood there, because I could see how excited she was. It made me feel light. But I didn't hug her. Of course, not.

I shake my head and go upstairs and take a long shower, thinking of a thousand ways I could've handled things better. Then I get into bed, only to toss and turn for another hour or so until it's just past midnight.

Then, right as I am about to fall asleep, I hear something. It's sharp, garbled. A second later, there's nothing. Maybe I was already dreaming.

Then there's another sound, muffled. I slowly sit up, listening and rubbing my face. And then suddenly I jump ten feet in the air when I hear it again and realize what it is and where it's coming from.

My sister is screaming bloody murder.

Part V
26 Days and counting…

The lights are almost blinding now as I trudge my way through the trees to the ambulance, completely out of strength. I slam my back against the ambulance doors, keeping her body clutched to my chest as I slide to the ground, extending my bad leg out. I pound on the door with my elbow. A young paramedic swings it open, alarmed. He sees me down here, then he shouts something I can't make out because I think I'm losing consciousness. He jumps down beside me just as another paramedic runs around from the front of the ambulance. They start examining her.

I fall onto my side, knee throbbing, watching her. All I'm able to focus on is the bracelet around her wrist. It has a real emerald in the shape of a heart, and it's sticky from her blood.

"I'm her blood type!" I yell, my words slurring for some reason. "She'll need blood!"

"No pulse," one says loudly to the other, and they take her from me.

I failed her. I failed.

Emil

A pounding sound wakes me, and I scramble to my feet, not even remembering where I am or who would be banging on my door in the middle of the night. Then I remember Sienna.

"Get up!" she yells. "Something's happening!"

I pull some pants on and don't wait to grab a shirt as I head out the door, racing down the hall after Sienna. We descend the basement stairs, and I hear some sort of screeching sound that's getting louder. I run to the screens, stopping my momentum by slamming my hands down on the desk. I lean in. It's not screeching. It's screaming. I've never heard anything like it, except from a few horror movies I watched years ago.

"No! No! Stop! Help! Help me!" It's Lyla.

I stare at the screen that shows the hallway.

"Come on, Will," I say through my teeth. My heart is pounding.

Sienna is almost hysterical. "I'm going over there."

"It's her nightmare, Sienna."

"What if it isn't?" She starts for the door.

"Wait," I say.

Will's bedroom door slams open on the screen and he bursts into the hallway and into Lyla's room. The screaming continues. But then we hear, "Lyla! Lyla, stop! It's just a dream! Wake up!"

Still, the screaming continues. Sienna lets out a breath. When I turn to look at her in grim relief, she leans back against the wall, sliding down it. Gun in her hand, she puts her face into her bent elbow.

"I can't do this," she says softly. The ring I put on her glints white. "I can't."

"Hey," I say gently, coming to her. But the screaming is like a sick soundtrack, so I stop and turn down the volume on the speaker.

When I turn back around, Sienna is getting to her feet and tucking her gun into the small of her back.

"I'm going to bed," she says flatly.

Then she's gone, leaving me here in the chill of the basement with the eerie echoes of Lyla's screams around me.

Lyla

Dogs rip at my back and neck, tearing through skin until I'm bleeding out into nothing. I feel helpless. I thrash and scream and try to fight back, digging at their faces and eyes to get them off me. Garbled words come up from my throat, screams like bubbles from my lungs.

And then, all at once, everything stops when my hands are pinned down and someone is yelling in my face.

"Lyla! Lyla, stop! It's just a dream! Wake up!"

A shadow is over me when my eyes snap open.

I scream, "Get off me!"

"It's me! It's Will. Relax!" He's breathing hard, and I can hear in his voice that it is my brother. I'm not outside in the woods, being attacked. It's Will.

"Relax, Lyla. It was a dream."

I am breathing so hard my lungs hurt and even though I'm aware that it's my brother and I'm being pushed down into my bed and my pillow, I am very confused and I don't want the dogs to be able to get to me since I'm held down like this.

"Get off! Let me go!"

He backs up and I can hear his breath coming in short spurts. The room is so dark I can't see his face or anything else.

"Turn the light on," I say frantically, and he does, groping the wall for the switch until he hits it, and everything lights up.

I scramble to the corner of my bed, curling my legs up, looking around for the dogs. I am caught in this half-reality and can't get out. Not until my brother sits down on my bed and wraps his strong arms around me and pulls me into him. I start to cry, choking on tears.

"No," I groan. "No, no, no. It's back." I try to control my sobs. "It's back! It's happening again."

247

"Shhh. It's okay, it's okay. Shhh."

I am so embarrassed and terrified of what he thinks of me.

"Shhh. Take a breath."

I sob into his shirt. He's holding me so tight. When has he ever done this before?

He lets out a big breath, his chest expanding against my cheek and releasing warmth on the top of my hair.

"The dogs –"

"There are no dogs in here," he whispers. "You're safe. I've got you, Lills."

He hasn't called me that in a very long time.

After a while of sitting like this, the yellow light breaks through the hair that's over my face as I slowly open my eyes. I see the bare wall beside the bed, the white of my brother's t-shirt sleeve, the curl of my fist in front of my face the way a child sleeps against their dad's chest. I miss my dad, my mom. I haven't really missed them for this whole trip because everything's been so exciting and wonderful. Except for Will sending Samantha home, and my fight with him. And now this – waking up to the old nightmare that I know so well, like a terrible old friend. Mom used to sing to me. I want to start humming the song now, but I'm afraid it'll make me cry even harder because I miss her and dad.

But actually, I feel very comforted right now. Like Will is a pretty good substitute for my parents. He's holding me tight, even rocking slightly. His hand moves in a comforting line, up and down on my back, even though it's bumpy from my scar. He usually avoids touching it like this.

I clutch him, starting to calm down, my heart beating more regularly and breaths slowing down. Minutes pass in quiet, and I realize the nights in this house are extremely different than back home. I haven't actually been awake to hear the tapping of the furnace, the soft gasps of the wind and waves outside the window. It's colder in here at night than in my room back home, and there are goosebumps down my arms because of it. The floors are wooden, not cozy like my white carpet. The room is nearly empty, not stuffed with the cheerful furniture and decorations and the dresser covered in smiley faces for when I wake up like this. They try to tell me with their little "u" mouths that everything will be okay.

There is nothing like that here. But even so…I do not want to go back home.

"We fought," I say lamely, sniffing.

"Yeah, we did. I'm sorry for sending Samantha home. You'll understand it someday."

No, I really won't, but saying that won't do any good. Not right now.

"Everything's going to be okay," he tells me.

"No," I cry, shaking my head. "No, it's not. It's not okay. Nothing's okay. I'm going back to normal. This is my old life. I don't want it."

He holds me tighter. "Shhh."

"I'm so scared."

The rumble of his voice in his chest is comforting when he says, "It was a dream."

"Don't leave me," I say.

"I won't. I'll stay on the floor tonight."

"But it's wood."

"It's alright."

I take a breath, shaking.

"I don't want to go home," I tell him suddenly.

He stops rocking and his hand stops moving. I squeeze my eyes shut again. I shouldn't have said that. He doesn't want me here. I swallow against the grief.

But he starts rocking again. "I don't want you to go home, either."

I blink, then move my hair back from my face and look up at him. "You don't?"

He shakes his head. "I want you to stay. We'll figure everything out. We'll fix things between us. Just…" He looks down at me. "Stay."

My face crumples again as I start to cry really hard. He laughs softly, rubbing my back again.

I'm now thinking about the time I slipped at the neighborhood pool when I was seven and smacked my head on the edge and fell in. Will jumped in so fast I didn't even know what had happened before I was in his arms as he yanked me out of the water and carried me home. He was sixteen, deep into his rebellious stage. I was surprised he even took me to the pool that day. He probably doesn't remember it, but I'll never forget it. It was the last time he held me like this.

Maybe this is the beginning of healing. Maybe we're coming full circle. I find that there is a tiny part of me that is glad this happened, even if it means the nightmares are back for good. If it hadn't happened tonight, I would've been on a flight home tomorrow. Maybe the timing is perfect.

I sniff and wipe my nose on my sleeve and finally start to sit up a little, looking past his arm at the room again. He moves the blankets and scoots over, letting his grip loosen slightly as we shift. He rubs his face.

"That was crazy," he says, "hearing you scream like that."

"I'm sorry." I touch the scar beneath my hair.

"You don't have to apologize." His blue eyes reflect mine – that's always been something we have in common – and we just look at each other for a second. I think we both know that there's been a change, a shift between us.

"It's going to be a long night," I say, grimacing.

"It's okay." He stands up, saying roughly, "I'll go get my blanket and pillow."

I shiver when he's gone, fighting the fear rising up in me. I try to blink the images out of my mind...and try not think about how this is me again. I'm back to being the girl who has nightmares all night, every night, and who sleeps in the day. My fingers press into the mangled skin on my neck and back, going numb.

When my brother returns, he lays his blanket down on the hard wood floor and squats down to smooth it out and get comfortable. I let go of my scar and wipe my teary face and neck, and we both lay back silently.

Awkwardness has been our norm, and I expect it as we try to fall back asleep in my brightly lit room. I drop another pillow down to him because I think his looks too thin.

"Thanks," he says, stuffing it beneath his own. "Good night, Lills."

"Night." *Love you,* I say in my mind.

I love you too, I imagine him responding.

And we both wait to drift off again, and it's not very awkward at all.

Emil

Alyssa Riley – or Samantha Foster – looks flustered as she enters the airport, ready for her pre-arranged flight. She's wearing jeans and that touristy shirt that she had on the first morning I spoke to her. She glances around, seeing me over by the wall.

Eyes widening, she walks in the opposite direction to get into line behind four people to check in to her flight. Just as she does, I sit down in a chair and get comfortable. I'll wait here as long as it takes to make sure she boards that flight. I thumb through my book to find my dog-eared place, and I start reading. I only glance up at her twice as the hour passes. Once when she finds a seat by the window, and then again when she gets in line to board the flight.

The entire time, she's stiff and nervous. Good. She's been the most annoying and yet entertaining part of this whole adventure for me, since the night Sienna arrived up until now.

Samantha follows the line of people out the door and looks back in my direction when she's outside and almost to the metal stairs. Her black hair is wildly blowing around her. People hold onto their jackets as they blow open and their hats as they threaten to get lost in the wind. It's going to be a bumpy ride.

She walks up the stairs, lugging her little suitcase, and then she disappears into the small oval entrance. Good riddance. She added more drama and stress to this whole situation than she could possibly know.

I close my book and tuck it under my arm, stretching. I won't be coming back to this airport, I know. Since my flight back to L.A. will be on my own dime, I'll do the long drive down to Grand Rapids. Back to guarding celebrities. I thought I would miss my old life, the excitement of clubs multiple times a week. Right now, it sounds daunting. This has been my home for five years. It's strange, thinking of Sienna living in my house now all by herself. Making her homemade tortillas and obsessing over every teenage boy who comes into Lyla's life.

But it isn't my house, and it never has been. This whole time, it's been owned by the Baileys, not me.

As I head out the front entrance of the airport, someone steps into my path after pushing off from the wall he was leaning against. It's a man I took notice of when I first walked in because he's wearing a black hat like a private investigator from a nineties' movie.

I nod at him and move to step past him, but he says in a low voice, "Mr. Alanovic. Can we talk?"

I study him, everything about him now. He's about fifty-five, graying at the temples next to where laugh lines form deep crevices around his eyes.

"And you are?" I say carefully.

"Charlie Haise," he tells me, taking a card out of his jacket pocket and handing it to me.

Looking at it, seeing who he works for, makes my heart pick up its pace. I meet his eyes again.

He nods. "I have an offer for you. But we can't talk here."

Will

Lyla is dead asleep with her mouth open when I stretch and stand up from the uncomfortable floor I've been on since midnight. All is still and quiet now. Peaceful.

Lyla's softly breathing, and I just watch her for a second. Then I leave her there and go into my room to get dressed, then quietly head down the stairs. Feeling guilty, I write out another note for her on a notepad on the kitchen counter, and I leave the house.

I get into my car quickly, my body aching from spending the night on Lyla's hard floor. I don't think I fell asleep until later this morning, but I can't remember. It's all a blur in my mind. I just waited around all night for the next wave of screams and thrashing to roll in. It finally stopped around four-thirty, and I had a few hours to lay there and think, to contemplate my life. My sister's life. Everything in me tells me that she suffers from these night terrors because something is off, but she doesn't even know what it is.

Like the fact that she's really a Bailey. And the fact that her brother is lying to her. And her parents. And she has two bodyguards living next door. I glare out through the window at their house that's set far back in the trees. All this time, Emil's been watching over me. Ridiculous.

I squint against the blaring beams of sun through the trees above me as I pull onto the small Lake Shore Drive. I'm not thinking very clearly after a long night of no sleep.

All I know is that it's time to come out of hiding. And there's only one person who can help me do that.

My mind reels. I don't know what I'll say. I don't know if she'll even want to be a part of this. She probably hates me. But like a lighthouse in the fog, only one thing is clear: I need to stop Samantha from getting on that plane.

The prospect of inheriting the Manor is gone now. At least, it will be when my parents find out what I'm planning. Forget it. Like Samantha said, it's all nothing in the grand scheme of things. It'll rot someday or burn away. Yesterday I was willing to put it before a relationship with my sister, and a relationship with Samantha.

Today, after a wild night of hearing my sister's screams fill my whole house, my perspective of things has shifted. Nothing else matters except the truth coming out. All night I would grab my sister's arms as she thrashed. I'd have to shake her firmly, saying her name until she snapped out of it. Then she would fall into my chest and cry about her life being back to normal now.

I don't want this to be her "normal" anymore. It's time for things to change.

I drive fifteen miles over the speed limit the entire way to the airport.

Samantha

My heart is pounding as I sit in my seat. This plane looks exactly like the one that brought us all here, and I wonder if it *is* the same one. I'm just as nervous as I was on that trip, but for a very different reason: I spotted Emil the second I first walked into the airport. He's here to make sure I'm really leaving town, just like he said he'd be.

I look down at my phone to check the time. Twenty-one minutes have passed since I boarded. Hopefully Emil's gone by now, since he watched me walk onto the plane. Hopefully he isn't waiting until it actually takes off.

Glancing around, I stand up and grab my big purse. A few people look up at me as I head to the tiny bathroom in the back of the plane. Closing myself in, I quickly grab the change of clothes from my purse and start taking off what I'm wearing, just like Nell and I planned.

It's very difficult to change in the small space. I bump my right elbow three times on the little sink and my knee hits the door hard enough to leave a bruise. People are probably wondering what on earth I'm doing in here.

Finally, I take the long pink scarf Lyla gave me out of my purse, and I drape it over my head. I toss one end of it over my right shoulder in a loose wrap, and then catch a glimpse of myself in the mirror. I look truly Indian. Nell says I look a lot like our birth mom. She doesn't know who my dad was. She never talked to her about things like that before our birth mom passed away. Maybe I'll never know.

Swallowing, I push the scarf down from my head and instead leave it loosely around my neck. Then I fold open the accordion door, stepping out. A few people glance up at me again, and I wonder if they notice that I look completely different than when I first went in there. I sit back down in my seat, buckling for no reason, and wait, tapping my fingers on the side of my leg. Three more minutes. Four. Then, just before the flight attendant goes to shut the door, I unbuckle my seatbelt and stand to my feet. I grab my purse and my carryon again and hurry towards her.

"I forgot something," I tell her frantically.

She's already shaking her head. "I can't hold the plane for you."

"It'll only take a minute."

She sighs heavily, glancing back at the door to the cockpit. "I can give you two minutes. But that's it."

"I have all of my things if you have to take off. I don't mind."

"Hurry."

"Thank you."

I go to the door, putting my sunglasses on, and then rush down the metal steps, lugging my carryon behind me and praying that Emil isn't still inside, watching this. I don't see him when I get back inside the small airport. Still, I carefully look around and press the scarf to my face as I head towards the rental car desk. I get the cheapest car I can, sign the paperwork, and take the keys from the young kid behind the counter. Still no sign of the bodyguard as I walk out of the airport and into the moist breeze. I watch the numbers painted on the rental car parking spots, counting up towards number 30, which is my number. A puny silver hatchback, but I don't care right now. I unlock it and open the trunk, putting in my luggage. And when I close it, I pause for a second, realizing I have no clue where I'm going. I'll have to call my sister and my mom, confirm with them that I'm not on the flight. But then what? Am I going to Will's house? Emil's staying right next door to him. I can't.

I'll call Will, I decide. Because no matter what happened between us, he's the only one I'm thinking of right now. He needs to know he has bodyguards. He needs to know that this is bigger than we thought.

And no matter what, I still feel things for him. I still care about him, even when I'm not sure if I should.

I start digging for my phone as I step over to the driver's side door, glancing around nervously for Emil.

That's when I see something I don't expect. Will's car is pulling into the airport parking lot. But maybe it's not him. Maybe I just wish it's him. I push my sunglasses up into my hair as I watch. The car parks. Someone gets out.

Will. It's him.

My brain, and all of the fear of the past few hours, comes to a complete stop.

Will slams the door and hurries to the entrance of the airport.

Why is he here?

"Will!" I call out to him. He doesn't hear me. "Will!"

He glances over, and then stops. He takes in the sight of me, and I can see him processing the fact that I'm still here. Does he want me here? Did he come here to stop me from getting on the plane?

He starts over to me, moving around the cars in the parking lot. His eyes don't break from mine. I can't read his expression as he gets closer, but I can tell that he's tired. His hair is messy, his eyes shadowed, his shirt only partly tucked in – half of it spilling over his belt.

He doesn't slow down as he comes to me. He practically slams into me…enveloping me, embracing me.

Will

She smells like flowers and everything that's good. I hold her tightly.

"I'm sorry," I say into her hair. "I'm so sorry."

"I'm sorry too."

I pull her back and look at her. Her cheeks are flushed. Both of us are breathing hard.

And I'm so glad she's not gone.

"I shouldn't have done that," I say quickly. "I shouldn't have brought you there. I didn't mean to lead you on...I just..."

"You wanted me to see your roots," she interrupts, tucking her hair behind her ears. "I get it."

I want to kiss her. "You didn't get on the plane," I say.

"I did, but I got off again."

I grin slightly, noticing she's wearing the pink scarf my sister bought her. "You didn't want this be over, either?"

"No, I didn't." There's concern in her light brown eyes. "But there's something else too." She takes a small step back from me, letting me go. "You have a bodyguard, Will."

I nod grimly. "I know. Two, actually. I just found out yesterday." I frown. "How did you find out?"

"Emil came by last night and had me sign a different gag order. Yesterday I accidentally signed it as Samantha Foster, not my legal name. And then today, he was here to make sure I got on the plane."

She glances around, fidgeting with the pink scarf.

My jaw flexes. "He'll be gone soon. I'm refusing protection. But Sienna will stay on."

"Why isn't she leaving with him?" Samantha asks.

I look in her eyes. "Because I asked Lyla to stay last night."

Samantha's eyes widen, and she studies my face. "You did?"

"That's why I'm here," I tell her. I run my hands through my hair. "I can't do it anymore. I can't keep the truth from her anymore. We fought last night, because I told her I sent you away, and she decided to leave. But then her nightmares came back."

Samantha's expression turns sweetly concerned.

"She's staying," I tell her. "And I want you to stay for a while too. As long as you can…"

She smiles. "Okay."

"…because I want you to write this."

Her expression freezes. "You…what?" she says, breathless.

I search her face, nervous about this decision. But I'm determined.

"If you do," I tell her in a low voice, "my parents will be forced to tell her everything."

Her mouth opens. "But…the gag order…"

I shake my head. "We'll figure it out. I'll pay the fine."

Pressing her fingers to her temples, she shakes her head. "There are a million other people you could get to write this for you, Will. Professionals-"

"I know," I interrupt, expecting her to say this. "But I want you to do it. You care about this story, and you've been in Lyla's shoes, in a way."

"And the Manor," she says, not listening. "They'll never give it to you if you do this."

I take her elbows in my hands and she looks up at me. "Forget the Manor. You were right. It's all worthless. Especially if it means keeping the truth from her." I swallow. "And losing you."

She searches my face with her light brown eyes, quiet, shocked.

I'm slightly confused by her silence, her reluctance. There's attraction between us, isn't there? I didn't just imagine it? As a few moments pass, I start to doubt.

But then…she takes my head in her hands and she kisses me.

I'm stunned, at first. But then I grab her face and kiss her back intensely. Her arms wrap around me. There is nothing between us, space or secrets. I dig my fingers into her hair, finally giving vent to my feelings for her. Her hands spread on my back. My heart pounds.

After a few seconds, she gently breaks off the kiss. We press our foreheads together, both of us breathing hard.

"I'm guessing that's a yes?" I say.

She gives me another quick kiss. "Yes," she says happily. "Yes, yes, yes."

My heart lifts.

"I've wanted to kiss you since Saturday night," I whisper.

She's smiling, beautiful. "Until you found out I was a stalker."

I shrug. "Minor detail."

Her eyes are shining. She backs up and keeps hold of my hands, looking down at them.

"What now?" she asks.

There's a small ring on her finger. I lightly twist it. Her fingers are delicate, while mine are rough and calloused.

"Lyla can't know that you're still here," I tell her, "or else Sienna would find out."

She thinks about it. "I could stay somewhere in town for a little while."

I shake my head. "Word might get around that you're still here if someone sees you." I grin slightly, scratching my head. "I know a place."

She eyes me excitedly. "Yeah?"

"Yeah. I think you'll approve." Her eyes are bright when I give her instructions as to where to go.

"You're not coming with me?" she asks.

I shake my head. "I don't think we should be seen there together yet, just in case."

She nods and looks disappointed.

"It's only temporary," I tell her. "How long do you think you'll need to write this?"

She shrugs. "I honestly have no idea. I've never done this before." She blushes.

I rub her fingers with my thumb. "I'll pay you for your time."

She rolls her eyes. "You're already giving me the opportunity of a lifetime, Will. You're not paying me. Besides," she says, brushing some hair out of her eyes, "you couldn't afford me."

I grin. "How much do you charge?"

"Someone like you? Two million an hour."

We laugh, and I kiss her again. She lingers for a second, hands still in mine, and then she reluctantly steps away from me and gets into her new rental car. She's back to being flustered as she looks up at me through the window. She smiles and blushes, touching her scarf as she starts the car. She gives a small wave, and I wave back, and she drives out of the parking lot.

I watch until her car disappears. Everything has changed between us. She knows who I am. Soon, she'll know *everything*. I can tell her all of it.

Excitement pounds through my chest as I head back to my car.

I decide to call my dad right now, instead of while I'm driving. I don't know what state of mind he'll be in after how we left things yesterday. Reluctantly, I pull my phone out and call him.

My dad answers, sounding guarded as he gives a simple, "Hey there."

"Hey…" I clear my throat, more nervous to talk to him than I thought I'd be. "She's gone," I tell him, ignoring the tightening of my stomach from lying.

"I know. Emil met her at the airport to make sure she left. He called me a while ago and said she was gone." He sighs. "Lyla will be on the next flight with Sienna."

"Actually…" I take a quiet breath. "I asked Lyla to stay last night."

My dad doesn't say anything for a few seconds.

"I don't want her to go," I tell him, swallowing. "She doesn't want to go either."

"That's…good," he says, surprised. "Good." He clears his throat.

Things go so quiet that I wonder if the call dropped. "Dad?"

"Then the deed's transferred, Will."

I blink and stop beside my car. "What?"

"The Manor is yours."

I stagger backwards. I can't think straight. "What? It's…What?"

"Do with it what you want, but of course your sister can't know about it. You probably can't do much with it while she's there."

I'm so relieved that I don't even get mad about that statement. "Thanks…Dad. I…" I can't believe it. "I'm…sorry for what I said yesterday. I didn't mean it."

Some of it.

"You're not the only one with regrets, son," he says, referring to everything, probably. The past. His relationship with me. How it is with Lyla.

261

I almost ask him, for the millionth time in my life, if there's a bigger reason that they aren't telling her the truth. A bigger reason why they gave everything up. But I already know what his answer will be, and I don't want to ruin this moment.

"I love you, son."

The words surprise me. Guilt rises up in me because now I'm the one lying to him. He has no idea what Samantha and I plan to do.

But I say, "Love you too, Dad," and we end the conversation…very differently than how we ended it yesterday.

I open the car door and toss my phone onto the driver's seat, then I turn around, hands in my hair. I can't believe it. Finally. Finally, it's mine. Without losing my sister first. Without losing Samantha.

Samantha. I want to call her and then go with her to Harbor Springs and we'll bust open a bottle of champagne, even though she doesn't like alcohol.

But instead, I realize I have to go there. To the Manor. I have to see it – for the first time ever – as mine.

It takes me less than fifteen minutes from Pellston, along the backroads through the trees. I turn onto the small road called Carson Lane and come to the gate, getting out quickly to unlock it and open it. I hate the long process of having to pull through and close it and lock it again behind me. We used to have guards here who did all that. Chuck and Merle and good ol' Parker. I wonder where they are now. Parker might not even be alive anymore.

I drive the curving paved road towards the cove and the house in the distance, letting myself finally imagine what all I'll do to it. It's mine.

Sadly, I think of Alexandra, but I push her out of my thoughts.

I pull up to the front steps and get out. The sound of my car door shutting sends a flock of birds out from a tree. I stare up for a minute, then climb the steps and unlock and open the front entry doors. Abandoned is the word you first think of when you walk in here, especially with the echo of footsteps and the crunchy tapping of leaves on the marble floor of the foyer. But soon it'll be teeming with people. It'll bring more tourism to Northern Michigan than they've seen in years. Like my grandfather wanted.

I picture Lyla walking in here, looking around with her big eyes, in awe. She might see it soon. There are some things I should do first. I could start right now, because I know she's still sleeping.

I head down the west hallway towards her nursery, feeling exhilarated…and more like myself than I have in years.

Lyla

A deep hunger pain in my stomach is what finally wakes me up. I slowly blink and then…remember. Letting out a long breath, I turn onto my side and curl up, clutching my scar and pinching my eyes closed. How embarrassing. My brother held me over and over, all night long.

They're back. My stupid life-wrecking nightmares are back.

I open my eyes and look at the clock on the nightstand. It's four o'clock. Must be in the afternoon. I try to think of what day it is. It's Tuesday, I'm pretty sure. I didn't eat dinner last night because of our argument, and I've also missed breakfast and lunch.

Turning onto my back, I lay here in my worn pajamas and stare at the ceiling, thinking of the first time my parents and I realized that the nightmares were not going to stop for a while, and that they might actually change my life. I stopped being able to keep up with public school. I only went to a few months of high school before that. I met Justin – a senior, when I was only a freshman – and then there was one terrible night where he made fun of my scar in front of everyone, and the bullying started. My stomach churns as I think about it.

Thankfully, my parents have never allowed me to be on social media, or else it would've been a lot worse. Still though, it hurt. It was the worst thing I had ever experienced so far. The nightmares started, too, maybe because of the bullying, and there was nothing I could do to stop them. I began to sleep a lot during the day, falling into depression and despair. My friends stopped coming around, and I realized they were never truly my friends anyway. Almost three years went by in a haze of darkness.

Then…I came to Good Hart. I met Christian, and Samantha, and got so close to getting her together with my brother that I really, truly thought it would happen. But then, in one night, everything came crashing down. I curl in on myself, my throat closing.

At least Will asked me to stay. At least there's a relationship with him starting. That's what I truly wanted out of all of this anyway. We'll start over.

Maybe things won't be so bad with the nightmares being back. Maybe it was just for one night, because of everything that happened. Maybe.

But even so, I'm too scared to hope for that.

Rolling out of bed and feeling like I'm carrying a thousand pounds on me somewhere, I make my way out of my room and head downstairs to see what Will is doing and if there's anything to eat. But the only thing on the counter is a note from my brother.

Running errands. – W

I stare at it. He didn't even say when he would be back. When did he leave? He's probably been gone all day long, like yesterday. Did anything change for him last night? He finally acted like a human being. Comforting, loving, concerned. Today, he's left me here again with nothing to do. No car, no internet or cable, no phone except his house phone, no friends. Nothing about that has changed from the usual, except *I* have changed. I've decided to not be okay with it anymore.

I'm going home.

Feeling sadness grip my stomach, I decide that I don't want any food right now and instead I head out the back door, barefoot and unsure of where I'm going. Tears streak my cheeks and become cold in the wind. I barely feel the water when I reach it, turning to the left and heading south for some reason. I just need to be out of his house because I am feeling very sorry for myself and just need to be alone in case he gets back.

The rocky sand hurts but I keep going. I start to wish I had put on shoes, but there's no going back now. The weight of everything seems to be pressing on me. I feel this way a lot after I wake up in the evening or afternoon after a long night of screaming. But this time, there's more to it.

Because something that I had is lost.

A life.

I thought this would be a great summer, an adventure, especially after my nightmares went away. I was wrong. I stop and stand on the beach for a second, thinking of dancing out here that first morning, meeting Christian. It seems like a lifetime ago. I was wearing a yellow dress that day, and now I'm in ugly pajamas. I had all these stupid plans to have a great life and make all these friends and get so close to my brother that we wouldn't want to ever be apart again. But I was so wrong about all of it. I think of playing fetch out here with Estes, of Christian holding me and asking me to go out on a boat for the first time ever. I start crying harder. I'll never see him again.

And then there's Samantha... But I push the thought of her away because I'll lose it completely if I focus on her.

I keep walking down the beach in the shallow waves. After a while, I realize I'm on other peoples' private property, but I don't even care. Tears slip down and I brush them away. I sniff and wipe my nose on my sleeve, feeling so pathetic.

My feet suddenly come to a stop when I notice someone ahead of me. It's the redheaded girl again. She doesn't see me because she's looking out at the water again, like she was the first time I saw her yesterday. I'm close enough now to tell that she's probably my age. She's all alone in shorts and a long blue shirt that moves in the breeze, like her red hair does.

I'm holding my own hair down so she won't see my scar, but I don't say hi to her yet because I'm embarrassed that I'm crying. And for some reason, I feel like I shouldn't say anything yet. Instead, I just watch as she stands there, hugging herself. She brings one hand up to her face, then her other hand...and suddenly, she is sobbing. I stare at her as she sinks down to her knees in the sand. My heart starts pounding. She cries harder and puts a hand down into the sand to steady herself. My throat closes up, but not for myself now. For her. What happened to her? Why is she so sad?

I don't know what to do, or what I should say to her, so I just stand here, watching...

Audree Tyler

This morning, my mom found me on Remmi's bed again. I wrapped myself in her sheets and surrounded myself with her stuffed animals. I wasn't crying yet, I was just breathing in the scent of my sister, trying to feel like she was there with me. My mom started crying when she saw me. She curled up next to me and we held each other like that for over an hour.

And now I find myself out at the water. I come out here to cry most of the time. I need to be strong for my mom when I'm around her, but out here, I can be myself. I can let myself feel the pain because my mom refuses to even come near the beach anymore, so I know I'll be alone. My sister's body was found washed up on shore a few miles from here. The lake itself reminds my mom of this.

I know I should probably avoid the water too, but for some reason, I don't. Sometimes I think it'll help me get over the loss faster, facing it. I come out here, think of her and how much I miss her, and then I cry for a while until I feel like I am going to die. And then, I go back inside. I have only been home for a few days, and I've already realized this is my new routine.

My stomach hurts because I am crying so hard now. I try to breathe. My knees sting from the rocks and the sand digging into them, but I hardly notice because the pain in my heart is much, much worse. I am only seventeen years old, but I've lost my little sister. My only sister.

And it's my fault she's gone.

Loss and guilt and shame choke me, and I try desperately to push the thoughts away, but I can't and now I'm sobbing harder. I keep thinking that if someone just knew...if someone knew how hard this is and how dark things are for me, it would make it better. I might be okay in the end.

But I feel very alone.

Christian's face fills my mind. I wonder how he's doing. My heart breaks all over again. Christian. He loved her. It was always the three of us. I haven't told him that I'm back in town yet. I can't. I can't face him. It's not fair. None of it is fair. I can't take it. Maybe I should just walk out into the water. Maybe it would make me clean. Wash my sin. And then I could just float away, like my little sister did. It would be easy, just one step after the other. Maybe I should. I feel the water on my hand – so cold. I sob harder and move to crawl forward...

But then, I jolt back suddenly...because there is suddenly someone beside me.

A girl gets down on her knees next to me. She reaches out and wraps her warm fingers around my hand. Tears stream down her face. She has long and dark, curly hair. Bright blue eyes. She's wearing gray pajamas. I have no clue who she is, so I just stare at her, stunned and clutching her hand.

She looks out at the water and not at me.

"What's your name?" she asks.

I gulp some air and hiccup as I try to get a hold of myself.

"Audree," I choke.

Her fingers tighten around mine.

"Audree," she says, "I saw you crying, and it made me sad for you." She wipes her cheeks with her free hand and looks in my eyes. "I thought I'd come try to comfort you, but I have no idea what to say."

I want to tell her that no one does. No one has any clue what to say to me, so I haven't told anyone that I'm back home yet after being in Denver for weeks. My mom doesn't want anyone to know, either. We plan to stay hidden at home for a while. My grandma goes to the grocery store for us, because no one knows her.

"I thought I'd just stay here with you for a while," the girl says, "if that's okay."

After a second, I find myself giving a small nod. The girl sniffs and wipes her nose and looks out at the lake again.

I am kneeling in the sand, crying and desperately holding hands with a girl I've never met before. This is really weird. But somehow, it isn't awkward.

I look out at the water too, wondering about this girl. A few minutes pass. Her knees must be really hurting by now because mine are really killing me. I gently let go of her hand and start to wipe at the streams of tears on my cheeks that lead down to my neck. Sand smears beneath my chin and I scrape at it. She's not crying anymore. Was she really crying for me? As I study her, I realize something.

"I saw you," I say. "Out on the beach yesterday."

She nods. "I almost came over to meet you, but you went back inside."

I wish I hadn't. Yesterday was a really bad day – only our second day home since the funeral a month ago. My mom and I still aren't used to being back here, having to face all the memories of my sister. Someone painted her name on a fence outside our neighborhood, and when I saw it, I burst into tears. It was worse, getting home. The whole house is like a box of memories that I wish I could stuff under the bed and only look at when I absolutely have to.

I push the thoughts from my mind because tears are streaming down my face again.

"Who are you?" I ask the girl.

She smiles at me. "My name's Lyla."

I nod, wiping my face, and now I don't know what else to say. But I search for something, because I don't want her to leave me.

"Do you want some tea?" she asks suddenly.

I sniff, and I'm already nodding. "Tea actually sounds great."

We get to our feet together and dust ourselves off, our knees dotted pink from the sand and rocks. Lyla has about twenty different types of teas, and she tells me about all of the flavors as we walk up the beach together. By the time we get to her stretch of beach, I realize I am completely done crying because I'm trying to pick a tea flavor. I tell her vanilla, and she stops and looks at me with her big eyes.

"You're kidding," she says.

"What?"

"That's my favorite kind! What are the chances?"

She laughs, and part of me thinks she's way too entertained by this, but it's kind of nice for some reason.

She turns and passes a fire pit with different colored chairs around it and heads towards a path through the trees.

I stop dead in my tracks when I look up at the house. I don't know why I didn't realize it before, when I saw her out on the beach yesterday, but this is Christian's grandma's old house. My heart starts pounding. I was six when I first met Christian on this very beach. My family just moved here, and I was out playing in the water with my mom and sister when we realized we went too far up the beach. Christian was swimming around, his grandma close by. He swam right up to me and Remmi, already confident at seven.

"Wanna play?" he asked us.

That's all it took. My sister and I didn't have any brothers, so this neighbor boy enthralled us. We built a fort that very same day on his grandma's property – *this* property. My sister was only five at the time, I was six, and Christian was seven, but the three of us were inseparable from the beginning, up until recently. My sister always wanted to be a part of whatever Christian and I did. I can still picture her standing close by us that first day, quietly fascinated as we pieced together a fort.

My throat closes up. The fort used to be somewhere to the left, in the trees. It's probably still there, forgotten and overgrown. I can't even look.

"I have to go," I say suddenly.

Lyla stops and looks back at me. She's only a few feet ahead of me.

"Oh," she says. "Are you sure?"

"Yeah, I...um, didn't realize..." I trail off, looking up at the house.

Lyla seems to catch on to what I'm saying.

"If it's my brother everyone's so worried about, he's not home right now," she says, and I wonder what she means. "He's running errands in town."

I do know who her brother must be. Will Brooks. Some of the high school girls used to drive by his house sometimes, just to try to get a good look at him and see if he was actually out of his house.

"It's not that," I tell Lyla. "I just..."

I just what? I don't want to tell her anything. I don't want her to look at me like everybody else does.

"We don't have to talk," she says. "We can just hang out and drink our vanilla tea." She smiles hopefully. "Tea can fix anything."

I feel my heart warming to her. She really wants me to stay. Despite everything, I can't hurt her feelings.

"Okay, yeah," I say quietly.

She is very excited about this but tries to hide it. And then, slowly and trying not to think too much, I follow her up to the house.

I am thankful that the inside looks almost nothing like it did back when I would come over to see Christian and his grandma, Dorothy, also known as Dee Dee. It's very sparse now, compared to how it used to look. Dee Dee used to have flower prints everywhere – the curtains, the couch pillows, the paintings on the walls. The only flowers in here now are in small water glasses on the coffee table and side tables, along with a few unlit candles. I'm guessing Lyla put them there. There are some twinkle lights that aren't plugged in, and white curtains. There's a big TV in the living room, missing cabinets in the attached kitchen, a guitar on a stand in the corner, and everything smells like sawdust, although it's pretty clean. And the fridge is in the living room beside the couch for the remodeling. I'm relieved because no memories have flooded back to me yet. Maybe this will be fine.

Lyla brings me over to the couch, sits me down, and puts a gray blanket in my lap. I am kind of weirded-out by this because it's a warm day, but I find myself cuddling with it, slightly comforted. Lyla goes into the kitchen and fills the tea kettle in the sink.

"Do you want a muffin?" she asks. "I bought some this weekend."

"Um, sure."

"Really? Okay that's great because we have too many."

I watch her as she moves around the kitchen, putting muffins on plates and grabbing two mugs for our tea. She's humming and smiling, yawning occasionally. She doesn't know that I'm staring at her. When's the last time I saw someone so happy around me like this? It was definitely before my sister died. Now, everyone's afraid to be happy around me, like everyone else should be miserable just because I am. I'll never understand it. It would be much better if people were like this girl.

I offer to help her with the mugs and the plates, but she insists I don't move. It takes her two trips, but she finally sits down next to me on the couch, handing me a plate with two muffins on it and my mug of tea, with the little string dangling down the side of it.

"Smell it," she says.

I do. I take a big whiff, and the scent fills me with some kind of...I don't know. Goodness or something. I am so happy all of a sudden to be sitting here in this strange familiar house, drinking tea with this girl and eating a muffin. Well, not happy exactly, but I'm relieved at least. Maybe even hopeful.

I expect that even though Lyla said we don't have to talk she'll still ask questions, like why I was crying. But she surprises me by being completely silent. She has a soft smile on her face as she pinches bits of muffin between her fingers and eats them. I sip my tea, liking the warmth that goes down through my chest and into my stomach. I realize we're in a comfortable silence together even though we've only known each other for twenty minutes or so. I read what her mug says on the side: *Tea makes everybody happy.* And I think, *maybe it does.*

Something tells me that this happened for a reason. This girl saw me on the beach at the perfect time. She came into my life right when I needed her, like a light in a blackout. An angel. I can't explain it, this change of events in my day, but I can't wait to tell my mom later. It'll make her smile, which is rare these days.

"Did you move here recently?" I ask.

Lyla shakes her head. "I'm just visiting my brother."

My heart sinks a little. "Oh. So...how long will you be here?"

She smiles, like she has a secret. "The rest of the summer," she says quietly.

I'm so relieved. Maybe I'll get to hang out with her more. For the first time in a very long time, I actually have something to look forward to. I am excited for this summer.

Lyla and I drink our tea quietly together, as if we've been friends for a long time.

Sienna

My feet are curled up under me on the office chair as I watch. My hand is pressed to my chest. Lyla made a friend. I must be tired and overdone by everything recently, because I want to cry. I am eating the popcorn I just made, feeling like I'm watching a movie play out before me.

Emil's asleep upstairs. I can actually hear his snoring through the walls. He's overdone, too. He hasn't had this much action in five years. And now, for him, it is abruptly over. He packed his things this afternoon quietly, seeming deep in thought the whole time. I felt a very sudden urgency to stop this change. He has to move out of this house. His home of five years. I almost reached out and touched his strong back as he looked through the fridge for something to eat between packing his weights and the rest of the workout equipment. Instead, I went downstairs, depressed that everything's over.

But now...Lyla's not leaving. I'll be staying here with her. Her parents were going to have to figure out something else if she insisted on coming home. But she isn't going home. She's staying. So am I. The Baileys agreed to send another three covert officers to watch her and follow from different locations once Emil is gone. I told Carlos I am unable to provide adequate protection by myself now, and he agreed.

I don't know what Emil will do...probably go back to L.A. or transfer to another job Carlos might assign him to.

As for me, Lyla needs me here.

Samantha
Harbor Springs Pier

Will said it's the fourth boathouse past the pier. It's the same color blue as his house, and I can see it now in the distance as I walk towards the path. I've never seen boathouses as big as these. Will's looks like something a family of ten could comfortably live in.

The path that leads to the boathouses, away from the pier, is closed in by a fence with a gate that has an access code – 9118. Looking around, I enter the code when I reach the gate and step through, closing it behind me. I glance around again, looking for any sign of the bodyguards. I know now why Will didn't want to risk being seen here with me. We'll have to be careful from now on.

There are not many people around today, a relief in the crowd from this weekend's music festival. I'm thankful that I can keep going down the path without being noticed. The boathouse has dark blue trim around its tinted windows. There's another code for the door – 6876 – and I enter it in and quickly open the door and step through. It beeps as it automatically locks behind me. It takes a second for my eyes to adjust in the dim expanse that has two large shapes filling it – one larger than the other. The first thing I notice is the smell – a light fish and motor oil smell. The sun streams in from the big garage door that's laden with windows. Gulls fly past. My eyes adjust, but even so, I reach for a light switch. It's a big industrial one on the wall behind me and flipping it causes a big clack.

I stare, my mouth open. Then I let out a laugh that echoes. Two polished black boats with gold trim float still in the water in front of me. No, not boats. One is a yacht, for sure. The other one, a speedboat. The yacht is named *Juanita*, and the speedboat *Little Nita*. I cover my mouth with my hands.

And then, of course, I call Nell and my mom.

"You were right, Nell," I tell her when she answers.

She gasps and calls for Mom. "He's got a yacht!"

I walk over to the side of it as I listen to them giggle and ask questions. There's a back deck where I can step onto it, and I feel it move just slightly and smoothly in the water beneath my weight.

"Do a video call thingy!" my mom says, and so I do.

I take them around with me, showing them everything I'm seeing at the same time. I feel like they're here with me, and I realize how much I miss them. But we're all too enthralled to think about it right now.

I show them the upper and lower decks, the living room, the kitchen, the bathroom with subway tiles all the way up to the ceiling. There are two bedrooms, the largest is in the back and it's clearly Will's. Everything has Will written all over it – the Bailey version of him. It's masculine and dark, mostly black and gold with navy blue accents. It's the exact opposite of how Lyla would decorate. Or me. But it is absolutely the most gorgeous setting I have ever been in.

I find that the best part about it is that it's been used, maybe even lived in, by Will. I wonder if this is what he sailed around in after he first inherited the money from his grandfather. My favorite things are little and intimate, like his toothbrush in a cup on the bathroom sink, the small bottle of a store-brand painkiller in the cabinet next to a black razor. The folded pairs of pants and hanging white shirts in the master bedroom closet. The map with wrinkled and marked pages sitting in the seat where you drive this whole thing. I don't point these things out to my mom and Nell. These are just for me.

I haven't told them that we kissed. I don't know why. I think I am still processing it, relishing it, and I am definitely questioning what will happen between us now.

But I did tell them, on the way here, that Will asked me to stay and write this. They both screamed, and I pictured them jumping up and down in the coffee shop together.

When we go to tour the speedboat, I decide that this is where I'm staying. Beneath the front deck there's a single small bed space that I have to duck to get into. It's much cozier, less extravagant. I lay back on the bed with my phone above me, smiling at the small faces of Nell – who looks just like me – and my mom, who looks almost nothing like me. We talk and dream about what it will be like in these next few weeks.

I am the one who gets to tell the Bailey's story to the world. Most importantly, to Lyla.

I can't believe this.

Lyla

Audree and I have been sitting quietly for a long time now. Our mugs are dry, our plates reduced to muffin crumbs. I asked her if she wanted more of anything a few minutes ago, but she said no. She looks pale as she gazes out the window beside us. She has a perfect amount of freckles on her nose. When she put her red hair up into a ponytail a few minutes ago, I found myself touching my scar beneath my hair, glancing at the flawless skin on the back of her neck. She could wear her hair up like that every day if she wanted to. She is just like the very pretty girls that Justin used to hang out with at school. It made me feel pretty too when they took me into their little group within the first few months.

But then Justin embarrassed me in front of everyone, and the comments started. Then the nightmares. Why am I thinking about it so much today?

I let out a small breath, forcing my hand away from my neck and still watching Audree, who seems like she might break into pieces at any second. I doubt she's ever experienced a moment of insecurity in her life, because she's gorgeous. But still, she's clearly been through something terrible.

I'm having a very hard time not asking her what it is.

Everything has changed. Before I saw her on the beach, I thought nothing could get me to stay here with my brother. But now, there's this girl who needs a friend. And I need a friend too. I feel like we're kindred spirits already, and I don't know why.

Another few quiet minutes pass, and then I remember something. Breaking our long silence, I ask, "Is your name spelled with two e's?"

Eyes flickering, she looks at me. "Yeah. How did you know?"

I set my mug down and get off the couch, walking over to the kitchen counter. Behind a few envelopes is the yellow wrinkled one that Christian accidentally left here the first day I met him. I bring it over to her and hand it to her.

"This is for you, I think."

She stares at it, not taking it from me. "How did you get that?" she asks.

"A guy I met accidentally left it here."

"What guy?" she says quickly.

"Um…" My heart speeds up as I watch her face change. She's almost frantic. I hope I didn't do something wrong. "His name is Christian."

"You know Christian?"

"A little. Yeah." I definitely don't think I should tell her how well I know him, that I was even questioning if he liked me before everything got ruined last night.

Audree suddenly stands to her feet, setting her mug down hard on the coffee table.

"I have to go," she says, looking around for her shoes.

"What?" I say, confused. "Are you sure?"

"Yeah, I'm sorry. I just remembered something my mom wanted me to do."

"Do you want the card?"

She grabs it at the same time she grabs her shoes from the floor beside the couch.

"Did I do something wrong?" I ask her, following her to the back door.

She turns and tries to smile. "No. I'm sorry. I just have to go. Let's…hang out sometime."

I study her. "Okay."

She opens the door but pauses. "Please don't tell anyone I'm here. People think my family is out of town, and I want it to stay that way for as long as possible."

"I won't tell anyone."

"Especially not Christian," she adds.

I nod, wanting so badly to ask her why. But I don't want to push her away.

"Thanks for…everything," she says quietly. Her chin quivers.

"Of course." I gather my courage to say the thing to her that has always helped me. "Everything will be okay," I tell her.

She stares at me for a second, eyes getting watery, and then she nods and swallows, looking away and walking out. She hurries down the path and heads into the trees. The yellow card in her hand looks like a broken wing.

I stand in the silent house, confused and worried for her and wondering what that was about. What happened to her? Why doesn't she want people to know she's here? And how well does she know Christian? Well enough for him to give her a card, I guess. I wonder what it says. I wonder if they have a history together. Audree is very, very pretty. I could see them being together. I don't know how to feel about that.

Before I have too much time to dwell on it, I hear a car door shut out front. Will's home. I sigh loudly, thinking this is terrible timing. I can't face him right now, not after all of that, and not after he left me here all day again. I'm still staying here, like we decided last night, but not for him. And I don't want to talk about it right now.

I go out the back door and walk quickly down to the beach. I stop by the fire pit, looking out at the water. I think of Sunday night, when Samantha was here with us and we all ate bratwursts together. My brother was quiet and already getting on my nerves at that point, but I was too naïve to see what was coming. I look down at the blackened wood in the circle of stones, wishing there was an actual fire right now, although it's warm out today.

I hear the back screen-door open and I tense up. I wish I could just run out into the water and swim away from him. Anything to not have to talk to him.

I hear him quietly walk up from behind and then go to the other side of the fire pit. I don't move, just keep staring down at the non-existent flames.

"We could make a fire tonight," he says quietly. "If you want."

I swallow, not wanting to cry in front of him.

"I probably won't be able to stay awake long," I tell him.

He sighs. "That's right. I forgot."

He slides his hands into his pockets. He's looking at my gray pajamas, and I realize I was wearing them last Friday, the day he first saw me. I've been in dresses ever since. Until now.

I glance away. "And are you sure you're going to even be here tonight?" I ask quietly.

"I'm sorry," he says. "I had a few things I needed to do."

I notice he doesn't tell me what those things were.

He sighs. "It'll be different now. I promise." He waits a second, then he says, "Are you still staying?"

I rub my nose, holding back tears. "You don't want me here, Will. You've made that very clear this whole time."

"What about last night?" he asks.

"You weren't thinking straight last night," I whisper.

He shakes his head. "I'm sorry you think that. But I meant it. I want you here."

I realize he's looking right in my eyes. Is this the first time he's done that? I guess he did it that first day, on my birthday. And then I hugged him because I thought I'd missed him. But I didn't really know him, not like I do now.

"I'm not used to being around people much," he says. "I know how I can come off."

I swallow.

"I'm sorry," he says. "Do you forgive me?"

He looks vulnerable for the first time ever.

And for the first time ever for *me*, I'm guarded against him, cautious. I don't have the urge to touch my scar, I have the urge to hug my arms like a shield around myself, so I do.

"I forgive you," I tell him quietly. "I just…I don't really get you. I don't get why you sent Samantha away. I don't get why people around here seem to be either angry with you, or afraid of you. I've met two people who don't even want to come inside your house."

His brow furrows. "Who?"

Remembering that Audree asked me to keep her secret, I say, "Never mind."

I look out at the lake again, not knowing what to say.

Will comes a little closer around the fire.

"I'll be around more," he says. "I promise. Whenever you're awake we'll do things together."

My arms tighten around my torso. "Like meet people? Your neighbors?"

He hesitates, looking over through the trees at the closest neighbor's house.

"Some of them," he finally says. "Sure."

I think of something. "Will you show me what's in the garage?"

He gives me a look, then says, "Fine. But...not quite yet."

I gather my courage. "And can I go out on a boat with Christian?" If he still wants to, I mentally add.

Will's surprised, but then he nods slowly. "If Dad says it's okay, then fine."

"He already said yes, but I wanted to ask you too. Out of respect."

His eyes soften.

Trying not to cry at this change I see in him, I say, "What else?"

He rubs his neck, thinking. "I might need your help to get things done around the house. I'm selling it quicker than I thought."

I almost smile.

"And," he says sort of nervously, "I'll teach you how to cook."

I stare at him. He grins slowly and walks by me towards the house. It takes me a second, but I follow behind him.

When I walk inside through the back door, my throat immediately closes up. Will has set the coffee table for a meal again, and even plugged in the twinkle lights. "I'll show you how to really cook a steak. And it doesn't involve a grill," he says.

What on earth is happening right now? This is something I've always wanted with my brother – an actual fun relationship – and yet it's happening for real and it doesn't feel exactly like I wanted it to feel.

It still feels pretty good, though.

"Also," he says, "I have something for you. I realized I never gave you anything for your birthday."

He hands me a little box. Inside, there is a very pretty piece of jewelry with a small dangling emerald, shaped like a heart.

"What is it?" I ask.

He frowns. "It's a bracelet."

I take it out and look at it. "It's kind of small. It's for a child, isn't it?"

He blushes a little. I've never seen him blush before. "I didn't realize that."

"It's okay," I say quickly, not wanting to ruin anything. "It's still pretty. I'll still keep it, if that's okay. Maybe I can get it re-sized."

"Read the inscription on the back."

The inscription says *Lills*. My throat is burning.

"Thanks, Will," I say softly.

He nods, swallowing. "How about those steaks?"

Then, for the first time, Will cooks for me. He sears the two steaks in a cast iron pan in some oil and then he adds garlic butter, meticulously spooning it over the steaks after they've browned. He also roasts some root vegetables in the oven, telling me the whole time why he's doing certain things, why it's the best way to do it. He is so very focused. I wonder where he learned to cook like this.

Even though Samantha is gone, and even though it's still mainly me who does the talking during the meal, Will is listening, even smiling sometimes, and I can't believe how different he is. He turns on the TV when we're done eating and starts the same football movie from my first night here. We sit back together, and he makes a few comments about the types of plays they're doing in the movie, and what the coach is saying. I already know all of it because I love football, but I let him talk. This is just what I wanted that first night – for us to bond.

After a while, I start to get tired again. I know I'll wake up screaming tonight, but even so, maybe everything is going to be okay.

Samantha was right. Behind a wall, my brother has a heart after all. Maybe even a good one.

To Be Continued...
25 Days and counting...

I failed her. I failed...

I'm alone now, on the cold dirt behind the ambulance. I hear others running up to me. Search dogs bark in the distance. Her emerald bracelet is on the ground. I pick it up and clutch it in my bloody hand. That's when I start feeling the pain rip through my side. I touch it and wince. His gun must have fired, too. I'm hit.

I close my eyes.

Everything goes black, and I welcome it.

The story continues in Book 2:

The nightmares are back...

The Manor sits waiting...

Some things must still remain hidden...

While the truth is about to come out.

It all unravels in the small town of Good Hart.

Continue on for discussion questions...

And visit www.LMarieThomas.com to join the Good Heart Community!

By signing up for the newsletter you'll receive insider information about the author's life, including behind-the-scenes research for the next books.

See you there!

Discussion Guide

We hope you enjoyed the story and characters of Good Heart.

There is much more fun and suspense to come!

The author is passionate about using her love of storytelling to encourage real-life connections and deep discussions. We encourage you to connect with someone through a book club or one-on-one meetings and enjoy getting to know people on a deeper level!

While writing Good Heart, themes began to emerge that were unplanned, but intricately woven into L. Marie's own life. Insecurity. Fear. A guarded heart. Unforgiveness. Even a little greed. And fun things, too, like the excitement of a new adventure, and a zeal for life.

She hopes these topics and discussion questions will help stir deeper relationships between you and someone you want to connect with.

Enjoy!

The L. Marie Thomas Team

Lyla

Character Review:
1. Describe your favorite scene with Lyla and what stands out about her.
2. Elaborate on her relationship with her brother throughout the book.
3. What do you think she wanted at the beginning of the book? Did she get it?
4. Describe Lyla's outlook on life before and after her nightmares go away at the beginning. Discuss any changes you see in her character at the end of the book.
5. Is Lyla a normal teenager in your eyes? Why or why not?
6. Discuss how Lyla perceives herself, and how others perceive her.
7. Discuss how you think Lyla might have turned out if her parents hadn't changed their lives to raise her to be "normal."

Seeing Yourself in the Characters:
1. In what ways do you identify with Lyla? How are you different?
2. Discuss how tiredness and fear kept her from thriving at the beginning, and how much that changed. Is there anything in your own life that keeps you from thriving?
3. A major theme of this book seems to be "If they really knew me, they wouldn't love me," since many of the characters are hiding something. Have you ever felt this way? Elaborate.

Will

Character Review:
1. What is your favorite encounter with Will and why?
2. Elaborate on his relationship with his parents.
3. Describe his lifestyle and what you think of it.
4. What do you think he wanted at the beginning of the book? Did he get it?
5. In what ways does he justify his actions and cold manner?
6. Discuss how Will perceives himself, and how others perceive him.
7. What is your favorite scene with Will and Samantha? And Lyla?

Seeing Yourself in the Characters:
1. In what ways do you identify with Will? How are you different?
2. What do you think motivates Will at the beginning of the book? And the end? What motivates you?
3. Will guards his heart against people – mostly his sister and Samantha. Have you ever done this in your life? Why do you think people do this?

Samantha

Character Review:
1. Describe your favorite scene with Samantha and what stands out about her.
2. Elaborate on her relationship with her mom and Nell throughout the book. Did you view these relationships any differently after you found out about Samantha's backstory?
3. What do you think she wanted at the beginning of the book? Did she get it, or did it change?
4. Discuss any changes you see in her character at the end of the book.
5. Discuss how Samantha perceives herself, and how others perceive her.
6. What do you think about the relationship that develops between her and the Bailey siblings?
7. Is the fascination she and her mom and sister have with the Baileys unhealthy in your eyes?

Seeing Yourself in the Characters:
1. In what ways do you identify with Samantha? How are you different?
2. Do you think she is crazy for following the siblings to another state? Have you ever done anything that might be perceived as crazy but ended up being the best thing you've ever done?
3. Another major theme of this book is about making a difference in someone's life in a seemingly small way, like Samantha did with Lyla and vice versa. Is there a time in your life when someone did this for you, or you did it for someone else?

Sienna

Character Review:
1. What is your favorite thing about Sienna and why? What is your favorite encounter with her in the story?
2. Elaborate on her relationship with Emil throughout the book.
3. Describe Sienna's initial opinion of her clients and whether or not it changed.
4. What do you think she wanted at the beginning of the book? Did she get it?
5. How does her past affect her ability to protect Lyla? Is she just overreacting, in your opinion?
6. What was her initial opinion of Emil and this new case she took on?
7. When did she first start to soften towards Emil?
8. What is your favorite scene with her and Emil?

Seeing Yourself in the Characters:
1. How do you identify with Sienna? How are you different?
2. Discuss how trauma and guilt can affect people. Have you had any personal experiences with this?
3. The Baileys live very differently than most extremely wealthy families, especially families Sienna has worked with. Discuss the differences.

Christian

Character Review:
1. What is your favorite encounter with Christian and why?
2. Elaborate on his grief and how he deals with it.
3. What do you think he wanted at the beginning of the book? Did he get it?
4. Describe Christian's outlook on life before and after meeting Lyla. Discuss any changes you see in his character at the end of the book.
5. Is Christian a normal teenager in your eyes? Why or why not?
6. What was the high point of the story for him? The low point?
7. Discuss how you think Christian might be different if Remmi had not died.

Seeing Yourself in the Characters:
1. In what ways do you identify with Christian? How are you different?
2. Discuss how guys may deal with grief differently than girls, and how teens might deal differently with grief and trauma than adults. How do you deal with it?
3. Unforgiveness is another theme of this book. We're not sure what exactly Christian is having a hard time forgiving Grant for, but it is definitely taking over his life. Has this ever happened to you? Have you ever reconciled?

Continuing Story Questions

1. What do you think will happen next?
2. What would you like to see happen with each of the characters' storylines?
3. What do you think is happening in the intermission scenes where each day is counting down? What do you think *will* happen?
4. What characters would you like to see more of?
5. Do you want the truth to be revealed about the Baileys once and for all? Why or why not?

We want to know what you think, and what your most intriguing answers are! We also want to know about what connections you've made with people over the book. A book club? Coffee with a friend? Dinner in a mentor relationship? We'd love to hear from you!

Go to www.LMarieThomas.com/contact today!

Note from the Author:

I hope you enjoyed the first book of Good Heart! I had SO much fun writing it, and I hope you had fun reading it. It's meant to be suspenseful and light-hearted, but I also hope that in a real way, it brings to life what it's like to hurt, feel alone, and have a guarded heart.

On that note, if you have ever felt like I have before – depressed, wanting to give up, ugly, full of fear and anxiety, wondering if you are truly worth loving or are even capable of love – if you've ever experienced any of this and want to know my story and how I was brought out of it, go to LMarieThomas.com and click on "About." Then click on the link in the last sentence of my bio.

Lastly, I want you to know that TRULY you are loved. TRULY there is a purpose for your life.

Sincerely, L.

Made in the USA
Las Vegas, NV
10 October 2021